The
LANGUAGE
of
SAND

The

LANGUAGE

of

SAND

A Novel

Ellen Block

 Bantam Books Trade Paperbacks   New York

A Bantam Books Trade Paperback Original

Copyright © 2010 by Brett Ellen Block
Reading group guide copyright © 2010 by Random House, Inc.

Published in the United States by Bantam Books,
an imprint of The Random House Publishing Group,
a division of Random House, Inc., New York.

BANTAM BOOKS and the rooster colophon are
registered trademarks of Random House, Inc.

RANDOM HOUSE READER'S CIRCLE and colophon is
a trademark of Random House, Inc.

Chapter-opener definitions are from *The Random House Webster's Unabridged Dictionary,* 2nd edition by Random House, Inc., copyright © 2001, 1998, 1997, 1996, 1993, 1987 by Random House, Inc. Used by permission of Random House, Inc.

Library of Congress Cataloging-in-Publication Data
Block, Brett Ellen.
The language of sand : a novel / Ellen Block.
p.   cm.
ISBN 978-0-440-24575-9
eBook ISBN 978-0-553-90761-2
1. Grief in women —Fiction. 2. Self-realization in women —Fiction.
3. Psychological fiction. I. Title.
PS3602.L64L36 2010
813'.6—dc22   2009052876

Printed in the United States of America

www.randomhousereaderscircle.com

9 8 7 6 5 4 3 2 1

Book design by Carol Malcolm Russo

For my parents.
With love.

The
LANGUAGE
of
SAND

a•be•ce•dar•i•an (ā´bē sē dâr´ē ən), *n.* **1.** a person who is learning the letters of the alphabet. **2.** a beginner in any field of learning. —*adj.* **3.** of or pertaining to the alphabet. **4.** arranged in alphabetical order. **5.** rudimentary; elementary; primary. Also, **abecedary.** [1595–1605; < ML *abecedāriānus.* See ABECEDARY, –AN]

◆   ◆   ◆

Never *was a word she didn't care for. Not because of the infiniteness* it implied or because it sounded so stubbornly unforgiving, but because it was, by definition, improbable. Improbability bothered her.

The consummate hyperbole, *never* was a nervy word, especially for an adverb. Limitless and indiscriminate, *never* did what few words could. It refused to be qualified, to succumb to rationality or be bridled by it for longer than a single sentence. *Never* defied logic, and for Abigail Harker, there was nothing more perturbing than that.

Logic was, in a manner, her job. She was a lexicographer. She edited dictionaries for a living. Greek in origin, the term *lexicographer* was a marriage of *lexicon,* meaning dictionary, and *graphos,* signifying a writer or writing. The pleasing precision of its etymology translated to the profession as a whole. It was a career in which Abigail's syllogistic nature served her well.

Facts, proof, and reasoning were her cardinal directions, while logic acted as the map with which she navigated the world, keeping her on course and helping her maintain her bearings. A compass could shiver at due north. A weather vane might waver in the wind.

Yet logic was as steady as stone. It could take Abigail wherever she needed to go, and on one crisp October day, logic—along with an actual map—took her from a quiet side street of a Boston suburb across six states and over eight hundred miles of unfamiliar highway to Bourne's Crossing.

Neither a city nor a town, Bourne's Crossing was merely a dock situated at a finger-shaped outcropping of the North Carolina coast. Wind undulated through the saw grass that had grown unchecked around the pilings, and the silvered timbers stretched into the water like a plank off a pirate ship. The nearby dock house, a shingled shed in desperate need of a new roof, was the sole structure for as far as the eye could see. The last bastion of civilization on a forlorn stretch of the coast, Bourne's Crossing served as the only means of getting from the mainland to the distant island of Chapel Isle. Which was exactly where Abigail was headed.

She drove her Volvo station wagon onto the dock, and the wooden boards let out a disconcerting creak. Uncertain if it was wise to pull forward any farther, she stopped and sifted through her purse for the brochure the real estate agent had sent her. According to the literature, the ferry from Bourne's Crossing ran every two hours on the hour. A departure was scheduled for four p.m. The clock on her dashboard read four on the dot. But there were no other cars, no people, and no ferry.

At the bottom of the last page of the brochure, Abigail noticed a minuscule notation she hadn't seen before: *Ferry hours subject to change off season.*

She sighed. "If there was ever a time for second thoughts."

Coming to Chapel Isle had seemed to be a perfectly logical idea when she was back in Boston. Now Abigail could see the decision for what it was: a monumental leap of faith. She worried that she might be too weak in the knees to make the jump.

As she got out of her car and headed for the dock house, a strong ocean breeze kicked up, sending eddies of sand skidding across the tract of asphalt road that ended right at the dock. The warm fall air was tinged with wetness, giving it an edge.

"Hello?" Abigail called, opening the screen door.

Inside the dock house was a small office furnished with folding chairs, a bulky wooden desk, and a TV topped by a mangled hanger acting as an antenna. A coffee mug was perched on a filing cabinet, giving the impression that whoever had been there just stepped away. Abigail stood around, growing more uneasy with each passing second. After ten minutes, she gave up and went outside.

The wind was waiting for her. It ruffled her clothes, heaved her hair, and rattled the screen door to the dock house as she wrangled it shut. To her right was the road she'd come in on. On her left was the wide expanse of the Atlantic.

"Well, what now?"

Squinting, Abigail searched the horizon, only to discover there was no horizon line. The color of the water and the color of the sky blended into an unbroken block of deep blue as solid as a wall. She couldn't tell if it was a trick of the light or if her eyes were failing after the long drive. Panic began to pluck at her. She was utterly alone at Bourne's Crossing, disarmingly alone.

"Fourteen hours on the road and delirium has officially set in."

Then a dark dot emerged in the distance, a fleck of contrast against what could have been ocean or air. Abigail stared until she could sense her eyes dilating. Soon the outline of a boat became clear. It was the ferry.

Even at a distance, it was obvious the vessel had seen better days. Too many seasons at sea had weathered the paint and lightened the ship's logo, a cresting wave capped by the words *Chapel Isle Ferry,* to a faint shadow. The wide, squared-off craft had rows of benches that rimmed the railings and room for more than a dozen cars on deck, though presently there were none.

As soon as the ferry docked, a lanky kid in an oil-stained sweatshirt and plastic sunglasses jogged from the wheelhouse to the stern and looped the lead lines to one of the pilings.

"You comin' or not?" he shouted over the drone of the idling engine.

"Oh. Right. Sorry."

Abigail hastened to her Volvo and steered on deck. Moments later, the ferry growled to life and was off again. She wasn't sure whether to get out or sit tight.

"You don't have to stay in your vehicle, miss."

Startled, Abigail's hand flew to her chest. The kid in the sweatshirt was standing at her window.

"I didn't know if it was safe," she said, adjusting her collar to pretend she hadn't been frightened.

"Hell, I don't know if it's safe myself. But it is a long ride. Wouldn't want you going stir-crazy in there."

He spoke in a sluggish Southern drawl, each syllable lagging behind the other as if they were freight cars in a slow-moving train. Abigail always took note of accents, slang, colloquialisms. Verbal affects were proof, from her perspective, of the capacity of the English language, the fortitude. It was a phenomenon in and of itself. The abuse it endured was awe-inspiring. Words were shortened, lengthened, plundered, and bastardized, yet they went on, ever resilient. Words had a strong constitution she envied.

"Round trip?" he asked.

"One way."

The kid gave her a dubious glance. "That'll be fifteen-fifty."

Abigail handed over the money with vigor to convince him, as well as herself, that she knew what she was doing.

"Out of a hundred," he said, eyeing the large bill. He peeled her change from a stack of tens and singles, counting each aloud tediously. She guessed he was about twenty-five, less than ten years her junior. Though she couldn't see his eyes behind the plastic sunglasses, what Abigail could see was that his clothes needed washing and his hair needed cutting, like a child who'd been left to fend for himself for too long.

"So," he said, "you a doctor or a lawyer?"

The odd question caught her off guard. "A doctor. Technically. I'm a—"

"Figured as much. If it ain't summer, folks don't come to

Chapel Isle. Not unless they're doctors or lawyers. Doctors for taking care of people. Lawyers for taking care of those the doctors didn't take care of right."

"You're saying *nobody* visits in the fall or winter?"

"Yup." His response was resolute.

Although the serenity of the island's low season was part of its appeal, this kid had Abigail envisioning tumbleweeds rolling through the center of town.

"What sorta doctor are you?"

"I have a Ph.D., actually. I'm a lexicographer, not a—"

"Oh, X-ray stuff. Gotcha."

Before she could correct him, the kid shoved his hand through the window, saying, "I'm Denny. Denny Meloch. I run the ferry. Pleased to meet you."

Abigail introduced herself and shook his hand. "If you run the ferry, Denny, who's steering?"

"That'd be my dad," he answered sheepishly. "It's his rig. Won't let anybody forget it. Least of all me."

The boat was picking up speed, and the revving engine filled the awkward silence that followed his comment. With the current growing more conspicuous the faster they went, Abigail realized she hadn't removed her seat belt. Denny, however, was unfazed by the waves. He kept his stance wide, taking in every roll placidly.

"You have a lot of stuff in there." Denny was giving her Volvo the once-over.

"It appears that way, doesn't it?"

Bags, boxes, and luggage were pressed against the windows. The car held the last remaining possessions Abigail had in the world. While packing, she'd tried to imagine paring down an entire house to fit into the station wagon. Deciding what was worth keeping versus what wasn't would have been daunting. Except Abigail didn't have the luxury of choice. The fire had reduced her life to the lean mass she currently carried.

"You moving to the island for good?"

"How long is for good?" she asked, making light of his serious question.

Denny shrugged. "Either you're here to stay or you're here to leave. No two ways about it."

"What do you mean, 'here to leave'?"

"Tourists. They start pouring in when the weather gets sunny. Run for the hills once it turns. Don't get me wrong. We need 'em. Couldn't get by without 'em. Summer business is the only business we got besides fishing. That don't mean we have to like 'em."

"Denny," someone yelled, interrupting him.

In her side mirror, Abigail saw a stout man peering from the wheelhouse. The brim of his cap cast his face in shadow.

"Is that your father?"

"Yup. That's him." Denny's cheeks flushed. "As I said, you don't have to sit in your car."

With that, he scuttled off, his parting statement issued half as fact, half as a challenge. If Abigail stayed in her car, she wouldn't last on the island. If she got out, she might be different.

The ocean was becoming choppier, the waves more brazen. Abigail unhooked her seat belt and her stomach instantly tightened. Was it seasickness or fear? She opted to believe it was the former.

A burst of clammy air caught her on the chin when she opened her door. Droplets of water seeped through her clothes, prickling the flesh beneath. Maintaining her balance for the short walk from the station wagon to the railing took effort. It was as though her body was drunk but she wasn't. The ferry slogged heavily through the water, and by the sound of it, the engine was battling to make headway.

Abigail got to the side, then plunked down on a bench, happy to have it hold her. As gusts of wind whipped her hair into her mouth and eyes, she brushed aside the strands, only to have them flung back at her, an exercise in frustration. She wasn't a let-the-wind-comb-your-hair kind of woman, not figuratively or literally. The free and easy spirit didn't apply to Abigail. Few things in the world were free and not many were easy, including getting from the car to the bench. Yet she had. It wasn't much. It would have to be enough.

The rocking of the boat made her dizzy, so Abigail fixed her eyes downward on the bench where she sat. A flurry of names, dates, curses, and epithets were carved into the wood, a roster of who had come and gone, trapped under layers of shellac. Swarms of hearts in every size were etched around initials, each crowding the other. She traced the outline of some letters, feeling the deep indentations in the wood and letting her fingertip linger along the craggy curve of a heart.

The need to be remembered was an instinct. No one wanted to be forgotten, to slip away, to be lost from memory. That was why people scrawled words on everything from benches to turnpike overpasses to wet concrete sidewalks. The scars they left made them unforgettable. Sometimes, though, remembering could be worse than being forgotten. Abigail knew that well. Remembering left a different kind of scar.

◆ ◆ ◆

The afternoon sun was buried under a bale of dull clouds, night poised to push the day aside. Abigail had lost track of how long she'd been sitting on the bench in the wind. Her clothes were damp, her stomach ached, and the horizon line remained absent. She needed to get out of the elements. There was an enclosed seating area behind the wheelhouse. Using the railing to reclaim her balance, Abigail forged toward the door, doing her best to keep her footing.

More benches and a measly snack bar awaited inside. The snack bar was closed, the glass candy case empty, save for three boxes of saltwater taffy that slid from one end of the case to the other in tempo with the waves. On the walls were posters of yachts and schooners, each yellowed with age, as well as a cork bulletin board speckled with bits of paper pinned under staples from signs that had been pulled loose. A handful of flyers remained. Some advertised half-priced fishing trips for Labor Day weekend. Others pitched holiday bicycle rentals, fresh corn, and strawberries. Another read, *Dinghy for sale. Will take best offer.* Vestiges of the bygone summer, the month-old signs were already obsolete.

Next to the bulletin board was a large map of the Outer Banks, framed and bolted to the wall with a protective sheet of plastic over the top. The dull sheen of smudged fingerprints gave the map a hazy glow. Hovering beneath the surface of the plastic was a string of barrier islands that fringed the coast, each dotted with towns that had names like Nag's Head, Whalebone, Frisco, and Ocracoke. The name *Chapel Isle* stood apart among them, its tenor starched, ringing primly in the ear. The reference to religion made it less adventuresome in comparison to the rest. That suited Abigail fine.

Beyond Chapel Isle's eastern shore was a dashed outline, *Ship's Graveyard,* written inside. An inscription hung below. Abigail couldn't make it out. The plastic covering the map had been rubbed thin there, touched by so many hands that the words blurred. She wiped at the spot with her sleeve and picked at it with her nail. The plastic wouldn't clear.

"I was worried you fell overboard," Denny said, surprising Abigail again.

"I needed a break from that wind."

He cringed. "If you think this is windy, you might not want to stay on the island after all."

Abigail thought she'd passed the first test. She wasn't prepared for another.

"What does this say?" she asked, tapping the obscured inscription on the map.

"Says, *Not at rest, but at peace.* The men who died in the Ship's Graveyard, who went down with their ships, they never got a proper burial. Never got to be put to rest, so to speak. Means they're at peace because they died at sea. The place they loved."

The explanation sent Abigail sinking into her memory. She struggled to stay in the present. Denny was oblivious. His gaze had slid down her body to her hands. He was checking to see if she wore a wedding ring. It dawned on Abigail that he was trying to impress her, that he found her attractive. She automatically tucked her left hand behind her hip.

"That's, uh, how Chapel Isle got its name," he continued, clearing his throat. "Since there weren't bodies to bury, the families would go and stand on the beach dressed in their black clothes and have the funerals right there in the sand. Wouldn't be no coffins. A preacher would just say the prayers. More proper, I s'pose."

Abigail could tell that her strange demeanor was starting to make Denny uncomfortable. Since the fire, she would sometimes slip into a sort of fugue, rendering her the opposite of a ghost, a body momentarily devoid of soul. That unnerved people. She couldn't help it.

"Chop's kicking a bit. Isn't much further 'til home." Denny shifted on his heels self-consciously. "I should get back to work."

"Okay," Abigail said, eventually recovering. "I wouldn't want to keep you."

"Okay," he echoed, then turned to go.

"Denny?"

"Yeah?" He spun around eagerly.

"Thanks for telling me about the map."

He held in a smile. "It was nothing."

The door swung closed behind him, wafting the briny odor of the ocean through the room. The smell summoned Abigail's childhood memories of summer weekends spent with her family on the shores of Massachusetts—picnics at the beach, pails full of shells, the sticky feel of the salt water as it dried on her skin. The scent had always been synonymous with happiness. That was one of the reasons she'd come to Chapel Isle. To see if it still was.

◆　◆　◆

Abigail returned to her car, her stomach in knots. Denny hadn't been exaggerating. The ocean was noticeably rougher, with whitecaps dappling the surface. The pitch and yaw made her queasier.

She took refuge in the station wagon, rubbing her arms to get warm. She was about to start the motor to run the heater, except a sign on the side of the boat ordered her not to: *Engines off until ferry is docked.*

Breaking the rules wasn't Abigail's style. She was chilly enough to entertain the notion but didn't want to make trouble for Denny. Of course, rules, like definitions, could have exceptions. She'd spent the better part of her adulthood in pursuit of definitions. To understand the exception was to understand the meaning. As she sat shivering in her car, Abigail chose not to turn on the motor. The posted rule could have been inconsequential. The consequences of breaking it may not have been.

Heat or no heat, the seasickness had gotten to her. A cold sweat was slinking along her neck, and her mouth was bone-dry. Abigail hitched her gaze to the bottom of the steering wheel, blocking any movement from her vision. Having set out before daybreak that morning, the journey from Boston had been grueling. She half-expected to find grip marks in the wheel from her fingers. The goal of getting to Chapel Isle in a single day made the trip slightly more bearable. With expectation pecking away at her, Abigail wished she'd asked Denny what time they would arrive. She purposefully hadn't checked the horizon since leaving the dock. When at last she looked up from the steering wheel, a dim line was separating the ocean from the sky.

"Finally."

The band of darkness in the distance broadened, a lapse amid the breadth of blue. It wasn't the horizon line. It was Chapel Isle.

As the ferry drew closer, the contours of trees and the silhouettes of rooftops came into focus. Abigail's gut cinched. This was no longer seasickness. This was anticipation.

Without warning, the ferry plunged between two deep swells. Abigail clenched the steering wheel as the boat bucked. She considered how ridiculous she must look, white-knuckling the Volvo's wheel while it sat, stationary, on the ferry's deck. Though she was happy there was no one to see her, the relief twisted into a twinge. She was very much on her own.

Chapel Isle was close, less than a half mile away. However, the ocean was making it difficult to reach.

"Should I take this personally?"

Another wave sent the ferry lunging.

"I'll interpret that as a *yes*."

Cold and nauseous, she did the one thing that would calm her. She recited Latin, conjugating verbs from rote and enumerating each tense in a monotone chant.

"*Sum, esse, fui, futurus.*

"*Habeo, habere, habui, habitus.*"

The verbs were transformed into a soothing hum, a distraction. She had picked up the practice as a young girl, from her father. A prominent surgeon specializing in patients with lung cancer, he'd helmed early research into the link between smoking and lung disease. "Gray is rarely a good thing," he would say in reference to the color of a patient's lungs, a philosophy he applied to most matters. He was a pragmatic man, unflaggingly precise, and he categorized life in terms of what was a *good thing* or a *bad thing*. For her father, there was rarely any room in between.

When the world did dim to a shade of gray for some reason or other, her father would retreat to his study and retrieve his beloved Latin textbook from his school days. In spite of its age, the book remained in pristine condition. The binding was slightly broken, the spine no longer stiff, but there were no torn pages, no dog-ears, no pencil marks in the margins. As a child, Abigail would peek in the doorway while he pored over the pages of the tome as if it were a photo album. She longed to see what he saw.

Once she was old enough to read, Abigail's father invited her into his study, sat her on his lap, and allowed her to open the book.

"I want you to listen to the words before I teach you what they mean," he had said. "That will make them easier to learn, my sweet. Trust me."

So began her Latin lessons, her father reading root upon root upon root. The rhythmic flick of the turning pages mingled with the

Latin to form a melody that became the background music of her youth. As if hearing a fairy tale in a foreign language, Abigail intuited meaning beneath the words, and her love of language took hold there in her father's study. It was a love that carried on through the books that filled the boxes cramming her station wagon. The chassis rode low because of the weight. She found reassurance in how heavy a book could be. Even paperbacks had heft in the palm. The fact that letters printed on paper could amass such gravity was a marvel. It made words even mightier to Abigail.

The books in the boxes were from her parents' house, the stored surplus and castoffs of a once-substantial collection spanning a gamut of subjects from fiction to history, classics to the esoteric, first editions and signed copies, a private library she had spent years assembling. These books were the lone survivors of her collection. They were all Abigail had left.

blan•dish (blan´dish), *v.t.* **1.** to coax or influence by gentle flattery; cajole: *They blandished the guard into letting them through the gate.* —*v.i.* **2.** to use flattery or cajolery. [1350–1400; ME *blandisshen* < AF, MF *blandiss-*, long s. of *blandir* < L *blandīrī* to soothe, flatter. See BLAND, -ISH²] —**blan´dish•er**, *n.* —**bland´•dish•ing•ly**, *adv.*

◆   ◆   ◆

As the ferry neared Chapel Isle, the picturesque vista of the island was marred by a troubling sight. One of the dock's pilings had buckled, and a broken plank dangled precariously over the water. The dock appeared on the verge of collapse.

"That doesn't look good," Abigail declared.

Studying language for so long had taught her that initial impressions weren't necessarily dependable. The spelling of a word and its pronunciation could be astonishingly irreconcilable. That was why every entry in the dictionary had a phonetic guide. Abigail willed herself to believe the same rationale would hold true for Chapel Isle.

"This is it. End of the road," Denny announced, ambling toward her car. The ferry's engine whirred to a stop while he wound the lead lines around an intact piling, then slid a ramp out to bridge the gap to the dock.

"Denny, what happened?"

"To what?"

"To this dock."

"Oh, yeah. Hank Scokes ran into it."

"Ran into it?"

"With his fishing boat."

"On purpose?"

"Naw, old guy was drunk as a skunk."

"Is the structure secure enough to drive on?"

"Plenty o' people have."

"How reassuring," Abigail mumbled. "When did this little 'accident' occur?"

Denny had to give it some thought. "'Bout a month ago."

"And nobody's fixed it?"

"That's a seriously messed-up dock. It's going to take a lot of fixing to get it right again. Don't you fret, though. I'll keep an eye on ya. Where are you staying?" he inquired with a suggestive tilt of his head.

"The lighthouse. I'm actually the new caretaker," Abigail replied, braced for some type of advance.

Instead, Denny's expression faltered. He pursed his lips to prevent himself from saying what he wanted to say.

"It can't be that bad," she joked halfheartedly. "The place isn't operational anymore, so I can't get in too much trouble."

"No, it's not that. It's . . . um, never mind."

After the lengthy trip, Abigail didn't have the energy to prod Denny into opening up. Whatever he was holding back would have to wait.

"I'm supposed to go and see the realtor first," she told him. "Can you give me directions to her office?"

"Lottie Gilquist's who you need. Ain't hard to find her. All you gotta do is listen."

Forgoing any further explanation, Denny went to unhook the chain that barred the front of the ferry.

Confused, Abigail pulled the station wagon alongside him. "Let's say my hearing's not very keen; how exactly would I find her?"

"You go straight."

"Okay, straight. What's next?"

"Just straight."

"If I just go straight, I'm going to drive into the ocean on the other side of the island."

"You'll spot Lottie's place before that'd happen."

A whistle rang out from behind Abigail's car. Denny's father was hovering in the doorway to the wheelhouse. He folded his arms in silent command.

"Take the main road," Denny instructed. "You can't miss it." He started to trot away, then stopped himself. "Oops. Promised I'd see you get onto the island safe and sound."

Abigail was glad he remembered, because she hadn't forgotten. "Thanks," she said, easing her foot from the brake.

"Maybe I'll see you around?"

"I think you will."

Denny broke into a wide grin, which made Abigail smile too. However, her smile dissolved the instant she let the Volvo inch forward onto the dock. The wood whinnied and groaned under the wagon.

"It's fine," he said encouragingly. "Go ahead. Really. It's solid as a rock."

Despite the squawking planks, Abigail drove onward while Denny waved goodbye. She would have waved back but couldn't pry her fingers from the wheel.

As soon as the car coasted off the dock onto a gravel lane, Abigail exhaled, grateful for solid ground. A placard at the side of the road read: *Welcome to Chapel Isle.*

"Some welcome."

The island's dock house was closed tight, and a nearby soda stand had been boarded shut. *See You Next Summer* was spray-painted on the plywood. The tourist season was decidedly over. Chapel Isle had gone into hibernation. The solitude of seclusion was another reason Abigail had chosen to move here, one she was beginning to reconsider.

"Careful what you wish for."

Her father had been the first to plant the phrase in her mind, a cautionary quip that stuck with her because it proved true more often than she cared to concede. Like when Abigail was eight and begged her parents for a cat. She'd spent weeks pleading and pledging to be responsible, then ultimately wore them down. The day they brought her home a kitten, Abigail broke out in a case of hives that was so severe, her father had to bring her to the hospital.

"Sometimes what you want is the worst thing for you," he'd pronounced, as Abigail's mother slathered her in cortisone cream. "Sounds like the stuff of fortune cookies, except it's usually true."

Lesson learned. At least about having pets. With only a gravel lane to guide her and not a single person in sight, Abigail wondered if she'd ever really taken the moral to heart.

◆ ◆ ◆

The road from the dock fed inland. On either side were wide expanses of salt marsh, punctuated by tidal pools. The tall grass swayed in the breeze, underscoring the cloudy sky with swaths of blond that bled into green.

Abigail caught passing glimpses of the coast where paths to the beach had been trampled through the dunes. The scent of the ocean was heady, tipped with a salty tartness. When she lowered the rest of the windows to let the fragrance fill the car, the sudden rush of air sent her books and boxes flapping frantically.

"That's enough wind for today," she said, as she raised the windows and blew a wayward chunk of hair from her forehead.

In the distance, a beach shack hunkered at the edge of the asphalt. Abigail slowed for a better look. It was another food stand, the serving window padlocked.

"The town has got to be somewhere."

A mile later, the languorous marshland was overtaken by trees and a strand of shingled cabins. Each one was identical to its neighbor, like a row of paper dolls. There were no cars in the driveways, no lights, motion, or noise.

"Summer rentals," she stated, imagining that if she were to open one of the cabin doors, she would hear the ocean the way one does when putting an ear to an empty shell that has washed ashore.

Ahead was a bend in the road. Rounding it, Abigail found her reward: a postcard-perfect cobblestone town square. The bay and the boats huddled at the pier provided the backdrop. The square was lined with shops, most of which had nautical names and specialized in fishing or gifts. They alternated between bait and tackle or keepsakes and collectibles, the marine theme a constant. What they also had in common was that they were all closed.

Abigail trolled through the square, noting a bank, a café, and a post office interspersed between the stores. But no real estate agency. The bay was fast approaching.

"You're about to run out of island."

That's when something caught her eye. Hemmed in at the end of the strip of shops was a dainty cottage. The patch of grass in front teemed with throngs of plastic pink flamingos, clattering whirligigs, spinning pinwheels, and a gallery of garden ornaments. It was a staggering spectacle, a conflagration of color and movement, the epitome of flamboyance. Smack in the middle of the gaudy mob of lawn decorations stood a freestanding mailbox, which sported its own miniature flag and the stenciled slogan: *Controlled Chaos.*

Abigail gawked. "If ever there were a more appropriate oxymoron."

The awning over the cottage door read: *Gilquist Realty.*

"This should be interesting."

She parked her car, then maneuvered along the cottage's obstacle course of a walkway, clicking through the synonyms for *chaos* in her mind, another habit for tempering anxiety. The alternatives ranged from the mild, such as *disorder* or *confusion,* to the manic, *turmoil* and *anarchy.* On a sliding scale, the exterior of Gilquist Realty ranked somewhere around *obnoxiously unruly.* What Abigail discovered indoors was closer to *pandemonium.*

Every inch of available space in the front office was jammed from floor to ceiling with an array of knickknacks—figurines of mermaids, a fleet of ships in bottles, stuffed animals, novelty salt and pepper shakers, ashtrays adorned with clamshells. Objects overflowed from each corner and crevice, dripping from the walls, brimming from the windowsills, and dangling from the light fixtures by the dozens. Abigail blinked, absorbing the bedlam.

"Not for the faint of heart, huh?" said a plump woman wearing a pastel sweatshirt airbrushed with the image of a dolphin. She was sitting behind a desk. Abigail hadn't noticed her among the clutter.

"My husband calls it 'Tchotchke Heaven.' Where bric-a-brac goes to die." The woman let out an unmistakable cackle that clanged like a bell. This was what Denny must have been referring to.

"Lottie Gilquist?" Abigail asked.

"That's me."

The floating heart pendant Lottie wore jangled as she laughed. Its soft, distended shape mimicked her frame. She had sloped shoulders, round fleshy cheeks, and a pouf of hair combed high into a bun and dyed the color of corn silk, the same shade as the countless dolls in display stands around the room.

"And you must be . . ."

"Abigail Harker. I'm here about the—"

"Oh, yes, I've been waiting for you. Wondered if you'd catch the ferry or not. Doesn't run again until tomorrow, so it's lucky you made it."

The brochure didn't mention that, nor had Lottie when they spoke on the phone earlier that week. Abigail wasn't sure what to think.

"Let me get your paperwork, dear."

Lottie propped a pair of purple-rimmed half-glasses on her nose and motioned for Abigail to take a seat. The chair cushion was covered with iron-on decals of starfish.

"I just need your signature, Mrs. Harker, then I can take you to see the property. Betcha can't wait."

"You can call me Abigail," she said, hurrying to correct her.

Lottie's stare leapt to Abigail's left hand, as Denny's had, too fast for Abigail to hide her bare ring finger.

"Okeydokey, Abby. Sign here."

Abigail recoiled slightly. She didn't go by *Abby*. She didn't dislike it. Yet the nickname didn't feel right on her. The informality didn't fit. As far as she was concerned, *Abby* was a different name altogether. Peppy, familiar, and easygoing, it was totally incongruous with her.

Once Abigail had thoroughly read through the rental agreement, Lottie offered her a pen. "Isn't this the cutest?"

Attached to the end was a fuzzy head with googly eyes that jiggled as Abigail wrote her signature. Using it to sign a legal and binding document left her leery.

"Remind me who referred you again, Abby."

"It was . . ." A lump formed in her throat. "A friend."

"Good enough," Lottie chirped. "I'll get the keys and meet you out front. You can follow me in your car."

If Lottie noticed Abigail's hesitation, she didn't show it. Abigail only wished *she* hadn't shown it.

◆ ◆ ◆

Distance was a measurable quantity, be it in millimeters, feet, or miles. What Abigail sought was something measurable to put between her and the fire. Time was also a measurable quantity, one she had no control over. She couldn't make the minutes go by faster, let alone the months. What Abigail could do was move away from the place she wanted to push from her mind. That was precisely what she'd done.

"Almost there," Abigail told herself, stretching her sore limbs. She was painfully stiff from the long drive. Muscle had memory, too, and by now, her muscles wanted to forget as much as she did.

Lottie pulled up beside Abigail's station wagon in a mammoth Suburban and tooted her horn merrily. "I can't wait for you to see the lighthouse," she called from her window. "Isn't this great?"

"Yes, yes, it is," Abigail sputtered. "It's . . . great."

Great was definitely not the first adjective that came to mind. While it aptly described the scale and magnitude of the decision she'd made, as well as the potential repercussions, any positive connotations had yet to be seen.

Along with her remaining possessions, Abigail had unwittingly packed a series of assumptions, foremost being that the inhabitants of Chapel Isle would be a staid breed, solemn by nature. She pictured stern, weathered fishermen and soft-spoken women with soulful faces. What she got instead was Lottie, who was undoubtedly the perkiest person Abigail had ever met. Her surplus of cheer seemed to portend that nothing terrible could happen on Chapel Isle. It was another assumption, one that Abigail hoped would prove correct.

Lottie led her into a web of gravel roads that fanned out from the center of town and split into narrower lanes. The style of homes varied in character from plain clapboard Cape Cods to Victorians with wraparound porches and fanciful gingerbread molding. Each lane was more enticing than the next. Some were even fronted by tangled archways of wild grapevines that draped from the trees, creating lacy sets of gates. Abigail bobbed her head from side to side, trying to absorb every ounce of the island as it streamed past. In spite of herself, she surrendered to the excitement.

Ahead, Lottie's Suburban was jouncing over sandy ruts as they delved deeper into the southern end of Chapel Isle. Fifteen minutes had passed. Abigail was going to be much farther from town than she'd anticipated.

"Any minute now. Any minute and you'll be there."

At last, the scrub pine broke, revealing a meadow. Beyond stood the lighthouse, singular and stoic, slicing a wedge through the sky. Abigail felt her heart lift.

Built on a scallop of shoreline with a jagged jetty of blue-black boulders separating it from the sea, the whitewashed lighthouse exuded a humble majesty, as though the surroundings had been ground down by the weight of the world and it alone endured, holding its head high.

However, alarm began to set in as Abigail drew closer. The whitewash that looked crisp from afar was actually cracked and peeling. The outermost layer of paint hung on like a sheet of skin about to molt. Attached to the lighthouse was the caretaker's cottage, which was even more dilapidated. The basic two-story brick box slouched up against the lighthouse, holding on for dear life. Its roof sagged and some of the shutters had come unhinged. None of it matched the photograph Lottie had faxed her. Abigail chewed her bottom lip, trying to tamp down her rising anger.

"Lottie will be able to explain this. She has to."

The Suburban stopped at the front door to the caretaker's house, then Lottie slid from the driver's seat to the running board into the overgrown yard. The vehicle dwarfed her and the high grass cut her off at the knees. Abigail might have seen the humor if she wasn't growing more furious by the second. She jumped out of her car, prepared to lay into Lottie for lying about the condition of the property. But Lottie got in the first word.

"I realize the place isn't how I described it, dear."

"No, not even remotely," Abigail agreed, barely concealing her irritation.

"I swear it's exactly what you're looking for, though," she trilled. "Quiet. Peaceful. You'll have the world to yourself here."

The sincerity in Lottie's eyes made Abigail soften slightly. She wanted to believe her. She also wanted to believe that the long journey here wasn't in vain and that this wasn't an enormous mistake.

"Okay. Let's go inside."

Together, they mounted the drooping front steps. Lottie inserted a key into the door, though it refused to open, as if warding visitors away.

"It'll work," Lottie said, struggling. "Never fear."

There was that word. *Never.* Annoyance bubbled in Abigail's brain as she watched Lottie fight with the knob until the lock finally relented.

"Allow me to show you around," Lottie panted.

As the door swung in, the stench hit Abigail like a slap. The house was permeated with the odor of rotting wood along with the musky scent of mildew.

"Lottie."

"Bear with me, dear. We'll open some windows and it'll be right as rain."

When she rolled up the shades, the waning sunlight illuminated a grim scene.

What had appealed to Abigail was that the caretaker's house came furnished. Much to her dismay, the décor left a lot to be desired. The front door opened into a main living and dining area. However, the terms *living* and *dining* could be only loosely applied. The couch was shabby and threadbare. The curtains were sallow with age. An assemblage of mismatched chairs, a pockmarked table, two moth-eaten rag rugs, and a soot-covered fireplace rounded out the room's furnishings.

"Lottie," Abigail repeated.

Pretending to be busy, the impish woman fussed with a window that wouldn't budge. She gave up, saying, "Let's take the tour, shall we?"

"Fine. Let's do that." Abigail was fuming.

Lottie motioned her over to the far side of the house and through a doorway. "Here we have a precious little kitchen."

A stunted alcove passed for that by virtue of having a sink and some appliances. The massive stove and one-door refrigerator were relics. As the house settled, the cupboards had shifted away from one another, giving them the look of gapped teeth. Warped wainscoting covered the lower part of the walls, while outdated floral wallpaper in white and cornflower blue wilted from the top.

"Needs a woman's touch to highlight the period details and—"

"Lottie."

"Don't worry, Abby. Everything works. The electricity is on. The phone's connected. Water's running. What more do you need?" She turned the faucet, and brown bilge splattered from the spigot before it ran clean.

Abigail glued her hands to her hips in a show of protest.

Lottie quickly skirted around her. "Let's move on to the second floor."

Trudging up the tight staircase behind Lottie, Abigail was eye to eye with her substantial rump. Each step squealed underfoot, and the handrail shuddered unsteadily. The staircase dead-ended onto a landing.

"To the left we have the master suite."

She showed Abigail into an ample room painted a chalky, medicinal green. Raising the blinds exposed a lumpy bed with a frayed quilt, which was backed by a pine headboard. A brass lamp sat on a dusty nightstand beside a modest dresser. A rocking chair cowered in the corner. The bedroom was as spartan as a monk's cell.

"I bet you could make this real cozy. Some throw pillows would do the trick."

"I think it's going to take more than throw pillows."

"Have a gander at the other bedroom," Lottie suggested, scooting away before Abigail could say more.

The next space wasn't much larger than a walk-in closet, and because the ceiling was low due to the pitch of the roof, Abigail had to duck as she went through the door. A diminutive writing desk, a stumpy bookshelf, and a twin-sized cot on a metal frame were what passed for furnishings.

"This was the watch room, where the lighthouse keeper would sit lookout for ships during storms. It was always a stag light, but I put a bed in here so the house would sleep more people."

"A stag light?"

"Means a lighthouse with no family living in it."

Although Lottie could not have known, her comment made Abigail's heart ache. The implication was wrenching.

"It'd make a perfect study for you, Abby. Or a guest room. You can count on having a million visitors soon as your family and friends hear you live in a lighthouse."

"I doubt it," Abigail said faintly. There would be no visitors, no need for a guest room.

"Then a study for sure. See, there's a desk. Ready and waiting."

The writing desk was elementary-school-sized. Abigail wasn't convinced she could get her knees in it. "It's sort of . . . small."

"That's because folks were much shorter in the olden days. We're giants compared to past generations."

It was an ironic comment, considering the size of the source. Abigail might have expressed as much if she wasn't on the verge of strangling the petite woman before her.

"It's true," Lottie exclaimed. "I saw a story about it on the news. They predicted that at the current growth rate we'll be gargantuan in fifty years. Tall as basketball players." Lottie was wide-eyed in amazement, and again she had managed to divert Abigail's ire.

"Last but not least, we can't forget the *pièce de résistance*," Lottie said, her lolling drawl flattening the French. "Wait 'til you get a load of this."

Displaying her best game show hostess wrist flick, Lottie presented the bathroom. By comparison, the study was spacious. The antiquated toilet was missing its lid, the fixtures on the porcelain basin were encased in rust, and paint was sloughing off the underbelly of the claw-foot tub in scabby sheets.

"Isn't the bathtub marvelous? How's this for authentic character?"

The only authentic aspect of the bathroom was that it was authentically awful. The mirror above the sink hung crookedly from a nail. The grout between the floor tiles was dark with dirt.

"The whole house really oozes charm, doesn't it?"

Abigail tried the faucet. The pipes moaned, then more brown sludge dribbled from the spout.

"It oozes something, all right."

Ignoring the remark, Lottie clapped her hands ceremoniously. "Now that you've had a gander at the place, let's get to business."

"Business?"

"The lighthouse, my dear. The lighthouse."

co•na•tus (kō nā´təs), *n., pl.* **-tus. 1.** an effort or striving. **2.** a force or tendency simulating a human effort. **3.** (in the philosophy of Spinoza) the force in every animate creature toward the preservation of its existence. [1655–65; < L: exertion, equiv. to *cōnā(rī)* to attempt + *-tus* suffix of v. action]

◆   ◆   ◆

Abigail had assumed the door next to the staircase was a closet. It wasn't.

"This is the entry into the lighthouse," Lottie explained. She opened the door, letting the last rays of afternoon sunlight pour into the living room from above. "Neat, huh?"

"Neat, indeed."

Abigail's batting average on assumptions was low and getting lower. In general, she tried to steer clear of them, as well as similar nouns. *Presumptions, conjecture, speculations*—they were sophisticated terms tantamount to guessing. To *hypothesize* had a scholarly air, to *postulate,* a scientific slant. They all meant the same. The subtleties of connotation were what differentiated them. *Guessing* sounded broad, risky, unreliable. Even an educated guess could be a shot in the dark. Abigail preferred to *deduce* or *infer.* Neither of which she'd been doing with any skill of late. So far she'd made scores of suppositions about the island and the lighthouse, most of which were wrong.

"I'd take you up," Lottie said, "but this darn sciatica won't let me." She rubbed her leg for effect.

Curious, Abigail poked her head through the doorway. A wrought-iron spiral staircase wound around the interior of the lighthouse tower, making for a dizzying view from the bottom, to say nothing of what the view must be from the top. The white-washed walls were checkered in a dazzling pattern of shadows cast by the stairs, creating a black-and-white kaleidoscope. Abigail was spellbound. While the rest of the house was an incontestable dump, the lighthouse was extraordinary.

"I can go later," she said casually. Still irked at Lottie for lying about the state of the property, she didn't want to let her renewed enthusiasm slip. Abigail had negotiated a discount on the rental rate after Lottie informed her there would be maintenance duties accompanying occupancy of the caretaker's cottage. Even with the reduction, Abigail thought Lottie should be paying *her* to live here.

"As I mentioned when we first spoke on the phone, the light-house is no longer operational," Lottie began. "Nonetheless, that doesn't diminish its beauty or significance." This was a pat introduction to the rehearsed speech that followed.

"The Chapel Isle Lighthouse was built in 1893. It took more than nineteen months to complete. Our magnificent spiral staircase has one hundred and two steps to the turret. We've got original Fresnel glass. Top of the line. Made specifically for lighthouses to ensure they'd have the clearest, longest beams. We're the twenty-third-oldest standing lighthouse in the country, and the number of vessels guided in safely while the beacon was in service is estimated in the thousands. The Chapel Isle Lighthouse is a bona fide piece of Americana."

Lottie folded her arms to signal she was finished with her spiel. Whether she was impressed with the lighthouse's history or with herself for remembering it was difficult to discern.

"Since you'll be acting as caretaker, you're going to be responsible for the working features of the lighthouse."

"A moment ago you said there were no working features."

"There aren't, exactly. But we have to keep up appearances, don't we?"

Abigail threw a glance at the living room's battered furniture.

"*Some* appearances. This lighthouse is a source of pride for locals; therefore, it's important to continue the traditions."

Lottie had her there. Abigail certainly didn't want to offend anybody. "What sorts of traditions?"

"I'm happy you asked." She unlocked a second door, which was situated under the staircase, but didn't open it. "You'll have to keep your eye on the water heater. It can be a touch finicky. 'Specially come winter."

If the water heater was a principal part of these alleged traditions, Abigail couldn't fathom what the others might be.

"What about the furnace?"

"What furnace?"

"There's no furnace? How do you heat the house?"

"The old-fashioned way." Lottie nodded at the fireplace, with its smoke-stained surround. Ash was heaped under the log rack.

The possibility that fire might be her sole means of heat hadn't occurred to Abigail when she agreed to rent the cottage. Fear began to roil beneath her ribs.

"I should also mention there's an old cistern in the basement built for underground water storage, what with the flooding we get. Oh, and you'll have to remember to check the generator, make sure it's running right. If the power goes out on the island, yours will be first to get cut."

Lottie prattled on about odds and ends related to the lighthouse and cottage, everything from how to open the chimney flue to how to prevent the pipes from freezing. The measures were as woeful as the events they intended to preclude. As the catalog of responsibilities mounted, Abigail was convoluting the do's with the don't's.

"Let me stop you, Lottie. Can we start with the basics? For example, where's the breaker box?"

"In the basement, dear."

"Then we should probably have a look around. Finish the tour."

"I . . . I . . . I can't go down there." Lottie was unconsciously backing away from the basement door. "I mean, my sciatica, it won't let me."

"I'll go. Just tell me where to find the breaker box."

"Now?"

"Why not?"

"Because we have other things to do. Tons of things. Tons. We have to go see the . . . the . . ." She scrabbled for an answer. "The shed."

"The shed?"

"Garden hoses. Rakes. Pruning shears. These are pertinent details."

Whatever had come over Lottie caused her face to turn crimson red. Abigail was willing to follow her anywhere if it would calm her. She gestured for Lottie to lead on, saying, "Let's see this shed."

"Excellent. This way, please." Lottie patted her heart, feigning she was fixing her pendant. Abigail noticed because it was similar to what she herself had done when Denny accidentally frightened her on the ferry.

"Are you all right, Lottie? You seem spooked."

"I'm fine, dear," she insisted, rushing for the door. "Really, I'm fine."

◆　◆　◆

Outside, birds heralded the setting sun while the crickets broadcast the temperature, quieting as the air cooled. Though Chapel Isle was on the same seaboard as Boston, the same continent, the same hemisphere, what made the island feel a world apart was the weather or, more specifically, Abigail's awareness of it. The wind currents were evident in how the seagulls wheeled in the sky and in the changing tides of the high grass she and Lottie were slogging through as they wended around the lighthouse.

"You must have noticed there's no TV. The house has an antenna, though. You can call the cable company on the mainland to hook everything up. You brought a television set, right?" Lottie asked, the grass shushing her with each step.

"No, I didn't."

Abigail's life had been on mute for months, the picture and resolution grainy. The volume was finally returning, and whatever she tuned in to was, at last, coming in loud and clear, so she didn't want a television.

Aghast, Lottie halted. "My word, Abby. Are you crazy?"

"That might be debatable."

"I'd absolutely perish without my soaps. I thank the Lord every day for giving us TV. What about a computer? You bring one of those?"

"Nope."

Her laptop had fallen victim to the fire too. Abigail appreciated her computer as a tool, but she could live without the Internet, email, even a cell phone, as long as she had a land line. There was a lot she could live without. There was much more she would have to learn to live without.

"I don't care for computers much myself," Lottie remarked. "I can play solitaire on the one my husband bought. That's about it. To me, it's a big paperweight. By the by, that's the fuel house over there." She pointed to a lean-to structure hunched at the base of the lighthouse. "That was where they stored the kerosene to run the lamp for the light. It's empty, so you don't have to worry about that."

One less thing on a growing list of hundreds, Abigail mused.

"My, my, my, Abby. What are you gonna do here by yourself without a TV or a computer?"

"I have my books."

"Hope you brought a lot, because you're going to need a whole mess of 'em. Me, I could read a romance novel a day. I go through them like Kleenex. You ever read those kinds? The racy stories about damsels in distress, hunky men with bulging biceps. Mercy me, they get my blood to swimming. I'll have to lend you some."

Abigail had no interest in Lottie's romance novels whatsoever. She kept her reply polite. "I wouldn't want to trouble you."

"It's not a bother. Not the slightest." Lottie had gone from a shaky wreck to her spunky self in a minute flat. "Here we are. This is the shed."

Hand-built with wood planks and large rocks from the shoreline for the foundation, it had the feel of an oversize safe. Lottie unlatched the padlock. "There's the firewood. And those are the kerosene lanterns. They're a must. We have shovels, buckets, a lawn mower . . ."

While Lottie itemized the shed's contents, the enormity of Abigail's decision hit her squarely in the chest. She was officially the caretaker of a lighthouse. Whatever needed doing, she would have to do. She'd romanticized the lifestyle, coloring it up with minor chores such as cleaning the glass on the top of the tower and pulling the occasional weed. The dingy little shed filled with dirt-crusted tools and aged containers of ant spray was a hint of how much Abigail had underestimated what the job of caring for a lighthouse—make that a run-down lighthouse—would entail.

"Are you getting this, Abby?"

"Every word."

She hadn't heard a syllable Lottie said.

"Merle Braithwaite over at the hardware store can help you with any other questions you might have."

"Was he the last caretaker?"

"Merle? Heavens, no. He's an islander. A native. Been looking after the place since the last caretaker left."

"When was that?"

"Dear me, I can't quite recall."

Abigail had no doubt that was a lie. She'd lost count of how many Lottie had already told.

"Takes a rare soul to care for a landmark such as this."

If "rare soul" was a euphemism for idiot, Abigail thought, then that was the first honest thing to come from Lottie's mouth since they'd met.

"I should be getting back to the office, leave you to your unpacking."

"Yeah. Sure. Okay." Abigail trailed her to the front yard in a daze.

Lottie hoisted herself into the Suburban and tossed Abigail a set of keys for the house. "Almost forgot these."

The key ring dropped heavily into Abigail's hand. There were dozens more than she could account for.

"Wait. None of them is marked."

"Whoopsies. Where is my head? I've had them forever, so I remember which is which. What I'll do is make you a cheat sheet and get you some of those round rubber doohickeys to put on 'em. I adore those. They're a miracle of science, they are," Lottie said, starting the engine. "Remember, Abby, call me if you need anything. Or talk to Merle. He knows this place inside and out."

With a parting toot of her car horn, she drove off, abandoning Abigail in the overgrown grass. She stood in the yard, alternating her gaze between the lighthouse looming above and the mass of unidentified keys in her palm. Abigail suddenly realized that since arriving on Chapel Isle, everything about her identity had changed. She'd gone from being a respected lexicographer to being the caretaker of a ramshackle lighthouse, from a suburbanite to a resident an island that was miles from nowhere. She'd been transformed from Abigail to *Abby,* a person with whom she was wholly unfamiliar, a stranger.

"Careful what you wish for."

◆　◆　◆

Dusk drifted down the skyline, enveloping the coast in pale gray, while Abigail doggedly unpacked her car. The air steadily grew colder, and there on the bluff, the wind was unremitting. She made trip after trip back and forth from the station wagon to the house.

Every time Abigail thought she was through, she would find more books hidden beneath the seats or tucked into crevices between the cushions. Once the car was empty, she thankfully went indoors.

The house was as dark as it was chilly. She flipped on the lights, and the brass chandelier in the center of the room flickered, brightening reluctantly. With her teeth starting to chatter, Abigail knew what she had to do. She had to light a fire.

"You can do this. You have to do this. Or you'll freeze."

She studied the fireplace intently, only to realize what was missing.

"No wood, no fire."

Abigail trekked to the shed, the wind hounding her along the way. She sorted through countless keys, cursing Lottie for relatching the padlock in the first place. The eighth attempt was the winner.

"This is a giant splinter waiting to happen," she declared, loading into her arms as much firewood as she could carry. Logs piled to her chin, Abigail slammed the shed door. Locking it with limited mobility was a feat. It took four tries.

The log rack grunted when she lumped the wood into the fireplace.

"You're not the only one complaining. Believe me."

Squaring off with the hearth, hands at her side gunslinger-style, Abigail said, "What's next? Matches."

A search of the kitchen drawers was fruitless. Most were stuck. Of those she was able to jimmy open, one held a dull set of silverware, another a tarnished eggbeater. The third was full of crumbs.

"Not too promising."

The upper cupboards were her last hope. Mismatched plates and bowls were stacked haphazardly behind the first set of doors. The next held a motley ensemble of mugs and glasses. There was one cabinet left. From underneath a mound of dinged pots and pans protruded a box of long wooden matches. Abigail shook the box and heard a rattle of salvation.

"You've got matches. You've got wood. You can do this."

Her hands shook as she opened the chimney flue and removed a match from the box. Right as she was about to strike it, Abigail stopped herself.

"Kindling."

She needed paper or newsprint, neither of which she had. The idea of ripping a page from one of her books darted through her mind. It was swiftly rejected. Scouring the kitchen cabinets and drawers again would be futile. As Abigail was eyeing the living room curtains as prospects, it came to her. She ferreted through her purse for the Chapel Isle tourist brochure Lottie had sent her.

"You're here. What do you need the brochure for?"

Kneeling in front of the fireplace, she pinched the match between her fingertips, but could not strike it. She simply couldn't do it. Defeated, she tossed the brochure aside, curled up on the couch, and shivered. Every ounce of her was cold, yet she was incapable of lighting the fire.

Abigail had thought she was dreaming that night when she opened her eyes and saw her own home burning to the ground. Support beams buckled and brayed. Windows bellowed as they blew out, exhaling the stench of scorched metal and chemical fumes. The roof roared as it tore from its moorings. The walls crumbled in a crescendo of screams. She had seen and heard and smelled it all as she lay in the street, barely conscious, muzzled by the smoke that had burned her throat, unable to tell the firemen that her husband and their four-year-old son, Justin, were still inside. As her house collapsed before her, the air filled with a swirling storm of burning cinders, a sea of stars cascading through the clouds of smoke as if the heavens had descended to earth for a single night. Neither her husband nor her child could have survived. There were no words Abigail could think of, no words she would have spoken, even if she could have.

She awoke in the hospital to the faces of her parents, her brother, and two policemen. Her father described her injuries, gave her the prognosis. Her windpipe was damaged, but in time she would be able to speak again. Her mother begged her not to try to talk. Her brother urged her to listen to the officers, who explained that the neighbor who called 911 had seen her husband, Paul, carry her out of the house, unconscious, her body limp. He'd laid her gently on the grass, then run back inside to get their son.

Abigail understood why Paul had saved her first. He was a mathematician and had been true to form. Justin weighed about thirty pounds. Abigail was four times as heavy. It was an easy equation. He'd decided to use what strength he had to bring her to safety first, then would go back for their son. He couldn't have calculated that the house would cave in.

The fire department made every attempt to rescue them; the officers assured Abigail of that. The inferno was too ferocious. It took fire trucks from three towns to quell it.

There was only one question Abigail had for the policemen, though the medication the doctors had her on made it slippery, almost too slick to get a grip on. The mix of anguish and potent sedatives was mentally obliterating. Laboring to stay conscious, she motioned for a notepad.

She wrote the word: *How?*

The officers traded glances with her father. Abigail felt her family bracing for her reaction. The source of the fire was a gas leak from the new oven that had recently been installed. A poorly fitted pipe allowed a stream of gas to bleed in between the walls, filling the shell of the house. Then something sparked the gas. The fire department couldn't pinpoint the exact cause. A power surge. A defective wire. Even the flipping of a faulty light switch would have been enough to ignite the gas that had leached into the structure. Despite the drugs, Abigail could comprehend what the officers were telling her, and instantly she knew.

She and Paul had purchased the oven a week earlier. They'd spent hours looking at a multitude of ranges, comparing features and prices. The oven Abigail was leaning toward was expensive, so she'd been open to other models. Paul wouldn't hear of it.

"Get the oven you want," he had said, taking her hand. "You deserve it" were his exact words. "Forget about the money. Think about that first batch of cinnamon sugar cookies. I can practically smell them."

Cinnamon sugar cookies were her son's favorite, so the morning the oven was delivered, Abigail went and bought the ingredients. She'd planned on baking them the following day. She wouldn't get the chance.

For a month, Abigail remained in the hospital. Her family and friends visited daily. Their company did little to console her. The drugs kept her too drowsy to do much other than nod if someone addressed her. Her injuries were slower to heal than the doctors had predicted. During the fire, Abigail had breathed in a combination of burning hot gas and smoke, scalding her lungs and scorching her throat. The mundane matter of breathing became a torture; swallowing, a misery. Abigail could feel the weight of air passing through her nostrils, making its journey through her chest. Although the medication made her thoughts gluey, she was grateful not to have to endure the brunt of the pain. Her grief, however, was an agony unto itself. It had degrees no thermometer could measure. The irony was that she had been burned on the inside of her body. The flames had spared her skin and burrowed deep inside her, leaving scorch marks that wouldn't heal.

The fire charred everything Abigail cherished, branding both her past and her future. The lawsuit her brother, an attorney, filed for her against the company that installed the stove would take months to settle, maybe years. Meanwhile, the money from Paul's life insurance policy was cold comfort. Though it meant she wouldn't have to work for some time, Abigail didn't care, because she loved her job. She was the lead lexicographical consultant for a company that produced electronic dictionaries for foreign markets, a plum position. But she no longer had the drive to work nor the strength to concentrate for very long. Whenever she tried to read, the words would scramble on the page. Snippets of old conversations with Paul would flare in her mind or, out of nowhere, she would have the sensation of running her hand through Justin's hair. He'd had cherubic curls that sagged into his eyes if allowed to grow too long. For an instant, she would sense the hair between her fingers, then the feeling would vanish. That was what was left of her family—memories that would blacken around the edges like burning paper and turn to ash.

◆ ◆ ◆

Darkness masked the view of the ocean from the cottage's windows. Abigail blew on her hands to warm them, then brushed a stray hair from her cheek, only to discover she'd been crying. She hadn't noticed.

Her watch claimed it was eight o'clock. It seemed much later. Abigail hadn't eaten in hours. An apple left over from the car trip was all she had in the way of food.

"It's that or the crumbs from the kitchen drawers."

Dinner in one hand and a duffel bag in the other, Abigail trundled up the staircase, carrying her luggage to the bedroom. Two steps from the top, the bag's handle caught on the railing, wedging her in the stairwell. She tugged and tugged, to no avail.

"Locked doors, stuck drawers, a scary fireplace, and now you want to give me a hard time?"

Abigail clenched the apple in her teeth to free up her other hand and gave the duffel a decisive yank. The strap ripped away from the railing, but the force of the bag coming back at her sent the piece of fruit popping from her mouth. She watched helplessly as it bounced down the filthy stairs. The apple spun to a stop at the front door.

"So much for supper."

Too tired to care, Abigail tossed the duffel bag onto the bed, sending a disheartening cloud of dust into the air.

"Ditto for a good night's sleep."

After stripping the bed, she replaced the unwashed quilt and sheets with the set of towels she'd brought, laying them in a patch-work pattern while saving some to use for blankets. She was changing into her pajamas when it became readily apparent the towels wouldn't be enough to keep her warm. The house was frigid. Abigail piled on another shirt and a sweater as well as a pair of sweatpants.

"I don't see how you're going to brush your teeth. You can't even move your arms with this many clothes on."

The same sludge that had run from the taps earlier that afternoon coughed from the faucet, spewing bilge into the basin. Abigail left the water running until she coaxed a clean flow from the pipes. Her reflection was framed in the lopsided mirror over the sink. She barely recognized herself. The extra clothing doubled her size, and her hair was wild from the wind, her eyes bloodshot, and her face puffy from crying.

Was this *Abby*?

If her full name stood for the person she'd been before the fire, what remained to be defined was who she would be now.

She shuffled to the bedroom, pining for sleep and rubbing her eyes, then remembered she had to remove her contact lenses. When she went back to the bathroom, the light was off. Abigail didn't recollect flipping the switch. Anxiously, she tested it, waiting for the smell of smoke or the *whoosh* of flames. The bulb dimmed and lit, the switch clicking. Convinced nothing was going to happen, Abigail shut off the light.

"You forgot your contacts. Again."

She turned around. The bathroom light was on.

"It's a short. A short in the wiring. This is an old house. It's just a short."

Abigail hastily took out her contacts and put on her glasses. After turning off the light switch, she held it down. The bulb dimmed, leaving her in total darkness. Crawling into bed, she nestled her head on the T-shirt she'd covered the pillow in, wrapped the towels around her, and trembled.

The wind was blowing stridently outside. While the brick house was impervious, the windows weren't. Each gust set the glass to quivering in the casements, a noise akin to bursts of static on a radio, random and aggravating.

"So much for peace and quiet."

dree (drē), *adj., v.,* **dreed, dree•ing.** *Scot. and North Eng.*
—*adj.* **1.** tedious; dreary. —*v.t.* **2.** to suffer; endure. Also,
dreegh (drēкн), **dreigh, driech, driegh.** [bef. 1000; ME;
OE *drēogan* to endure; c. Goth *driugan* to serve (in arms)]

❖   ❖   ❖

Abigail awoke to the sensation of warmth on her face. She bolted up in
bed and sniffed the air, seeking the source of the heat. A few heart-
pounding seconds later, she realized it was the dawn light from the
window that had roused her.

"Get a grip, *Abby.*"

During the night, the towels she'd improvised into blankets became tangled, and she had to unlace them from her arms and legs.
Since the fire, Abigail slept fitfully. She tossed and turned and
writhed, twisting her bedding into knots. Often she woke to find
wrinkles pressed into her skin, evidence of her late-night wrestling.
Rarely did she remember what she'd dreamed. The marks on her
body were battle scars from a war she'd waged in her sleep, so she
was thankful not to recall the fight.

The floor was icy underfoot, piercing right through her socks.
Abigail slipped her shoes on. The bedsprings whined when she
stood.

"My feelings exactly."

Her entire body cried out with soreness, and her eyes were dry
from sleeping on the dusty bed. There were eyedrops in her toiletry

bag. As soon as she opened the bedroom door, she could see that the bathroom light was on again.

"It's definitely a short," she insisted. "What you have to do is go see Lottie and tell her this is unacceptable. You can't have lights popping on and off in the middle of the night. She needs to send an electrician here immediately. And a cleaning crew."

Aside from the light, the bathroom was as Abigail had left it. Her toothbrush was on the edge of the sink, next to a travel-sized tube of toothpaste. Her contacts case rested on top of the toilet tank. Once she had her contacts in, she reinspected the switch. Nothing appeared amiss. Abigail snapped off the light.

Halfway down the hall, she turned back and flipped it on again.

"This way there won't be any more surprises."

Downstairs, Abigail found the brochure and the box of matches by the fireplace, evidence of her failure. Whenever she exhaled, she could see her breath. Starting a fire would have been smart. She wasn't up for it.

Habit prompted her to go to the kitchen and make herself a cup of tea.

"Except you don't have any tea. You may not have a teapot either."

A search of the cabinets yielded a scuffed kettle bearing a dented belly.

"One out of two."

Abigail wandered into the living room and checked her watch. It was a little before six a.m. She hadn't been awake this early in ages, not since Justin was an infant. She would stir at the sound of his soft, insistent crying and pad into his room, the carpet muffling her footsteps, then scoop Justin into her arms, and his crying would cease. It was gratifying that her touch could quiet him, that it had so much power. She smiled, then trembled from the cold, shaking off the memory. Abigail rubbed her arms, wondering what to do.

"The lighthouse."

Why Lottie kept the door locked was a mystery as well as a redundancy, given that the front door was as secure as a vault and practically impossible to open even with the appropriate key. Abigail didn't get it, which was for the best. Grasping Lottie's logic would have meant she'd relinquished her own.

A few steps up the spiral staircase, the iron risers began to growl ominously. Abigail froze, afraid the stairs might not hold. To assess their strength, she shook the railing and jumped on the lower landings. The wrought iron held fast, so she cautiously began to climb. Halfway to the top, Abigail made the mistake of glancing over the handrail. The staircase snaked around the walls vertiginously, bottoming onto a concrete slab.

"Note to self: Don't look down."

The tower acted as a giant megaphone, amplifying her words into an echo that swirled through the lighthouse like a coin in a drain. Abigail couldn't resist trying it again.

"Oh, say, can you see," she sang.

The bar of the song ricocheted off the walls, vibrating impressively.

"Watch out, Celine Dion."

For as much as Abigail had been talking to herself, this was the first time her voice wasn't being filtered through her own ears. The echo didn't match what she was accustomed to hearing. There was a gap between how she thought she sounded and how she *really* sounded. That was why Abigail always made Paul leave the message on their voice mail.

His voice wasn't especially deep or distinctive, yet there was a dignified quality to his speech. Each word was enunciated to perfection, which was what Abigail first noticed about him when they'd met in graduate school. They were in the library and she'd taken a seat at the same study table. When the girls at the next table began to talk too loudly, Paul noticed it was bothering Abigail.

"Could you lower your voices, please?" he asked.

His intonation said volumes. The girls promptly stopped, then Paul flashed Abigail a glance. She smiled to thank him and he smiled back. Though that wasn't what hooked her. It was his voice as well as those six short words he'd spoken.

Abigail returned to the library every day for a week to see if he'd be there. He was, sitting at the same table, in the same spot. Neither had enough nerve to approach the other, until one rainy evening when Abigail bumped into him in the vestibule of the library and he struck up a conversation. She was so enthralled by the purposeful manner with which he talked that she couldn't absorb a sentence he was saying. Meaning peeled apart from the nouns and verbs, stripping them to a chain of syllables, a pure resonance. Paul's voice was like a snake charmer's pipe, enchanting beyond reason. Abigail could have fallen for him with her eyes closed.

They began seeing each other, then continued to date as Abigail completed her linguistics thesis and Paul finished his doctorate in applied mathematics. Initially, the subject seemed dry and impenetrable to her. To hear Paul discuss it, she would have sworn he was describing a piece of art. His passion for numbers was rivaled by Abigail's passion for words, his exuberance infectious. He would transform as he sketched a theorem for her, growing more animated with each sign he scribbled onto napkins or place mats or newspapers, whatever was handy. Abigail had been captivated by his descriptions of math and by his unparalleled respect for it. If he could love numbers with such ardor, she couldn't imagine how it would be to have him love her.

After they'd earned their respective degrees, they moved into a three-room apartment together. They were both low on the totem poles at their new jobs, scrimping on food and essentials to get by. Abigail had been employed by an online research company. Paul worked at a think tank. Since their positions' potential outweighed the starting pay, they were willing to make do. Plus, Abigail's father slipped her cash when she would let him. He was so proud that she'd chosen to pursue a career in lexicography, he would tell people it was the equivalent of having the eldest son in a Catholic family enter the seminary. Flattered, Abigail made it clear to her father that she wanted to make it on her own. He acquiesced by sending smaller checks less frequently. She didn't mind going without as long as she had Paul.

One night, as they walked to their favorite Chinese take-out restaurant to order the cheapest entrées on the menu, Paul pulled Abigail aside.

"I've got an idea. I think we should rob the place, take the money, then run off to Las Vegas and get married."

Abigail knew he was kidding, but he wouldn't drop it. Paul dragged her into the tiny shop and dug a pointed hand into his pocket, pretending to conceal a weapon. "Follow my lead."

"Paul," Abigail protested.

When she wrestled his hand from his coat pocket, he produced a velvet ring box. Paul got on one knee and opened the box, revealing a delicate engagement ring.

"I could never love anyone more than I love you, Abigail. Never. Will you marry me?"

The cooks and clerks looked on expectantly. Abigail was speechless. She wiped her eyes and managed to get out a single word: *yes.*

Paul was everything she wasn't—spirited, fearless, unflappable. He was capable of the unexpected, and being with him made her feel as if, maybe, someday she might do something unexpected herself.

Abigail would never hear her husband's voice again, a fact that echoed in her heart as she clung to the iron handrail and allowed her gaze to fall into the well of the lighthouse, disregarding her earlier warning. The stairs wound downward, uncoiling away from her like her memory.

She climbed the remaining steps to the top of the lighthouse, which was crowned by the lamp room, a circular turret walled with windows that created an enormous lantern. Access to the lamp room was gained through a trapdoor-style hatch. The massive lamp squatted in the middle of the room, encased in thick plates of glass, each covered in raised concentric grooves, similar to those of a record. While running her hand along the glass and circling the lamp's pedestal, Abigail tripped over a tin pail she hadn't noticed, sending it clattering around the room cacophonously.

"If I wasn't awake before, I am now," she said, righting the pail and setting it aside.

The view from the lamp room was breathtaking. The ocean stretched infinitely to the east while the silhouette of the island's trees and marshes sprawled to the west. As the sun bulged over the horizon, it radiated golden light into the clouds, tinting the undersides pink. This was the quintessence of a sunrise.

Abigail stepped onto the parapet, mindful not to let the door to the lamp room close, in case it locked. She couldn't afford to get trapped out here. She was a newcomer on Chapel Isle, and hardly anyone was aware she'd taken up residence at the lighthouse. Who would think to look for her? Who would miss her?

The sentiment of *missing* was constant for Abigail. She missed her husband. She missed her son. She missed the life she was going to have with them. She was already beginning to miss the person she'd left behind on the mainland, the woman she had been before she went from Abigail to Abby.

A low railing encircled the lighthouse's parapet, too low to hold. She skimmed it with her fingertips, grappling with the impulse to categorize the sunrise, to apply adjectives to it, sculpting it into a class and rank. She wished she had a camera.

"A picture *is* worth a thousand words."

Abigail detested that cliché, the implication being that language was insufficient, imperfect. For her, it was the ultimate insult. However, during the fire, she had seen that the adage could hold true. It wounded her to admit there were instances when words were heartrendingly inadequate.

Descending the spiral staircase, she realized it was far scarier going down than coming up. Some of the steps whimpered under her weight, others yowled, iron gritting against iron. Abigail counted the noisy stairs to maintain her composure. By the bottom, the total numbered more than one hundred. Woozy, she flopped onto the couch in the living room, which expelled a puff of dust.

"Charming," she said as she choked.

The house was in dire need of a thorough cleaning. But Abigail firmly believed Lottie ought to have taken care of that. It was still too early to go into town and haggle with her for another discount on the rent or to request a complimentary maid service. Even if Lottie agreed to compensate her somehow, who knew when she would get around to it? Abigail couldn't handle another night's sleep on towels and decided to tackle the laundry before she unpacked. Lottie had mentioned a washer and dryer. There was only one place they could be.

◆ ◆ ◆

The basement door was under the staircase. Lottie hadn't unlocked it as she had the one to the lighthouse, so Abigail spent ten minutes sorting through the panoply of keys on the key ring. It struck her that an inordinate amount of her time was being consumed by locked doors.

"This is turning into a full-time job."

Once she got the basement door open, she was walloped by an unsavory smell—a potpourri of must, mold, and another scent she couldn't quite discern. She flipped the light switch.

"At least this works."

If there was a short somewhere in the house, the bulbs might illuminate or snuff out at will. Getting caught in an unfamiliar basement in the dark was not an ideal way to start the morning.

"Please stay on," Abigail implored, taking a tentative step. "Please stay on."

The stairs creaked beneath her in turn.

"Does everything in this house squeak?"

The next riser screeched in reply.

"It was a rhetorical question."

Two light fixtures bracketed each end of the basement, and there was a small window, but years of grime acted as a shade. The first light was by the stairs. The second was at the far side of the house, under the kitchen, creating a forest of murky shadows in between. A pale square form was glowing dimly from the opposite corner of the basement. Abigail thought it must be the washer. While navigating through the darkness, she hit something, knocking her shin hard. She had to squint to see that she'd walked into a stack of dust-coated crates.

"More dust. How lucky can a girl get?"

Feeling her way along the wall, Abigail inched forward. The stone was cool and gritty to the touch. The unusual smell was growing stronger. She couldn't place it. Soon she came upon the water cistern Lottie had spoken of. A vast cavern built into the earth, it was large enough to house a compact car. This was the source of the foul odor.

While stepping away from the cistern to catch her breath, Abigail backed into something cold and solid—a deep porcelain sink. That was what had been glowing. Next to it stood an old-timey washtub with a hand crank to wring out clothes.

"I should have known. This must be what Lottie meant by a washer and dryer."

The bulb overhead flickered.

"And that's enough of the basement for today."

In a dash for the stairs, Abigail collided with another mound of crates, slamming her other shin, then ran upstairs into the living room, which was mercifully bright and free of obstacles for her to sideswipe.

"What a bonus. Matching bruises," she griped, massaging her lower legs.

Her discarded apple was lying on the floor, reminding Abigail that she needed a cup of coffee, some food, and, most important, she had to pay Lottie a visit. Maybe the café she'd spotted in town would be open for breakfast and someone there could tell her where to find a laundromat.

The dusty linens she'd shucked off the bed the previous night were draped on the rocker in the master bedroom. Abigail gathered them and the towels into a ball. Given the amount of clothing she had to wear in addition to her pajamas to stay warm, laundry threatened to become a real issue.

"So help me, there had better be a laundromat on this island. That ancient washer in the basement isn't going to cut it."

Abigail got dressed in reverse, removing the clothes she'd slept in before she put on a pair of khakis and a knit top from her duffel. Even though she wasn't overly concerned with her appearance, she did notice that the house didn't have a full-length mirror. The puny one in the bathroom was the only mirror in the entire place. Abigail had to wonder if, after a while, she would forget how she looked from the neck down.

e•lide (i lid′), *v.t.,* **e•lid•ed, e•lid•ing. 1.** to omit (a vowel, consonant, or syllable) in pronunciation. **2.** to suppress; omit; ignore; pass over. **3.** *Law.* to annul or quash. [1585–95; < L *ēlīdere* to strike out, equiv. to *ē–* E- + *–lidere,* comb. form of *laedere* to wound]

◆　◆　◆

Morning's low tide exposed a forbidding cluster of boulders at the coastline, a natural seawall that protected the lighthouse. Strewn along the shore like the fallen walls of a fortress, not even the pounding surf had been able to wear the massive rocks away. The seawall was a testament to perseverance. Abigail took heart in its presence as she stood on the front stoop of the caretaker's cottage, attempting to find the right key to lock the door.

"Three down. A dozen to go."

The sandy, uneven roads made for slow passage into town. She tried to memorize landmarks as she went. The meadow, a listing telephone pole, a barren tree. The names of the streets and small lanes were confoundingly similar. *Bayside Drive, Beachcomber Road, Breezeway Avenue.* They were easy to mix up.

"According to your lease, you have twelve months to learn them."

Her family had tried to dissuade her from moving. North Carolina was so far from Boston, a year was so long. Between her savings and the pending insurance settlement, there was no pressing need to get a job, nothing tying her down. If Abigail hated Chapel

Isle, she could always move home. In spite of the sorry state of the property and Lottie's misrepresentations, she didn't want to hate the house or the island.

The dewy seaside air left a wet sheen on the cobblestones of the town square, which was deserted except for a trio of men loading coolers into a pickup truck and a woman with a cane inching across the sidewalk.

"Wow. Four people. It's practically a mob scene."

Compared to Martha's Vineyard, Nantucket, and the more-popular islands in the Outer Banks, Chapel Isle was a relatively unknown destination. It showed no hallmarks of overcommercial-ization or overcrowding. Chain restaurants and pricey luxury bou-tiques would be out of step here. The allure of the island was its lack of pretension. Store windows were spruced up with handmade posters, and the awnings were wind-frayed. The door to a café called the Kozy Kettle had a crack in the glass. Above the crack was an *Open* sign, which was sufficient invitation for Abigail.

A bell chimed when she entered. The café had the feel of a road-side diner. Red-checked oilcloths were stapled to the undersides of the tables, and the wood paneling was burnished by decades of wear. This was one place where the town's ad nauseam nautical theme wasn't in evidence. Perhaps the locals had had enough of it.

Two elderly men, both in John Deere caps, were seated at a booth in the corner. Another man, in a canvas jacket, was nursing a cup of coffee at the counter. A waitress was standing by the register, refilling sugar dispensers.

"Have a seat wherever, hon," she said. "Be with you in a minute."

The men in the booth followed Abigail with their eyes as she took a spot at the counter. She offered them a friendly smile but got frowns in return.

"Tough crowd," she whispered.

"What was that, hon?"

"Nothing."

Because the fire had temporarily robbed her of a voice, Abigail would often talk to herself. Doing it when other people could hear her, however, was probably not a smart approach, especially for a newcomer. She'd have to curb that.

"Coffee?"

"That would be terrific."

A pair of bifocals dangled from a chain around the waitress's neck, and her polyester apron was festooned with buttons and brooches. She appeared to be in her sixties, yet Abigail could tell the woman had been a true beauty in her youth.

"Here you go. It's a fresh pot."

She gave Abigail a menu, simultaneously pouring her a brimming cup of coffee. As soon as Abigail took a sip, she almost spit it out. The coffee was scalding hot.

"Burned yourself, huh?" the waitress asked.

In more ways than one, Abigail was thinking.

"I'll get you some ice water."

The waitress delivered her drink. The water came in a jelly jar. It was another country touch that reminded Abigail she wasn't in the big city anymore.

"Decided what you want?"

"Scrambled eggs and wheat toast," she lisped.

"You got it, hon."

Whisking away the menu, the waitress disappeared into the kitchen. Abigail chugged water to cool her taste buds, as the men in the corner continued to watch her closely. Uncomfortable under such deliberate gaze, she turned to face in the opposite direction, toward the register. A smattering of photos was taped to its side. Most of the snapshots featured a local baseball league, the guys dressed in matching uniforms and sporting matching toothy grins. Abigail was glad to see this side to Chapel Isle, a side where people actually did smile.

"That's our team," the man in the canvas jacket told her proudly. "Took the pennant last year in the playoffs."

"Good for them," Abigail replied, thrilled that at least someone was willing to converse with her.

The man removed a picture from his wallet and slid closer to show her. "These are my sons. They played right and left field. This was years ago, mind you. They're grown. Now their kids are playing Little League ball like they did."

The old photo was a family group shot from a backyard barbecue. The man had his arm around his wife, who was wearing a floral shift, and the two teen boys on either side of the couple were in bell-bottoms.

"Handsome kids," Abigail said.

He stared at the picture for a moment. The gratitude on his face told Abigail he hadn't received a compliment in a while.

"That's because they favor their mom," the man answered, with a self-deprecating shrug. "We had some fun times, we did."

That's when Abigail smelled the alcohol on his breath and noticed how he'd missed a button on his flannel shirt, causing it to hang crookedly from the collar to the tails. She had a guess who he might be.

"Breakfast is served."

The waitress set down a plate of food, intentionally intruding. The man tucked the photo into his wallet, tossed two dollars on the counter, and retreated to the door, with a parting nod to Abigail as well as to the waitress.

"Take it easy, Hank," she said. The bell on the door tolled his exit. "Thought you might want to eat in peace."

"Was that Hank Scokes?"

"You heard of him?"

"Sort of. Wasn't he the person who ran into the ferry dock with his boat?"

"Indeed he was."

If there was more to the story, the waitress wasn't willing to say.

"Boy, your cook works fast," Abigail remarked, ham-handedly changing the subject.

"Food's done quick if you come at the right time. You would've had to wait if you'd been here earlier."

"Earlier?" Abigail thought she was early.

"Lord, yes. Before the men head to sea for the day, they eat standin' if they have to. Ain't an empty seat in the house."

It hadn't occurred to Abigail that the island was so quiet was because most of its citizens were on fishing boats, making their livings. This revelation was a load off her mind. Chapel Isle wasn't as desolate as it initially appeared.

"First visit, I take it."

"Is it that obvious?"

"We don't see too many new faces after Labor Day."

The bell above the door rang again as a woman rushed in, hair wet from a morning shower, her oversize sweatshirt faded from too many spins in the washer. "Can I have a coffee to go, Ruth? I got the kids in the car and I'm running late as it is."

"Sure thing, Janine."

Abigail poked at her scrambled eggs. They tasted fine, but it hurt to eat. If the soft eggs were problematic, she wasn't sure she should take a crack at the toast. When she took another sip of water, she found Janine visibly sizing her up. The woman's eyes dove to Abigail's left hand, making her the third person in less than twenty-four hours to check for a wedding ring.

"Here you go." Ruth was putting a lid on the paper cup. "Tell Clint and the kids hey for me."

"Will do." Janine shot Abigail a withering glare on her way out.

"Excuse me. Ruth, is it? Did I offend that woman somehow?"

"Who? Janine? Hon, you could've been sitting there in a nun's habit and she would've looked at you funny for not having a wedding ring on."

Abigail was impressed. She'd caught everyone else looking at her hand. She hadn't caught Ruth.

"Am I missing something?"

"Chapel Isle's got two kinds of men: married men and old men. A single woman arrives in town, might as well be a wolf waltzing through a henhouse. Feathers tend to get ruffled."

"That would make me the wolf?"

"Yup. See, island folk are the same as diesel engines. Takes 'em a spell to warm up, especially to out-of-towners. Once they do, they're as reliable as rubber on a tire. That Janine Wertz, though, I wouldn't count on her warming up, period."

With that, Ruth went to top off the John Deere twins' coffee cups, while Abigail managed a couple more bites of her eggs, abandoning her toast and coffee altogether. In under an hour, Abigail had endeared herself to the town drunk and unwittingly provoked a woman she had yet to formally meet.

"Must be a land speed record."

"You say something, hon?" Ruth asked, tallying Abigail's bill.

"No. I mean, yes. Can you tell me where I could find Merle Braithwaite?"

"At his store, Island Hardware. If the door's locked, knock real hard or go 'round back. Shop doesn't open until ten, but he's usually in there, puttering about."

"Thanks. Again, that is." Abigail noted the total on the bill, paid, and dropped the tip on the counter, double what was due.

"Don't you worry, darlin'," Ruth said with a wink. "A new face is never new for long."

Long was a relative term. At this rate, Abigail wasn't certain how much longer she would last on the island: the twelve months of her lease, twelve more days, or twelve more hours.

◆　◆　◆

Her footfalls resounded coldly against the cobblestones in the empty town square. Even the shops that were open looked empty. Denny *had* warned her about this on the ferry.

"Cue the tumbleweeds."

The door to Merle's store was locked, as Ruth had mentioned it might be. Like Lottie's realty agency, Island Hardware had once been a private residence. Where the squat bungalow's original living room window had been, a large pane of plate glass now stood, the business name foiled onto it in gold and green. Beyond the glass, the interior was dark. Abigail knocked on the door and waited. Then knocked harder. There was no response, so she went around to the rear, following Ruth's suggestion, and discovered the back door ajar.

Nudging it open, she said, "Hello? Is anybody here?"

The door led into a kitchen littered with tackle boxes, fishing supplies, and Styrofoam coolers. Abigail could see straight through the bungalow to the front door she'd been knocking on.

"Hello?" she called.

Suddenly a giant man in a navy shirt-coat appeared from around a corner. Abigail jumped, letting out a yelp.

"Cardiac arrest, here we come," the equally startled man said, fanning off the fright. He had an immense build and was practically eye to eye with the crown molding, dwarfing everything in the room. "You trying to kill me, lady?" he asked, running a massive palm over his wispy gray hair to collect himself.

"I scared *you*?"

"Pardon me for not expecting some woman to be sneaking around the kitchen at too-damn-early o'clock in the morning."

"I'm sorry. Truly, I am. I knocked on the front door. There was no answer, and this door was open, so . . ."

"You figured you'd give an elderly man a heart attack."

"You don't look elderly to me."

"Now you're just trying to butter me up."

"Is it working?"

"A little," he admitted. "Store's not open yet, but you're welcome to come on in if you can hack a path through this junk."

The kitchen was a shrine to fishing. Rods were propped in every corner, and cans of dried bait were stacked on the floor beneath dozens of colorful lures that hung from specially crafted shelves. Photos of prized catches were affixed to the wall wherever there was space.

"Listen, I apologize for barging in. I'm Abigail Harker. The new caretaker at the lighthouse."

"Should've guessed it," he said, warming to her. "I'm Merle

Braithwaite. Proprietor of Island Hardware, fishing aficionado, and Chapel Isle's 'Tallest Man Contest' winner for over fifty years running, at your service."

She put out her hand and Merle shook it gently, wary of his own strength, as if it was not entirely under his control.

"Lottie told me you might be stopping by. I'd say have a seat . . ."

Each of the chairs was piled high with issues of fishing magazines, topped with spools of line.

"That's all right. I can't stay. Too much to do. I just came by to ask a few questions about the caretaker's cottage."

"Shoot."

"Well, the light in the bathroom keeps switching on and off. I'm concerned there might be a problem with the wiring. If you could recommend an electrician—"

"Wiring's fine. Checked it myself last week."

"Maybe you should check it again, because—"

"Wouldn't do a bit of difference if I rewired the whole house," Merle said, towering over Abigail. "He always messes with that light."

"*He* who?"

"The caretaker."

"I thought I was the caretaker."

"You are. Now."

"Then who's *he*?"

"Name's Wesley Jasper."

"Lottie didn't mention another caretaker."

"Naw, I bet she didn't."

"Why do you say that?"

"Because Mr. Jasper isn't exactly the caretaker anymore."

"I don't follow."

Merle leaned heavily against the refrigerator, clearly annoyed that he had to deliver this news. "Ma'am, to put a fine point on it, the lighthouse is haunted."

"What?" Abigail was convinced she'd misheard him.

"Haunted."

"Come again."

"Haunted," he said, enunciating. "It ain't that highfalutin a word."

"I understand what haunted means. But you're kidding, right?"

"Gotta give it to Lottie. That woman could sell lizard skin boots to a *T. rex*. Not a shock she didn't mention the ghost before you signed on the dotted line."

Abigail couldn't believe her ears. "Look, Mr. Braithwaite——"

"Call me Merle. Nobody calls me Mister anything anymore."

"Fine, *Merle,* if this is some sort of initiation for nonislanders, let's get it over with. I had an arduous drive, no sleep, and I burned my tongue on my first cup of coffee today, so I'm in no mood for pranks."

"*Arduous*——now that's a tad highfalutin."

"It means——"

"Oh, I know what it means." Merle began to empty the ice packs from the coolers into the freezer, as if nothing was wrong. "Just not the kinda word you hear often in these parts. I like it. Think I'm going to use it more. 'I had an arduous morning fishing on the bay.' Or 'I had an arduous day working at the store.' Has a ring, don't it?"

Before Abigail could answer, he went on. "Burned your tongue, huh? Must've smarted. Ruth Kepshaw does keep that coffee molten-lava hot. Tell her to put an ice cube in your cup next time."

"Mr. Braithwaite——Merle, let me get this straight. You're telling me the reason my bathroom light continues to come on is because of the ghost of the lighthouse's old caretaker?"

"Pretty much. And don't mind the smell of pipe smoke. Supposedly that's how you can tell Mr. Jasper's around."

That was the scent Abigail had caught a whiff of while she was in the basement by the cistern——sweet pipe tobacco mixed with the incense-thick odor of decay.

"He won't bother you as long as you keep the lighthouse as it is. Been said for years he's a bit of a stickler. Which is why he doesn't care too much for Lottie. 'Cause of how she's let the place go to pot. You can ask her yourself. She's convinced Mr. Jasper tried to push her down the basement stairs."

"Excuse me?"

"Lottie went to inspect the cistern after we'd had a storm. She was halfway down the steps when the basement door slammed shut. Frightened the bejeezus outta her, and she 'tripped.' Sent her ass over elbow. She won't go near the basement anymore. Has the door locked. The entry to the lighthouse too. You couldn't get her up that spiral staircase if you dangled a thousand-dollar bill at the top."

"I get it. I get it. You're having a laugh at my expense. Frankly, it isn't very funny."

"I've been accused of a lot of things in my day. Being funny isn't one of them. Scaring small children at Halloween, that I've got covered. Comedy, not my bag."

Abigail folded her arms indignantly. "Can you honestly tell me you believe there's a ghost in the caretaker's house? Honestly?"

"Could it have been the wind that shut that door on Lottie? Would make sense. Or maybe it wasn't. Me, I can't say for certain. But it really ain't that big a deal," Merle assured her. "I been taking care of the place for going on twelve years, and—"

"Twelve years!?! It's been twelve years since there was a real caretaker?"

"More, actually. Last guy was here almost twenty years ago. He was this hippie type who drove a Winnebago with feathers in the windows. Claimed he was writing his memoirs and needed a place to 'connect' with his spirit. He connected with a spirit, all right. Stayed a whopping two days. Don't think Mr. Jasper was very fond of him. Maybe he tried puttin' them feathers in the windows of the caretaker's cottage."

"What do I do if this Mr. Jasper isn't fond of me?"

"Why wouldn't he be? You seem nice enough. Little high-strung perhaps."

"I am not high-strung. I'm . . . conscientious."

"Right. Look, whenever I go to check the pipes or whatnot, I say my hellos and tell him I'm there to make sure the lighthouse is shipshape. Show him a little respect. He'll show you some back. It's that simple."

Nothing about what Merle had said was simple, though, and Abigail had reached her limit. She went charging through the kitchen to the store, past aisles of tools and shelves full of parts, toward the front door. Merle shouted after her, "Where're you going?"

"To see Lottie. I want some straight answers."

She tried the door. It wouldn't open. Abigail pulled and pulled at the knob until Merle lumbered over to unhitch the bolt.

"If a straight answer is what you're angling for, Lottie's the last person you should pay a visit to. Don't get me wrong, I love her like a sister. Well, more like a sister-in-law of sorts, seeing as she's married to my second cousin. Fact is, Lottie's not one to fess up to a fib. And she's not one to lose a tenant if she can prevent it."

Merle was being earnest. Nonetheless, Abigail's feet were moving faster than her brain. She stormed out the door on a collision course for Lottie's realty agency.

"Oh, and don't move the oil pail in the lamp room," he called. "Mr. Jasper prefers it just so."

But Abigail was already gone.

fan•tod (fan′tod), *n.* **1.** Usually, **fantods.** a state of extreme nervousness or restlessness; the willies; the fidgets (usually prec. by *the*): *We all developed the fantods when the plane was late arriving.* **2.** Sometimes, **fantods.** a sudden outpouring of anger, outrage, or a similar intense emotion. [1835–40; appar. *fant(igue)* (earlier *fantique,* perh. b. FANTASY and FRANTIC; *–igue* prob. by assoc. with FATIGUE) + *–od(s),* of obscure orig.; see –s³]

◆   ◆   ◆

A strong breeze was coursing in off the bay, sending a discarded soda can skittering across the square and fluttering the flag mounted outside the Chapel Isle post office. Abigail was too infuriated to feel it.

The cavalcade of pinwheels and whirligigs was yammering away on the lawn in front of the realty agency. Inside, the lights were off. Outside, the door was locked. Abigail pounded and yelled, "Lottie. It's Abigail Harker. We need to talk."

A note was taped to the window. *Closed* was underlined repeatedly in pink ink.

"Isn't that convenient?"

Abigail stomped down the steps and stood amid the spinning lawn ornaments. The patience she'd afforded Lottie the day before had evaporated into pure outrage.

"Hold on," she told herself. "Some stranger tells you a campfire story and you're ready to run for the hills? He's probably the local nutcase. You're about to take runner-up for standing here on the sidewalk yakking to yourself."

She sidestepped the garden gnomes positioned like sentries

along the path and returned to her car. The pile of laundry was waiting for her in the backseat of the station wagon.

"I forgot about you guys," she said to the bedlinens and towels.

Abigail swung by the Kozy Kettle to ask where she could find a working washer and dryer. The John Deere twins were still at their booth, sitting guard. Ruth glanced up from a newspaper she was perusing.

"Back so soon, hon? Food here ain't that good."

"Please tell me there's a laundromat on Chapel Isle, or I'll be washing my sheets in the bay."

"We may be a backwater town, but this isn't Mayberry. We got a proper laundromat. Go up the street about a block. You can't miss it."

Since it was a short distance, Abigail bundled the laundry and decided to hoof it. After repeatedly traipsing past the same set of gift shops, her arms were getting tired and her aggravation was piqued.

"For pity's sake, where is this place?"

Abigail was ready to wave the white flag—or rather the white pillowcase—when she spotted an alley between two stores. Hanging over the gap in the storefronts was a plank of wood with the word *Laundromat* routed out in script.

"Of course. Can't miss it. How silly of me."

At the end of the alley sat a repurposed garage lined with coin-operated washers and dryers, hidden like a speakeasy for cleaning clothes. Abigail was starting to feel as if Chapel Isle was some sort of private club and she hadn't been taught the secret knock. She dumped her laundry onto a sorting table and was sifting through the pile, separating the bedclothes from the towels, when she heard somebody behind her announce their presence with a cough.

"Here to do your laundry?"

Standing at the threshold to the laundromat was a man wearing wide-wale corduroy pants pulled high around his stout waist. He had the prominent under-bite of a bulldog and was a whole head shorter than Abigail.

"Um, yes. Yes, I am."

"Nothing beats clean clothes."

"Agreed."

"You're going to need soap. You have any?"

"No, now that you mention it, I don't."

The man cocked his head ruefully. "Can't do laundry without soap."

"You've got me there."

"I could lend you some," he said, emphasis on the word *lend*.

"Really? I can pay you for it." Abigail reached for her purse.

"Don't want the money." The intimation was that he wanted more soap in return. The man tottered over to a closet and retrieved a hulking container of detergent, which he heaved onto the sorting table.

"Think you have enough?" she quipped.

His brows pinched as he poured the detergent into paper cups for her. Deadpan, he answered, "You can't have enough soap. Bring some next time you come. That's all."

"Will do."

She went to put the first load of towels into the closest washer, and the man clucked his tongue in disapproval. She tried the next. He did the same. Once Abigail took a step toward the third, he nodded his consent. As she started to put the second load into another washer, the man clucked at her until she picked the correct machine.

"You got quarters?"

Abigail dug through her wallet. She didn't have enough for both loads. "Isn't there a change machine?"

"I'll make change for you."

He took her singles and fished through his pocket, producing a fistful of quarters.

This was too weird. Abigail couldn't resist asking, "Are you the owner?"

"Who me?" he replied, flattered. "Nah."

"You just like laundry?"

"You could say that. If you want, you can go. I'll mind your wash."

"Thanks. I think."

"Twenty-five minutes for the cycle. You'll need to be here to switch the loads into the dryers."

This was more an order than a suggestion. Giving a final glance to the peculiar man with the under-bite, her defenseless laundry already churning in the machines, she grabbed her purse and left.

◆ ◆ ◆

Twenty-five minutes wasn't much time to properly explore, but Abigail could at least take in a bit of the town. Anything would be preferable to staying at the laudromat. The calls of seagulls beckoned her toward the pier. Many of the boats she'd seen the previous day were gone, though some remained. There were no yachts or pleasure cruisers, merely a handful of skiffs and sloops that showed their age, each bobbing serenely. How enviable to be so blithe, Abigail thought, so imperturbable.

She strolled along the pier. The tide was coming in, and the barnacles that clung to the pilings below would soon disappear. The mottled white masses stood out starkly against the dark timbers. Abigail rolled the word *barnacle* around in her mouth, like a wine connoisseur would to sample the flavor. A bumpy noun, it crowded inside the cheeks, rattling against the teeth. That was the beauty of language. Sound made words, which made meaning. Love wasn't love without those precise consonants and vowels. The same was true of fear. Abigail was well versed in both. She knew how each made her breath quicken, her skin tingle, and her head swim. Love and fear required just four letters; however, there was a world of difference between them.

Years before Abigail ever set foot on Chapel Isle, she knew how it felt to go rafting in the ocean there, to pick shells from the waterline, to have the pristine sand sifting between her toes. She even knew the color of the sunset as it stained the sky. Paul had told her everything about the island where he'd spent summers during his childhood—this island. His boyhood reminiscences had filled Abigail's mind as though they were her own. She could almost hear the ocean lapping at the shore. Imagination could take her only so far. They'd planned to spend their honeymoon on Chapel Isle, but Abigail's parents treated them to a trip to Maui as a wedding present instead. Afterward, Paul promised to take her there on vacation when they had enough money. Once they could afford to go, though, plans were continually diverted by circumstance. The timing wasn't right.

In the months leading up to the fire, Abigail began to pester Paul about taking a trip to Chapel Isle, citing Justin as incentive. She wanted their son to have the same special childhood experiences he'd had. Despite his busy schedule, Paul put in for two weeks off in August so they could go to the island as a family. Then he could show them the sights he'd loved in his youth. One in particular was the island's lighthouse, a memory Paul held on to as a treasured souvenir. Every time he spoke of it, a smile would inevitably form on his lips.

"That was the most amazing sight I'd ever seen," he would say with boyish reverence. "It seemed like there was nothing bigger in the whole world. I would dream that the lighthouse still worked and that I lived there, guiding the boats in through rough seas. Getting the sailors home safely. Those were some of the best dreams I ever had."

Paul's dreams became Abigail's. She would wake up having spent the night with fictional stranded sailors at a lighthouse she'd never seen. It was the same dream she had the night before his funeral. Scant remains of her husband and son could be recovered from the fire, little more than charred bones. Abigail had ordered two caskets for burial anyway, one for an adult, one for a child. In Justin's coffin, she placed a toy truck he'd accidentally left at preschool. In Paul's coffin was her wedding band.

◆　◆　◆

The seagulls that had drawn her to the bay were what brought her around from the grip of the past, their cries snapping her into the moment. Abigail found herself standing at the very end of the pier, dangerously close to the edge. She didn't remember how she'd gotten there. Thirty minutes had disappeared, unnoticed.

Since the fire, she occasionally had incidents similar to sleepwalking. Minutes, let alone hours, could completely blur. The knowledge that she could abandon her body and it would act on its own, perhaps against her will, unnerved her.

When she returned to the laundromat, the man with the underbite was gone. Her towels and bedding lay in wet mounds on the sorting table. He had taken them out for her.

"At least *he's* not a ghost."

"I do that too."

Flushed, Abigail spun on her heel as the man appeared from inside a storage closet.

"Do what?"

"Talk to myself. Shouldn't be ashamed. There's no better listener than your own set of ears."

"That's . . ." She had to think of a sentiment that wouldn't be insulting. "Not untrue."

"I got you some dryer sheets."

"These'll be fine without—"

The man wagged his finger. "Wouldn't recommend it. You'll get static. As much as twelve thousand volts. The sheets have a lubricating effect."

"Wow. Who knew?"

He proffered the dryer sheets as if to say: *I did, and so should you.*

"On the house?" Abigail asked.

"On the house."

As she prepared to shove the sopping bedding into a random dryer, she deferred to him first. "Can you suggest the dryer du jour?"

Beaming, he began, "In my opinion, number eight is by far the best for sheets and blankets; not ideal for delicates. I've had trouble with the calibration. Runs real hot. For your towels, I'd go with number eleven. Heat stays even."

"Number eight it is." Abigail loaded in the soggy laundry under the man's watchful eye.

"Be ready in forty minutes," he informed her.

"Got it. Can you tell me where I might find a supermarket?" She didn't want to talk voltage and heat settings with him the whole time and needed groceries badly.

"There's a general store up the street on the right-hand side. You can't miss it."

"Can't miss it, huh? I've heard that before."

◆　◆　◆

A billboard-size sign for Weller's Market was propped on the roof of a barn-style building a block away. Abigail's new pal from the laundromat was right. She couldn't have overlooked it unless she was blindfolded.

The market had the feel of a makeshift country store. Rows of plywood shelves and display stands stacked on overturned crates gave it the vibe of a traveling show, ready to be dismantled and moved to a new location at a moment's notice. Even though the registers in front were vacant, Abigail could hear shuffling somewhere in the store. She picked a cart and cruised from aisle to aisle, lamenting that she hadn't written a list.

"Doesn't matter. You need *everything*."

One of the wheels on her cart was wobbly, making it troublesome to maneuver. The broken wheel bleated monotonously, and the front end kept veering into the shelves. The more she filled the cart, the more strenuous it was to steer. Since Lottie was AWOL and Abigail couldn't get her to have the place cleaned yet, her top priority was cleaning supplies. She couldn't stand all the dust for another night, so whichever products claimed to be the most powerful and abrasive got thrown into her cart.

"The stronger, the better."

She also chucked in any provision that caught her fancy. Hunger had that effect. Her cart on the verge of tipping, Abigail was ready to check out.

Slouched at the register, engrossed in a paperback romance, was Janine, the woman from the Kozy Kettle. Abigail unloaded her groceries, thinking Janine might not remember her. Unfortunately, she did.

"You got coupons?" Janine snapped.

Abigail hadn't been food shopping since before the fire. Her purse lay in the cart's children's seat, suddenly reminding her of Justin. The jolt of sadness made her entire head buzz for a second.

"I said, you have any coupons?"

"Me? Coupons? No, no, I don't. Not that I don't use them," Abigail stammered, worried Janine had mistaken her confusion for condescension. "I just don't have any with me. I'm new here. I got into town yesterday and I haven't even unpacked and I didn't get a good night's sleep and I...I...I'm going to stop talking now."

Janine narrowed her eyes, then rang Abigail's items in silence. When Abigail started to bag the groceries, Janine stopped her.

"I can do that."

"I thought I'd help."

"Well, don't."

Abigail's face burned with embarrassment. Unable to devise a sharp retort, she bided the minutes until Janine finished bagging and announced the total. It was higher than Abigail expected. She'd gotten extra cash for such expenses before leaving Boston and handed over three large bills, providing Janine with another reason to dislike her.

She thrust the change at Abigail. "Have a nice day."

"I will."

It was a lame comeback. Plus, it was hard to look triumphant pushing the wobbly shopping cart from the store to her station wagon.

"Where does that woman get off?" Abigail railed as she shoved the grocery bags into her car. "I've barely met her and she hates me. How can you hate somebody you haven't even been introduced to?"

Then Abigail caught sight of the John Deere twins from the

Kozy Kettle standing on the corner, staring as she talked to herself. She blushed.

"Morning," she said with a wave.

The men toddled away as fast as their arthritic legs could carry them.

"Terrific. Everyone you've met so far either hates you or thinks you're crazy. Speaking of crazy, it's time to get your laundry."

◆　◆　◆

Abigail arrived at the laundromat to discover the man with the under-bite folding her sheets.

"Gotta get them while they're hot or else they wrinkle," he explained, smoothing the fabric and patting down the creases. "Same goes for towels. I did those too."

"I don't know what to say. I mean I *really* don't know what to say."

Having him touch her sheets and towels was disconcerting. She had to squelch a grimace.

"Here. I couldn't remember what brand you preferred." Abigail had bought a container of detergent and a box of dryer sheets for him at the market.

He blinked at the offering. "These are the fancy kind. Top of the line. You didn't have to."

"It's no big deal."

"Thank you."

"Don't mention it."

Seriously, she thought. *Don't mention it.*

This experience had gone from bordering on bizarre to flat-out freakish. Abigail was eager to return to the refuge of the lighthouse. She collected her laundry and began to back out the door.

"I've got to run. Things to do. People to see."

"Okeydokey, you have yourself a nice day."

On the ride home, Abigail replayed the morning's events, wondering if she should bother unpacking. She could break the lease and pay the difference. Except that would mean admitting defeat.

For months, Abigail had felt defeated. The fire was an ambush, and grief had overpowered her, trouncing her spirits. Some days she would wake up thinking she was in someone else's body. Other days, she'd pray she was. She would stare at her fingers, unable to recall if her nails had always been so short. Or she'd look at her freckles in a mirror, uncertain as to how long they had been there. Her arms seemed clumsy, her legs gangly, her rib cage too small for her, stuffed tight with her swollen heart. Abigail had been losing the battle to reclaim herself and couldn't afford to be beaten.

She was passing the meadow, the marker that indicated she was halfway to the lighthouse, when a flicker of color caught her eye, a strand of blue-gray in the sea of vibrant green reeds. A heron was wading through the grass. The sheer beauty of the bird's slender body made Abigail slow the car. The heron stepped elegantly through the meadow hay, until it strode into a thicket and out of view.

Abigail decided to take the sighting as a sign. Paul had loved Chapel Isle. She was going to love it too.

"You're staying," she insisted. "This is exactly what you need."

Telling herself was one thing. Believing it was another.

gam♦mon³ (gam´ən), *Brit. Informal.* —*n.* **1.** deceitful nonsense; bosh. —*v.i.* **2.** to talk gammon. **3.** to make pretense. —*v.t.* **4.** to humbug. [1710–20; perh. special use of GAMMON¹] —**gam´mon♦er,** *n.*

G

♦   ♦   ♦

The noon sun was leering over the top of the lighthouse, casting a wide shadow that engulfed an entire side of the caretaker's cottage. Abigail pulled into the gravel drive, intentionally parking outside the scope of the shadow. She leaned into the steering wheel and peered upward at the lighthouse. The once magnificent sight, which had engraved itself in Paul's heart, had fallen into extreme disrepair. That saddened Abigail deeply.

She unloaded the car, dumping the heavy grocery bags onto the floor and setting the clean laundry on an edge of the table she dusted with her sleeve. The conversation with Merle came racing back to her. Abigail paused, examining the living room for any sort of change.

Everything was as she'd left it.

"What did you expect? A ghost in a white sheet?"

She wasn't sure what to expect. That was what bugged her.

Though the refrigerator needed cleaning, Abigail had to get the food in before it spoiled. The dry goods could wait, because the cupboard shelves had to be wiped down first. She assembled her brigade of cleaning products on the counter, saying, "This will be a change for the best."

Change was part of life and part of language. Abigail's predecessors in the field of lexicography had dropped superfluous letters from the American dictionary, like the *u* in *honour* or the archaic *k* in *musick,* on the grounds of utility, efficiency, and aesthetics. Her goal today was not nearly as magnanimous; however, utility, efficiency, and aesthetics were her prime objectives as well.

Dealing with the cupboard drawers and shelves would be relatively easy, but the generations-old appliances would be backbreaking. Abigail was especially anxious about the oven. She hadn't thought to bring a microwave, which she regretted. That would have solved myriad problems. The sole piece of electronic equipment she'd packed was a small combination radio and CD player, a dated model taken from her parents' garage.

"Some music might make this more palatable," she said, retrieving the radio from amid the pile of boxes in the living room.

No matter what direction Abigail twisted the antenna, static was all she got, so she grabbed a classical CD from her suitcase and popped it in. As the house filled with the warm melody of a violin concerto, she put on her new rubber dish gloves and advanced toward the cupboards, as if preparing to pull a tooth.

"Don't worry. This won't hurt a bit."

The music did make the work go faster. It didn't make it any less grimy. Abigail estimated the kitchen hadn't been given a thorough scrubbing since the last caretaker was there.

"Twenty years. It's past due."

She emptied the shelves, raining a cascade of grit onto the counter, and took stock of the contents: cracked plates, warped plastic cups, and crippled cookware.

"Suffice it to say, you're not quite ready to host a dinner party."

As she spoke, the CD skipped. Abigail was about to check the player when Merle's story about Wesley Jasper resurfaced in her mind.

It's nothing, she told herself.

The concerto recommenced, and she finished scouring the cupboards inside and out. Next came the refrigerator, where mold in a rainbow of hues had taken up residence, and the freezer, which had an inch-thick layer of ice glazing the interior. Abigail chipped at it with a serving knife while dousing the frost with tap water. Finally, she had to face the oven. Compared to the rest, it got a cursory cleaning. Even handling the range's knobs made Abigail nervous. She decided to focus on the countertop and backsplash instead.

"This entire kitchen could stand a new coat of paint," she mused. "And this wallpaper has got to go."

The CD skipped again, violins halting mid-beat. Abigail swallowed hard and waited. Seconds later, the music restarted.

See. It was nothing.

Emboldened, she gently picked at the wallpaper, which peeled away obligingly.

"See, the paper is damaged. The glue's shot. Removing it and putting on fresh paint would be a world of improvement."

This was part statement, part proposal. She readied herself for the CD to skip. It didn't.

You're delirious with hunger. So delirious you're making decorating suggestions to a ghost you don't believe in.

Abigail hadn't eaten since breakfast at the café, when she'd barely touched her food. She washed a plate and made herself a sandwich. Turkey, tomato, and mayonnaise was hardly haute cuisine, yet the fact that the sandwich would be easy on her burned taste buds made it sound divine.

Having moved the dishware to the dining table in order to clean the cupboards, Abigail had to clear a section so she'd have room to eat. When she sat on the only chair that didn't look like it would collapse, the cushion released a burst of air as if she'd come down on a whoopee cushion.

"Very attractive."

Her tongue was still sore from the scalding coffee. She was too famished to care. Since the fire, she'd been eating purely for sustenance and because her parents forced her. If they hadn't put meals right in front of her, Abigail would have forgotten to eat altogether. Food no longer seemed necessary. She was constantly full, glutted with feelings nobody would crave.

The chore of eating complete, Abigail picked up where she'd left off. Instead of putting the dry goods in the cupboards, she stored them on the table along with the dishware. Why bother if she was going to paint, she reasoned.

Abigail hated to leave the living room in such a state—cluttered with boxes and grocery bags, the furniture stacked with overflow from the kitchen—but if she was going to do this, she was going to do it right. She started in on the wallpaper, attacking it where the edges had come free. Although the blue and white flower pattern might have had country quaintness when the paper was first applied, the yellowy paste now showed through the white sections, turning them a pallid shade and adding to the sense that the kitchen was permanently dirty.

"*Au revoir,* floral wallpaper."

Not every sheet came down willingly. Abigail picked at loose corners until she broke both thumbnails. Forced to resort to a butter knife for the stubborn sections as well as the glue that streaked the wall, she redoubled her efforts. A haze of paper shavings drifted in the shafts of sunlight shining through the kitchen windows.

As the afternoon wore on, Abigail caught herself waiting for the CD to falter, yet the music played on uninterrupted. She began to hum, losing herself in the buoyancy of the violins. Paul had favored cello music. They would often debate what they should listen to in the car, vying over symphonies and comparing the virtues of each stringed instrument as if arguing political positions. For Paul, the cello spoke to the soul, with its mellow, sonorous voice. Abigail preferred the lighter, loftier range of the violin. The low tenor of the cello was too melancholy for her taste, well before she knew what true melancholy even felt like.

Strips of wallpaper plopped at her feet in growing mounds, while bits of paste speckled her clothes and the tips of her fingers took on a bluish cast from the cornflower color in the design. Eventually, the butter knife bent under the pressure of scraping the calcified glue. Only belatedly did it occur to Abigail that, as a rental tenant, she had no right to remove the wallpaper. The lighthouse wasn't her property.

"Way to go. That's playing it safe."

What was done was done, and nobody—not even Lottie—would disagree that the kitchen appeared more spacious minus the dated paper, a supreme achievement in light of its dimensions. Abigail considered it a victory. She took a break to open the windows and let in some air. The breeze seemed to rustle the paper-thin curtains in tempo to the music. Dust had collected in their lace trim, making the edges appear mealy.

"You've got to go too," Abigail announced, snapping off the curtain rod. Then she heard a bump.

It was the curtains. No, it wasn't that close. Was it upstairs? Relax. You're overreacting.

Abigail dismantled the other set of curtains to see if it would happen a second time. The violins played on and there were no other noises.

"You're losing it, Abby."

Yeah, you're definitely losing it if you're calling yourself "Abby."

After her assault on the kitchen, it looked as if it had been looted. Empty drawers hung open. The cabinet doors were swung wide, the shelves bare. What mattered was that everything was clean. Abigail had removed years of grease from the appliances and decades' worth of dirt from the sink. Beyond the slanting shelves and dislocated counters, she could imagine how the kitchen had once been: homey, pleasant. Perhaps it could be that way again.

◆　◆　◆

The master bedroom was next on Abigail's agenda. She laid the freshly laundered towels and linens on the rocker, preparing to make the bed. Stripped, the sunken crater in the middle of the mattress looked like a pothole.

"Maybe the other side isn't so . . . concave."

Flipping the mattress took muscle. Deadweight, it teetered, then collapsed onto the box spring, sending a piece of paper fluttering to the floor as a plume of dust fogged the room.

"Some people keep money under their mattress. Or dirty magazines. Here you have"—Abigail bent over to check—"a newspaper article."

The news clipping was amber with age and had been cut rather than torn out. The edges were neat, purposeful. The bold-type headline said: BISHOP'S MISTRESS SINKS, ENTIRE CREW LOST.

Before Abigail could read on, she was overcome by a coughing fit brought on from the wave of dust constricting her tender throat. She dropped the article on the nightstand and went to the bathroom for water. A sip from the tap and she was fine, albeit shaken.

"Here's a headline: *Woman Chokes to Death on Dust While Cleaning.*"

Abigail put the fresh sheets on the bed, along with the fabric-softener-scented quilt, which was prettier than it originally appeared. Handmade with squares of blue and yellow material and worn soft through the years, someone had put their heart into the blanket. Abigail admired that.

After carting the mop and bucket she'd bought upstairs, she swabbed the bedroom floor. The wood boards were actually a different color without the film of dirt darkening them.

"From mahogany to honey maple. Somewhat appalling. Yet somewhat impressive."

The water in the bucket rapidly went from clear to murky. She had to dump the waste down the tub's drain again and again before she could proclaim the floor clean. Neither the nightstand nor the dresser changed hue as did the floor, but each had new luster due to soap and a rag. Once she'd dusted the insides of the dresser drawers, Abigail unpacked.

The closet was minuscule by modern standards. The refrigerator downstairs was roomier. Five wooden hangers hung from an unfinished dowel acting as the closet rod.

"This Mr. Jasper must not have been into fashion."

None of Abigail's clothes had survived the fire, so her mother ordered her a new wardrobe in bulk through catalogs while Abigail recovered in the hospital. A kind gesture, her mother's intention was to be helpful, to give Abigail one less thing to worry about. However, as Abigail hung the tops in the closet and folded the jeans and khakis into the drawers, she had the distinct sense she'd picked the wrong suitcase off the luggage carousel at the airport and wound up with a stranger's clothes. The necklines on the tops were too high and the sleeves were too long and the pants had too many pleats. Even someone as close as her mother didn't know exactly what Abigail would want. Sometimes Abigail didn't either.

Standing in front of the closet, she felt a pang of longing. She missed her old clothes. The silk blouses and designer wool slacks she'd amassed over the years were hardly haute couture; however, they meant a great deal to her. Whether she was going to a consulting job or lexicography conference, tweed skirts and tailored shirts were her customary garb. On her salary, high-quality versions of such items were difficult to come by, so Abigail religiously combed the discount racks. Her persistence sometimes paid off, as it did when she came across a pure cashmere sweater on sale for forty dollars. It was a luxuriously soft turtleneck in a shade of burgundy that always garnered her compliments. Abigail envisioned the sweater hanging in her former closet, alight with flames and falling to pieces from the hanger. With a sigh, she ran her fingers across the collection of cotton knits and oxfords, resigning herself to the new *Abby*.

She opened the windows to air out the bedroom, which was somehow brighter despite the bilious green shade of paint and the jaundiced polyester drapes.

"It's a start," Abigail said to herself as she went to empty the last bucket of dirty water, having totally forgotten about the newspaper article on the bedside table.

❖ ❖ ❖

The sun was sinking, the temperature was falling, and the violin quartet was playing its umpteenth round of the same concerto. Abigail shut off the CD player. The music evaporated instantly, as though sapping the warmth from the room. If she didn't want to freeze, she would have to make a fire.

Abigail didn't need any more firewood. The log rack was already full. But going to the shed to get more delayed the process she was dreading. As she tromped through the tall grass, Abigail mulled over what Merle Braithwaite had told her.

"Why didn't you mow the lawn if you're so concerned about keeping Mr. What's-His-Name happy, huh? How about that?"

She opted not to dwell on what Merle had said that morning. Diverting herself with housework had been an intentional measure. What she couldn't distract herself from was the threat of spending another night in the bitter cold. Abigail unlocked the shed and the hinges sobbed.

"Take a number. You're not the only squeaky thing around here."

The firewood had been quartered, making one edge especially sharp. Her forearms took a beating as she bunched the logs.

"There has got to be an easier, less injurious way to do this."

While searching for a container to carry the wood in, Abigail spied a flashlight behind a phalanx of kerosene lanterns. Seeing how unreliable the house's wiring was, a flashlight could come in handy. She reached for it, inadvertently disturbing the delicate balance of firewood, and the logs proceeded to tumble to her feet.

"This is going swimmingly."

Hands now free, Abigail switched on the flashlight. Nothing. She gave it a shake.

"I guess I should put batteries on the shopping list along with primer, rollers, sandpaper . . ."

She hunted through the shed for painting supplies. The brushes she found were rock hard, bristles petrified with paint. Another visit to Merle's store was in order.

"Won't that be a treat?"

Flashlight and logs gathered in her arms, Abigail kicked the shed door shut, leaving it unlocked.

"Time to start a fire."

With the wood set on the log rack, the match ready and waiting, Abigail remembered she still had no kindling. Lottie's brochure was buried somewhere in the mess, and she had no pad or paper except for the register in her checkbook and her checks. There was the newspaper article from under the mattress. Except Abigail didn't feel right about burning it. The article had survived too many years to meet such a fate. Paper bags, which she had in abundance, were the best bet.

Fighting her trepidation, she struck the match. Abigail tried to stare down the flame but lost her nerve. She lobbed the matchstick into the fireplace, the flame caught on the bags, and the wood took.

"The first time is always the hardest," she told herself.

Abigail was well aware, though, that *any* time she had to start a fire it would be hard on her. She shuddered at the cold as well as the thought that she might have to do this every day from here on in.

Since the fireplace had no screen, she stayed close, holding vigil at the hearth and contemplating the fact that the word *fire* was almost as ancient as what it signified. Its ancestry spanned the millennia. The Greeks baptized it *pyr*. In Old English, it was labeled *fyr*, in Old High German, *fiur*. Fire was elemental to life, hence to language. The fear of fire was equally elemental. Abigail's fears had been justified. She had a right to them.

"Maybe you'll get used to this," she said. "Probably not."

◆   ◆   ◆

Night drew itself up along the shoreline as Abigail sorted through the boxes of books strewn across the living room floor. It was high time to find a home for them in the study upstairs. She doused the fire with a few mugs of water, then grabbed a box. The staircase sung a dissonant scale of screeches with every step.

"Yeah, yeah, yeah. I hear you."

The second floor was blindingly dark. Abigail hurried to switch on all the lights—the overhead fixture in the study, the bulb in the bathroom, and the lamp in the bedroom. Once they were lit, Abigail could breathe easier and concentrate on unpacking.

Several flights of stairs later, the study was filled to capacity. Boxes were piled on the desk, the cot, and the floor. Shelving the books was a project Abigail relished. Her packing process had been hasty, done without regard to order; hence, opening each package was like opening a gift. For her, the sprawl of bland brown boxes rivaled Christmas. As she organized, she allowed herself to read the first few pages of each book, tasting the story or sampling a morsel from a text. It was as if she were bumping into an acquaintance on the street—Abigail couldn't simply pass them by.

She was a fraction of the way through the project when the growling in her stomach told her it was time to eat again. Despite the ample selection of groceries she'd bought to prepare herself a proper meal, such as chicken cutlets and rice and fresh green beans, Abigail had no inclination to cook. Because it would mean she would have to turn on the stove.

"I'm hungry. But I'm not *that* hungry."

Instead, she made herself another sandwich, laid it on a paper towel, and took it to the study with her. She ate while thumbing through a Hemingway novel she'd found in her parents' attic, a first edition of *The Sun Also Rises* that her father ran across at a garage sale and gave her as a present.

Time drained away as Abigail lost herself in the first chapter. The weight of the novel in her hand anchored her, the pages supple as suede. She had a clear vision of the day her father brought the book home. It was summer. She'd recently turned fourteen. She remembered lying on her stomach on their porch, reading that first chapter while the crickets hissed in the heat. Abigail could have sworn she felt the porch boards under her elbows and smelled the chlorine from their neighbor's pool, though in reality she was wedged into the little desk in the study.

All of a sudden a thump came from above, reverberating through the house's brick walls. Abigail jumped.

It was nothing. It was nothing. It was nothing.

The phrase repeated in her mind, syncopated with her breathing. She tried to stand. Her legs wouldn't budge.

"Sitting is fine. Sitting is good. I'll stay right—"

Another thump resounded through the house, this one more distinct. It was loud and hollow. Whatever was making the noise wasn't solid.

The oil pail.

Abigail's thoughts corkscrewed back to that morning, to climbing the spiral staircase, entering the lamp room, and accidentally kicking the tin pail. What had Merle said as she'd left his shop? He'd told her not to move it.

Except that was ridiculous. There was no ghost.

Rational thought couldn't thaw Abigail from her position, frozen at the desk. She deliberated whether to go up to the lamp room and investigate or to leave it for tomorrow, when she had daylight on her side.

"It's dark. You don't have a flashlight. One false step on those stairs and . . ."

She preferred not to ruminate on what could come after *and*.

If the bedroom door had a lock, Abigail would have used it. She changed into her pajamas and considered climbing into bed and hiding under the covers, but she hadn't brushed her teeth or removed her contacts.

"Forget brushing your teeth. Being scared beats oral hygiene hands down."

She sprinted into the bathroom and plucked out her contacts in record time. When she slammed the bedroom door behind her, it sent a gust of air coursing through the room, setting the newspaper article on the nightstand aloft. The paper came to rest under the bed. Too tired, Abigail left it there. She pulled the quilt over her shoulders, thinking back to the nights when Justin awoke with bad dreams. She and Paul would comfort him, rub his head, kiss each cheek, and tell him that the kisses would keep the nightmares away.

He believed you.

Abigail had cherished that unconditional trust, the whole-hearted faith only a child, her child, could bestow. It was an incomparable honor. And it was gone. This time, she didn't bother stopping the tears when they came.

Amo, amare, amavi, amatus.

Oro, orare, oravi, oratus.

Wrapping her arms around herself to keep warm, Abigail hummed Latin verbs until they lulled her to sleep.

ha•mar•ti•a (hä´mär tē´ə), *n.* See **tragic flaw.** [1890–95; < Gk: a fault, equiv. to *hamart–* (base of *hamartánein* to err) + *–ia* –IA]

❖ ❖ ❖

Sunrise was different by the ocean. It came on fast and was impossible to ignore. Abigail groped the nightstand for her glasses so she could read her watch, which said it was after six. She felt harried, as if she'd overslept, but there was nothing pressing she needed to do, nothing that awaited her. Her arms ached from her cleaning rampage and when she rubbed them, she could feel the indentations left on her skin by the bedding. Deep valleys and ravines crisscrossed the flesh, a topographical map of where her dreams had taken her during the night.

Abigail slid her sneakers on in lieu of slippers and made the bed.

"What an attractive sight you must be. Bleary-eyed in pajamas, two sweaters, and a pair of tennis shoes. Thank your stars there *isn't* a full-length mirror here."

As she tucked in the sheets and straightened the quilt, it struck her that she didn't have to make the bed or look presentable. She lived alone now. There was nobody to see her. What she did need to concern herself with was the lighthouse and the slew of duties that came with it.

Two weeks after being released from the hospital, Abigail had searched out Lottie's real estate agency and consented to lease the caretaker's cottage before Lottie even faxed her a photo. It was easily the most impetuous act of Abigail's life, one she was second-guessing.

She poked her head into the hall, praying that the bathroom light wouldn't be on.

It wasn't.

Warily, she made the rounds of the second floor, on alert for the slightest difference. Her contacts case sat beside the faucet in the bathroom, unmoved. Mounds of books lay on the desk in the study, her shelving effort cut short. She questioned whether or not she'd imagined the noise last evening.

"There's only one way to find out."

The trip to the lighthouse turret went faster this morning than it had the previous day. Abigail was less circumspect, though just slightly. She noted the numbers of the squeaky steps from memory.

"Sixty-seven . . . seventy-one . . . seventy-nine."

That small practice comforted her. She preferred knowing what to expect. Upon reaching the lamp room, Abigail steeled herself for what she might see.

The oil pail appeared to be right where she'd left it.

Because she'd righted the pail after stumbling on it, Abigail couldn't tell if it was in exactly the same spot as before. She wanted to be certain. The rim of the pail was squared with a plaque soldered onto the base of the light. Rusted over, the plaque was illegible except for the year inscribed at the bottom—1893, the date the lighthouse was erected. Abigail took a mental picture of the pail's placement, then nudged it away from the lamp base with the toe of her tennis shoe, so the pail no longer touched any part of the plaque.

"This is merely a test, a test to see if . . . I've lost my marbles or not."

She hoped she would pass.

Abigail wound her way down the spiral staircase. From the

bottom, she stared upward at the lamp room, the mesh ironwork a sieve for the sun's gauzy rays. Maybe what had happened the night before was a fluke. Maybe it wouldn't happen again. The word *maybe* meant that something was possible or probable yet uncertain. It was the uncertainty that got under her skin.

◆　◆　◆

The sight of the kitchen in the bright morning light was sobering. Seeing the room in glaring clarity made her want to go back to bed. It was clean, but with the splotchy walls and slumping cupboards, it wasn't pretty.

"Caffeine might make this more tolerable."

She set the kettle on the stove to boil water for tea, but the burner wouldn't light. She could hear the gas hissing. The pilot light was out.

"Great."

Relighting a gas burner was a household chore Abigail always abhorred. Vacuuming couldn't hurt you. Neither could scrubbing the bathtub. Or waxing the floors. Once she'd waved clear the gas that had wafted into the air, Abigail struck a match. The gas instantly snatched the flame, sending her backpedaling. She doubted she would ever become accustomed to the fright that leapt through her as the match caught fire. Yet here in the caretaker's cottage, she would have to face that fear again and again, whether she was accustomed to it or not.

Abigail let the water come to a boil, pulling the teapot off the burner before it could whistle, a habit she'd adopted from living with Paul. For years she'd risen a half hour earlier than he did and conducted her morning routine in silence, careful not to wake him. She would shower, then make toast and tea, taking the kettle from the stove at just the right moment to prevent it from blowing. That was no longer necessary. She could allow the teapot to whistle if she pleased. Or she could leave the bed unmade or her hair unbrushed. There were a lot of things Abigail could do but ultimately wouldn't. She hadn't lived alone since college, but now that she was by herself,

Abigail wondered if, in time, her routines from when she was a wife and mother would disintegrate and morph into new habits. Single-person habits. Maybe they already were.

Two botched attempts at making toast in the oven made Abigail give up. Both times the bread turned coal black despite the temperature setting. As with the rest of the lighthouse, the stove had its own fussy personality, to which she'd have to acclimate.

Breakfast was a yogurt. Afterward, she busied herself by taking out the trash and tidying where she could until it was late enough to go into town to the hardware store.

"No small talk this time. No chitchat. No tall tales. Supplies and that's it."

❖   ❖   ❖

Finding a parking spot in the town square was about as difficult as finding hay in a haystack. There were more parking spaces than people. Abigail chose the same spot from the prior day, for no reason other than that it was familiar.

It was after ten, and the front door to Island Hardware was locked tight. She went around to the rear. Merle was sitting at a picnic table, gutting a large fish.

"Morning. It's, um, Abigail Harker. From yesterday."

"Morning, Abby."

That name again.

She gritted her teeth into a smile. "Yes, it's me."

Merle was carving out the fish's innards with a curved knife and flicking them into the grass. "She's a beauty, ain't she?" he said, cracking his catch open like a magazine. "Eight-and-a-quarter-pound Southern flounder. Got some hogchokers and whiffs too. This was the pick of the litter."

"Not to be rude, but is there something wrong with your fish?"

Amazingly, its eyes were on the same side of its head, so when Merle flipped it, one side was blank except for gills and a crescent of mouth.

Her remark gave Merle a chuckle. "Flounder are in the flatfish family," he explained. "They have real lean, compressed bodies and they swim on their sides, so their eyes are on the side that faces upward. That side's usually dark and the underside's white. Some are left-eyed, meaning their left side faces up. Others are right-eyed."

"Any particular reason for that evolutionary quirk?"

"Dunno. Maybe it's the same as some people being right-handed and some being lefties. That's how nature created them."

This was the sort of statement Paul might have made, boiling down the vast peculiarity of the universe to a plain, blunt fact, incontrovertible simply because that was the way it was.

"Well, I'm here because I'd like to buy some things from your store. Primer, sandpaper, brushes."

"Please don't tell me you're—"

"Painting? That's precisely what I'm going to do."

"Can't say I'd recommend it."

"Merle, the house is a disaster. Everything's falling apart. It looks terrible. How am I supposed to live like that?"

"Disaster? Don't you think that's a smidge harsh?"

"The place hasn't seen a scrub brush *or* a paintbrush since the hippie split."

"I'll admit the interior needs improvement. That said, allow me to propose two reasons why it might not be wise for you to paint. First, you're not allowed to. Says so in your lease. Second, what if Mr. Jasper doesn't take kindly to you messing with his lighthouse?"

"I've had enough of this nonsense, Merle. I don't want to hear about Mr. Jasper or any ghosts or any . . . anything that isn't normal."

"If you came to Chapel Isle for normal, Abby, you came to the wrong place."

He flopped the fish closed, so both of its eyes were facing skyward, and walked inside.

Under her breath, she said, "You may be right about that."

Abigail followed him into the store to the paint aisle.

"Any specific colors you fancy?"

She hadn't planned that far ahead and quickly skimmed the selection. "I'll take the light blue, the butter yellow, and the white."

"Is that it? How 'bout a new refrigerator? Big-screen TV?"

Abigail rolled her eyes. "Batteries. I need some for the flashlight I found in the shed."

"Don't bother. That flashlight's busted."

"You were holding on to it because . . . ?"

"Never got around to throwing it in the garbage."

"All righty. Here's another question I'm sure I'll regret asking. Why is the firewood in the shed? Shouldn't it be stored outdoors to keep it at 'outdoors' temperature or something?"

"Not much of an authority on wood, are you?'

"Does it show?"

"I put the logs in there so nobody'd steal them."

"Who'd steal firewood?"

Merle brought her cans of paint to the register, saying, "You'd be shocked what people'll steal. 'Specially here. Most of the houses on the island are rentals, occupied three or four months out of the year tops. And they're chock full of televisions, radios, small appliances. Ripe for the taking. Lottie's husband, Franklin, has me doing security at night on his properties so he won't get robbed blind."

"Security?"

"I drive around. Check each of his rental properties. See if anybody's broken in."

"Has that happened?"

"Three nights ago. East end of the island. Summer cottage got its window busted. They took the microwave, the toaster, and one of those video game machines."

"Maybe I should get in on this. I could use a microwave and a toaster."

"Not a joking matter if it's your stuff being stolen."

Abigail felt bad about the remark. Of all people, she was thoroughly acquainted with the anguish of losing possessions. "Should I start locking my door at night?"

"You? Naw, nobody'd come near that lighthouse."

"Why? A ratty couch and chipped soup bowls aren't good bur-glar bait?"

"No, because they'd be afraid to."

The insinuation irritated her. "Merle, if this is personal or terri-torial or you don't like me, so be it. However, you should know that if you're trying to get me to leave the lighthouse, to scare me away, it won't work."

"I didn't say I didn't like you, Abby. Contrary to your landlord, I'm trying to give it to you straight."

In her heart, Abigail believed that Merle meant well and that he was looking out for her best interests, which was what worried her.

"Then give me my paint so you can finish your filleting."

Merle rung her up and tossed in a plastic flashlight for free. She got out her wallet.

"You don't have to pay me now."

"Why not?"

He shrugged. "That's how it is here."

"What is it with this town? Yesterday I traded detergent to cover the cost of doing my laundry, and now you won't take a cent for more than a hundred dollars in merchandise."

"Met the Professor, eh?"

"If that's what you call him."

"It's not what I call him. That's what his students at MIT called him."

"Pardon me?" Abigail was stunned.

"Name's Bertram Van Dorst. He taught astrophysics at MIT for twenty years. He was born on the island, and when he retired, he moved home."

"You're telling me that man is a rocket scientist?"

"He is a wee bit eccentric, I'll grant you."

"That's putting it mildly."

"Bert's the smartest guy to ever live here. Won awards. Worked with NASA. If a guy as brilliant as him wants to come back to Chapel Isle, must mean Chapel Isle's worth coming back to."

Merle's pride reminded her of Denny and how he'd encouraged her to stay. Abigail suddenly saw Chapel Isle as a pretty girl who wanted to be appreciated for more than her looks. To most, the island was a summer destination, an escape. To the people who lived here, Chapel Isle was their world.

"So you'll run a tab for me?" Abigail asked.

"Depends on if you'll be sticking around."

"You know where to find me when you need me to pay. I'll be there."

"With this much painting to do, you definitely will be." He opened the store's front door, holding it for her as she hauled out the paint cans and supplies. "You want a hand getting to your car?"

"No, I've got it." Although straining, she was determined to do this on her own. "Oh, wait. I need more matches."

Merle slid a box into one of the bags Abigail was juggling, another gift.

"Good luck," he said.

"I might need more than luck."

"That you might."

in•stau•ra•tion (in´stô rā´shən), *n.* **1.** renewal; restoration; renovation; repair. **2.** *Obs.* an act of instituting something; establishment. [1595–1605; < L *instaurātiōn-* (s. of *instaurātiō*) a renewing, repeating. See IN-², STORE, -ATION] —in•stau•ra•tor (in´stô rā´tər), *n.*

❖   ❖   ❖

Luck *was a word Abigail knew a lot about. The term was derived from* the Middle English *lucke,* and from the Middle Dutch *luc,* short for *gheluc.* It meant an event, good or ill, affecting a person's interests or happiness, which was deemed casual, occurring arbitrarily. Depending on how she chose to view it, Abigail had been short on luck of late, having lost her family, or long on it, because she survived. So she was loath to leave anything but luck to chance.

Not taking Merle up on his offer had been a mistake. Her sore arms felt as though they were going to break off at the elbows. Abigail was packing the supplies into the station wagon, ready to head back to the lighthouse, when she recalled the other errand she had to do in town.

"Lottie."

A new note was taped to the door of the real estate agency. *Gone to the mainland,* was written in cursive. The *i* in *mainland* had a heart for a dot. Abigail ripped the note from the door and tore it to pieces as the gaggle of gnomes clustered along the front path smiled at her gleefully.

"Wipe those grins off your faces or I'll kick you in your little gnome teeth."

"Not very nice to threaten somebody one-tenth your size," a male voice cautioned.

A man in an official-looking uniform was studying her from the sidewalk. He wore gold-rimmed sunglasses, and what was left of his hair had been buzzed into a brush cut.

Abigail's cheeks went red. "That probably sounded a little . . ."

"Wacko?"

"Inappropriate."

"In these parts, we take bullying small ceramic men pretty serious."

The man's expression was unwavering.

"I'm just pulling your leg," he said after a moment's pause.

"Oh. Oh, yeah. I knew that."

"You here to see Lottie too?"

"Trying. Second day in a row."

"She's making herself scarce until the ink on your deal as caretaker at the lighthouse is dry."

Abigail's jaw genuinely dropped. "How did you . . . ?"

"It's not intuition. It's the old-fashioned grapevine. Denny Meloch told me he met you."

"No wonder everyone seems to know everything about everybody around here."

"There's plenty to wonder about on Chapel Isle, believe me. If you ever stop, means you haven't been here long enough."

Exactly what I need, Abigail thought. *More illogical platitudes.*

"Thanks for the tip."

"I'm Caleb Larner. I'm the sheriff."

"Abby Harker." She shook his hand, astonished that she'd introduced herself as *Abby*. She wrote it off as a subconscious slip.

"Pleasure to meet you," he said. "It's nice to have somebody minding the place. The lighthouse is the closest we've got to a monument."

There was that island dignity again. However, if this was how the locals maintained a landmark, historic preservation obviously wasn't a priority. So what was? Abigail wanted to ask.

"How are you settling in so far?"

She sensed more than interest in the sheriff's tone. He was probing. For what, she couldn't tell.

"Fabulous. Love the place," she lied.

"Glad to hear it."

An awkward gap in the conversation followed. They were on to each other.

"What are you here to see Lottie about, Sheriff? Has she committed any crimes—say, swindling her tenants?"

"Hardly. I came to talk to her about the robbery a few nights ago. I have to send the serial numbers on the stolen items to the mainland. I was making sure she had hers on file."

"The mainland? Why?"

"They check the pawnshops. See if any of the numbers pop up, people trying to sell what they stole."

"Should I be—"

"Nervous? No. Cautious? Yes. These guys seem relatively harmless. Strictly breaking in to take property. Still, you can never be certain."

That wasn't reassuring coming from the town's sheriff.

"Well," he sighed, "I'll be seeing you."

"Yes, you will," Abigail said, forcing a smile.

Sheriff Larner started to walk off, then turned back. "Hey, you should swing by bingo tonight."

"Bingo?"

"Thursday is game night at the fire station."

According to Abigail's brochure, Chapel Isle was rife with must-see places and must-do activities, the verbiage emphatic. The fire station wasn't at the top of the brochure's list or Abigail's. Neither was an evening of playing bingo.

"It's fun. Most of the town'll be there. Give you a chance to meet the natives."

"I'll try to stop in."

"Hope to see you there," he said, departing with a wave.

Despite his effort, the gesture wasn't in sync with the sheriff's inflection. Language was like water. It could carry meaning fluidly, be frozen solid by a change in cadence, or simmer into pure desire by a twist in tone. Abigail decided it wasn't a coincidence that she and the sheriff had bumped into each other. He was sniffing around for something. The question was what.

♦   ♦   ♦

On the ride home, Abigail mulled over her encounter with the law. Was it a pretense or should she take the meeting at face value? In lexicography, taking words at face value could amount to being shortchanged. Even the commonest of them could have multiple meanings, differing depending on usage. As a noun, *run* could signify a journey, a course, a sequence, or a cycle. As a verb, it meant fast movement on foot, to operate, to manage, to circulate, or to compete as a candidate. The first impression of some words was unreliable, a quality Abigail respected because it alluded to the intricacy of language. Was her first impression of Sheriff Larner reliable? Only time would tell. However, her initial impression of the lighthouse confirmed that some books can be judged by their covers.

Returning to the caretaker's cottage, she moved all the furniture on the first floor to the center of the living room and opened the windows in preparation for painting.

"You forgot to buy drop cloths. Then again, if you get paint on anything, it'll be an improvement."

Abigail turned the radio on and played with the tuner, locking in on the syrupy chords of a country ballad. Another spin of the dial snagged a snippet from a news station broadcasting from the mainland. Yearning for some contact with the outside world, she spent ten minutes dragging the radio around the room and adjusting the antenna until the station came in clearly. The reception was best with the radio positioned on the stairs, the antenna pointing straight up like a dagger. She made a mental note to move the radio once it got dark.

"God forbid you want a glass of water in the middle of the night. You could trip and get skewered. There's a gory headline."

Although she'd been racking up imaginary news captions, what Abigail was interested in were the real ones. While the broadcast recapped the important stories locally and across the world, the living room took its first casualty of the day. She removed the faded curtains from each window and stuffed them into a garbage bag.

"Buh-bye. Bon voyage. See ya."

As she taped off the windowsills, she listened to details about gunfights, car wrecks, and court cases. So much trauma and tragedy; Abigail was totally out of touch. The reports were eventually replaced by a discussion program where pundits contested the merits of senatorial candidates. Abigail wasn't paying close attention. Instead, she let the contributors' voices fill the room with human sound as she cracked the first can of paint.

The political discourse began to get heated, but Abigail was happily going from wall to wall, rolling on the warm yellow hue she'd chosen. Another coat was a must. The walls were so thirsty for change that they sucked up the paint and the color dried too pale.

Abigail was considering a second pass around the room when the next radio program started. It was a topical phone-in chat show hosted by a gravelly-voiced man named Dr. Walter. What his degree was in wasn't mentioned.

A woman phoned in to complain about the closing of a gun shop, saying, "Guns don't kill people. People kill people."

To which Dr. Walter replied, "Thank you for your highly original comment. Please do call back as soon as you've mastered the obvious."

That made Abigail laugh out loud, something she hadn't done in a while. Feeling guilty, she shut her mouth and locked her teeth together to prevent it from happening again. She was supposed to be in mourning. People in mourning didn't laugh. Or so Abigail presumed. Bereavement was her new job, a position for which she was unqualified and untrained. Whether this would be a lifelong career or temporary employment remained a mystery.

One after another, callers parried with Dr. Walter, who dismissed most of their comments as asinine and plowed onward with the show. Meanwhile, Abigail was reviving the windows and trim, care of a crisp coat of white, which she cut in with precision that would make her surgeon father proud. With the moldings painted, the dingy ceiling begged to be done as well. Because the chairs had proven unsteady, Abigail commandeered the table, rolling paint onto one section of ceiling at a time by standing on the table and pushing it from one side of the room to the other until she was finished.

"A first-rate job, if I do say so myself," she pronounced, touring the space from corner to corner.

The living room had been rejuvenated. Abigail, on the other hand, was spent. She'd been painting for hours, and the smell was giving her a headache. Being cooped up inside made her long to be outdoors. She was also starving.

Choosing a picnic on the beach rather than a meal at the now footprint-splotched dining room table, Abigail packed a sandwich and grabbed her keys, which she'd placed on an end table beside the house's old rotary-model telephone. Seeing the phone set off a spasm of guilt. Abigail had promised to contact her parents once she was settled. She'd been avoiding the call. The conversation would undoubtedly be fraught with staged questions about the island and the lighthouse, each intended to gauge her mental state, to determine if she was in immediate need of rescue. Abigail gave the big black rotary phone a final glance, opened the door, then locked it behind her.

◆ ◆ ◆

The sun was leaning low by the time she reached the strip of shore she'd passed the day she arrived on Chapel Isle. She parked next to the boarded-up snack stand, hiked over the dune ridge, and took a seat on a sandy crest above the tide line. From her perch, Abigail ate her sandwich and watched the waves slide up the beach languidly. The island was magnificent. She understood why Paul had loved it here. She could picture him walking along the water, holding Justin's hand. She could almost hear the splashing of their footsteps, Justin giggling as water sloshed over his tiny legs. The images were palpable. They felt real. Abigail could see Paul and Justin anywhere if she let herself. They could appear across from her in a room, riding in the car with her, beside her in bed, everywhere and nowhere at once.

As dusk descended on the coast, it grew too cold to stay by the water. Abigail had been crying and unconsciously churning her hands through the sand, as if to dig herself out of her misery. When she stood and brushed herself off, she thought of how similar sand was to language. A single grain or a single word meant little compared to the effect it had in concert with its own kind. Millions of granules made a beach; millions of combinations of words, a language. The whole would cease to exist without its parts. *Grief* was a word, a grain, Abigail wished she could separate from the whole, but that wasn't an option.

She wiped the sand from her hands and returned to her car.

jer•e•mi•ad (jer´ə mi´əd, –ad) *n.* a prolonged lamentation or mournful complaint. [1770–80; JEREM (AH) + –AD, in reference to Jeremiah's *Lamentations*]

❖　❖　❖

In the absence of streetlights or porch lamps or the glow from a neighbor's window, the night was overwhelmingly dark. So was the caretaker's house. Abigail had forgotten to leave any lights on. She fumbled for the front door. Inside, she groped at the switch. The living room looked better than she remembered, and the smell of paint had faded.

"That's because you left the windows open, genius," she scolded. "Didn't Sheriff Larner tell you to be 'cautious'?"

The thought of criminals prowling the island for empty houses to plunder was unsettling. Apart from Abigail's presence and her car in the drive, the caretaker's cottage could definitely be mistaken for vacant. It was an easy mark.

"On the bright side, the paint does look excellent. You, on the other hand, must look atrocious. You smell atrocious too."

Abigail hadn't bathed since she arrived. She'd been putting off cleaning the bathroom and had run out of excuses. Stepping over the radio on the staircase, a bucket of cleansers in hand, she said, "If *you* want to get clean, *it's* got to get clean."

A single swipe with a paper towel revealed that the bathtub was covered in a patina of dust. Though the tub could be wiped with minimal effort, the rust on the sink was less cooperative. The toilet put up a fight too, but the floor was the most intractable. Deeply ingrained, the dirt refused to be roused from between the tiles, until Abigail assailed it with a caustic soup of products that made her eyes water. Only then did the grime finally relent.

The mirror was last to be cleaned, and Abigail's reflection made her gasp.

Drops of white paint—some crusted with sand—dotted her face, and her hair was matted with sweat and flecked with yellow. Her clothes were splattered from shoulder to shoe. She hardly recognized her own visage. Abigail ran the bathwater, letting the tub fill almost to the top.

"Too bad you don't have any bubbles. Or steel wool. Because that's what it's going to take to get this stuff off you."

An image of Justin in the bathtub, clapping bubbles between his hands, floated into her mind, unbidden. Abigail closed her eyes, shutting the emotional door as a barrage of memories rattled the hinges.

Nolo, nolle, non vis, non vult.

Celo, celare, celari, cela.

Steam rose from the hot water waiting in the tub. She hadn't taken a bath in years. Showering was faster, simpler. Before, she didn't have time for a bath. Now Abigail had no choice in the matter and more time than she knew what to do with. If the claw-foot tub had been in better shape, it would have been quite grand. In its current state, the tub was ready for the salvage yard. Abigail felt the same way.

As she lowered herself into the bath, the water went spilling over the sides onto the floor. Out of practice, she had filled the tub too high.

"It appears you'll have to clean the floor *again*."

Despite a bumpy start, the steaming water soothed her aching muscles. A pass with a soapy washcloth had her feeling clean and, at least, somewhat human.

"This whole bath concept is actually really pleasant."

Her words bounced between the bathroom tiles, interposed by a staccato thump. Abigail sat up, covering herself with her arms. After seconds of silence, she made an announcement.

"If that was . . . somebody, I'm in the bathtub. I'm kind of naked. Could we do this whole banging and bumping act later?"

The house was still. Was that her answer? If not, Abigail didn't plan to wait around for another reply.

Scrambling from the tub, she grabbed a towel, scurried into the bedroom, and slammed the door. Wet, shivering, she addressed the ceiling: "I'm, um, going to leave for a while. Give you a little private time. You can have the place to yourself."

She threw on clean clothes and tore down the stairs, then stumbled over the radio. Abigail sailed through the air, missing the last three steps and landing on her hands and knees. Her palms stung from the impact. Her legs were wobbly.

"Ouch," she groaned, more in shock than in pain.

Abigail hobbled out the front door to her Volvo and sat there deliberating what to do. Her hair was dripping, soaking her shirt. She had nowhere to go.

"There's bingo," she sighed. "Why not? This night couldn't get much worse."

◆ ◆ ◆

To find the local fire station, all Abigail had to do was follow the line of parked cars that trailed from the center of town along a side street. She tied her wet hair into a bun and tucked in her shirt as an effort to appear more presentable. Having left in such a hurry, she'd forgotten to put on socks, and her shoes squished when she walked.

"Some first impression you'll make. You have your own sound effects."

The fire station was an unembellished cinder-block building, two stories tall. A sandwich board propping open the station's main door read: *Bingo Thursday Nights.* Abigail smoothed a wet tendril of hair behind her ear and marshaled her strength.

"Here goes nothing."

A large meeting hall spanned the entire second floor of the fire station. It was packed with rows of folding tables and chairs. Nearly every seat was full. The smell of popcorn and roasting hot dogs seemed to warm the air. Adults and children alike were flocked at the tables, gabbing. Abigail overheard people talking about the burglaries. They were the hot topic at each table, everyone speculating about who the culprits could be. Some thought it was a bunch of teenagers. Others believed it was lowlifes boating over from the mainland at night. The only one not discussing the robberies was a barrel-chested man in suspenders standing at the front of the room. He was too busy announcing numbers into a microphone as he plucked plastic bingo balls from a spinning cage. The plywood bingo board behind him lit up whenever he called a new number.

Abigail was standing by the door, feeling self-conscious and contemplating heading home, until she heard a familiar voice shouting her name.

"Hey, Abby! It's me, Denny Meloch. From the ferry. 'Member?"

He was pushing through the crowd toward her, a hot dog in one hand, a cup of beer in the other.

"Oh, hi. Of course I remember you."

Denny's eyes brightened. "Really? How ya liking it here so far?"

"It's been . . . colorful."

People were giving her passing glances. She was a stranger and she stood out. The women at the table in the far corner were doing more than looking, though. They were staring bullets and whispering.

"Why do I get the feeling I just walked into Salem with a pointy hat and a broomstick?"

Denny's face was blank, the reference lost on him. "Wanna sit down?" he asked, chewing his hot dog. "I can get you some cards, teach you how to play."

"Um . . ."

"There you are, hon. I saved you a seat." Ruth Kepshaw was motioning to her from a nearby table, supplying Abigail with a welcome excuse.

"Thanks, Denny, but Ruth already . . . Uh, you don't mind, do you?"

"No, that's cool. That's cool."

"I'll talk to you later, okay?"

"Sure. Later. Awesome." He gave her the thumbs-up. Uncertain how to respond, Abigail gave him the thumbs-up, too, then snaked through the crowd to Ruth's table.

"Thanks for—"

"Rescuing you from Denny? Don't mention it."

Ruth had a dozen bingo cards spread before her, which she was skimming and daubing with an ink marker with the smooth speed of a seasoned pro. She gave four of her cards to Abigail, along with an orange dauber.

"Take some of these, will ya? I got a hot one I have to keep my eye on."

"I haven't played since I was about eight."

"It's not chess. It's bingo. Now, mind those cards."

"Yes, ma'am."

Between numbers, Abigail scanned the hall. There were so many people, so many unfamiliar faces. She spotted Sheriff Larner three tables to her right. He saw her too and gave a nod.

Halfway through the round, she became aware that the clutch of women in the corner was keeping tabs on her. One gestured right at her. Janine Wertz was among them, sullenly smoking a cigarette.

"Oh, brother."

"What is it?" Ruth asked.

"Those 'hens' you told me about—they aren't too pleased that I'm here."

"Why? What are they doing?"

"They're ogling and pointing. I don't understand. I didn't do anything."

"Well, they're probably ogling and pointing because I told them your husband dumped you and ran off with his secretary."

"What? That's not—"

"True? Didn't think so. I took the liberty of concocting that little yarn to stop them from running you off the island. Now they can pity you instead of hating you."

If they knew what really happened, Abigail thought, *they* would *pity me*.

"Take it as a compliment. If you were as ugly as an ox's ass, none of 'em would give a care."

"That's a creative interpretation."

"I try."

A girl in braids on the other side of the room called out, "Bingo!" and Ruth cursed, crumpling her cards.

"That brat. I was one N-31 away."

"We could mug her for her winnings. She's small. I bet you could take her."

"Don't think I hadn't thought of that."

Round after round came and went as Abigail allowed herself to get absorbed in the game. Every time someone would shout "Bingo," Ruth would carp about the loss, then slide a new set of cards to her. When each game ended, people would decamp to the bar at the rear of the hall, where the food was served and a handful of men were stationed on stools.

"Our next round will be an X formation," the bingo caller announced, swirling the ball cage. He was about to pull the opening number when Hank Scokes, the man Abigail had met at the Kozy Kettle, staggered in the main door, knocking over a sheaf of folding chairs. The clatter echoed and heads turned.

Hank was swaying, visibly drunk. He was wearing the same clothes Abigail had seen him in the day before. "Sorry," he yelled in a mock whisper, before slipping on the chairs and falling to the floor.

Sheriff Larner leapt from his seat, prepared to drag Hank from the fire hall, but one of the guys from the bar came rushing to his aid. He was younger, the brim of his cap covering most of his face. He hauled Hank to his feet and was guiding him to the exit when Hank's eyes locked on Abigail.

"Hey. I know you," he said, as if she was a long-lost friend.

Now heads were turning toward her.

Then his tone changed on a dime. "Whaddaya think you're looking at," he sneered. The guy at his side squinted at Abigail, as though she was the one insulting Hank.

If Abigail could have willed herself to dematerialize, she would have.

"Nat, get him out of here," Larner ordered.

The caller spun the ball cage again and tried to get everyone's attention refocused on the game. "Check your cards, folks. Like I said, this game will be an X formation."

Abigail was shaking, she was so humiliated. "That was . . ." she began, but didn't finish because she couldn't decide whether *degrading* or *demeaning* was the optimal adjective.

Ruth chose for her. "Sucky. That was sucky."

"What's wrong with him?"

"Heart trouble," Ruth replied.

"Don't you mean liver trouble? He was plastered."

"Hank's wife passed away about six months ago. That's his heart trouble."

"Oh" was all Abigail could say. She experienced an abstract sympathy for the man, unwilling to associate herself with him or acknowledge that she had anything in common with a nasty drunk who made a scene. "Was that his son with him?"

Ruth scoffed. "Lord, no. That's Nat Rhone. He works on Hank's fishing rig. Bounced from boat to boat because nobody wanted to take him on full-time."

"Why?"

"He has a helluva temper."

"So why did Hank hire him?"

"There aren't many people as ornery as Hank Scokes. Nat makes him seem like a pussycat."

"Is Nat an islander, a native?"

"Nope. Came here about four years ago. Nobody knows where he's from. Way I heard, last person who asked wound up with stitches."

"Friendly guy."

"Somewhere, sometime, somebody did Nat wrong. He's never forgotten it."

"Maybe his husband divorced him and ran off with his secretary."

"Touché," Ruth retorted. "The real bummer is, Nat Rhone's the only decent-looking man on this island. Only it'd take a U-Haul truck to carry his emotional baggage."

"Is that your clinical diagnosis?" Abigail teased.

"Mind those cards, missy."

The men from the bar were collecting the fallen chairs and making a racket the bingo caller had to shout over.

"What are those guys doing at a bingo game if they're not playing?"

"Most are members of the volunteer fire crew. They volunteer because they get to drink here for half price two nights a week."

"How altruistic."

One of the men, the tallest of the bunch, was offering to lend a hand clearing the chairs. The others waved him off. He was almost as drunk as Hank, teetering on his heels.

"Uh-oh. We might have an instant replay."

"That's Clint Wertz. You be careful around him," Ruth warned.

"Any particular reason?"

"He's got what a lady might call a 'wandering eye' and what I'd call a real lack of zipper control. Gives Janine good reason to be as surly as she is."

"That's Janine's husband?"

"See why she wasn't real sweet with you? To her, you're bait."

Clint Wertz wove toward the bar and ordered another round. Abigail caught Janine watching him with a wistful gaze, equal measures anger and remorse. Her expression reminded Abigail that missing what was still yours could be as painful as missing what was lost.

"Tonight's final game will be a jackpot round," the caller announced into the microphone. "The cash prize is worth three hundred dollars."

At that, the noise level in the hall dropped to a hush. Ruth rolled up her sleeves, as though priming herself for hand-to-hand combat. "This is the biggie, hon, and it's got my name on it. Granted, I say that every week. This time I mean it."

"What do you want me to do?"

"You watch them cards like a hawk."

Abigail gave Ruth a salute and did as she was told.

With each number called, the tension in the fire hall mounted. Even the men by the bar grew quiet. Abigail had two cards to tend. Neither showed much potential. Ruth could have handily played them herself, but she was acting like she needed a partner, a gesture Abigail greatly appreciated. For a change, she was useful. She hadn't felt useful in what seemed an eternity.

"Bingo!" a bald man in a sweater vest yelled.

"Aw, damn." Ruth mashed her cards into a heap.

"The guy's about seventy," Abigail said out of the corner of her mouth. "You could pick his pocket and he might not notice."

"That senile Elton Curgess would enjoy it if I went rummaging around in his pockets. Let's get out of here before I strangle the old fart."

Together, Abigail and Ruth fell into line with the crowd as everyone filed from the fire station to their cars. Sheriff Larner caught up to them outside.

"Nice to see you made it," he said to Abigail.

"Yeah, it was fun. I haven't played in ages."

"No? Well, you've got an expert teacher in Ruth. Best of the best. If there's anyone here who could show you the ropes, it's her." Larner was laying the "down home" kindness on thick.

Ruth donned a fake grin. "That's me. The bingo master."

"You girls drive safe," he told them as he strolled off.

"Is he always . . . ?"

"In your business and actin' like he ain't? Yup. But he's all the law we have on the island—him and his deputy, Ted Ornsey. Thing about Caleb Larner is, he doesn't miss a trick. Makes him a damn good sheriff. Also makes him a pain in the rear."

That confirmed Abigail's earlier suspicion. The sheriff wasn't merely being hospitable. He was feeling her out.

"Caleb's had more right to be a pain lately," Ruth continued. "He has a daughter in Raleigh. She's twenty-six. Got pancreatic cancer and not much medical coverage, so the bills keep mounting. His wife's been staying with her for months. Caleb helps how he can. Works overtime but can't get to the mainland to visit her much. Scary, her being young as she is."

Abigail barely knew Sheriff Larner, yet her heart went out to him. There was no perfect way to say it, no phrase that wasn't flimsy or clichéd. "That's sad," she said.

"It certainly is."

"Do you want me to walk you to your car, Ruth? I hear there's a criminal element marauding around the island."

"Those robberies. Talk of the town. Everybody's blabbing and nobody has a clue. Would be handy if somebody blabbed about who's actually doing it." She shook her head. "Thanks for offering to be my bodyguard, but I'm parked right here."

Ruth had scored a space directly in front of the fire station.

"Lucky you. I parked so far from here I should have left my car at home."

"It's not luck if you come an hour early."

"Whoa, you're dedicated."

"I believe you mean *deranged*."

"They're not technically synonyms, but sometimes they're the same."

Ruth settled into a vintage sky blue sedan bearing an *Impeach Nixon* bumper sticker. There was a slot for an eight-track cassette on the dash, and the powder blue leather seats were in mint condition. The car looked as if it rarely left the garage.

"This is some ride. Drive it much?"

"Hon, I live on an island. Ain't too many places to go."

"I'm beginning to realize that."

Ruth started her car. "Nice to see you out and mingling, Abby."

Abigail hadn't told Ruth her name. Though she wasn't surprised she knew it.

"Don't worry. Merle gave me the scoop on you. And I promise your coffee won't be so hot next time."

Watching Ruth drive away, Abigail wondered whether Merle had been gossiping about her or if he was trying to protect her again. Abigail hadn't come to Chapel Isle to make friends, but between Janine, the John Deere twins, Hank Scokes, and his pal Nat Rhone, she seemed to be making enemies. She hoped Merle didn't have it in for her too.

♦   ♦   ♦

"I'm back," Abigail announced, hesitantly sticking her head in the front door of the caretaker's cottage. It was a relief not to come home to complete darkness, as she had the previous evening. Then she realized that she hadn't left the lights on intentionally. In her haste, she'd forgotten to shut them off.

With the windows closed, the acrid odor of paint and cleaning products had congealed into an overpowering stench. Nonetheless, Abigail could still smell last night's fire. It was a scent she couldn't forget, even when it wasn't there.

"Listen, I've had a pretty rough day and I'd appreciate it if there weren't any more noises tonight. Please," she added, righting the overturned radio as she climbed the stairs.

She changed into two layers of pajamas, removed her contacts at a record clip, and hightailed it out of the bathroom, making sure the switch was off. Twice. Abigail glanced back to check before shutting her bedroom door. The light was out.

"Now if only it would stay that way."

kith (kith), *n.* **1.** acquaintances, friends, neighbors, or the like; persons living in the same general locality and form‐ ing a more or less cohesive group. **2.** kindred. **3.** a group of people living in the same area and forming a culture with a common language, customs, economy, etc., usually en‐ dogamous. [bef. 900; ME; OE *cȳth,* earlier *cȳththu* kin‐ ship, knowledge, equiv. to *cūth* COUTH² + *-thu* -TH¹; akin to Goth *kunthi,* G *Kunde* knowledge]

❖   ❖   ❖

Abigail opened her eyes the next morning to find herself facedown between her pillows, with the bedding knotted around her arms and legs as though she were in a straitjacket. She wriggled free, her limbs tingling with the renewed rush of blood.

"What on earth were you dreaming about?"

No matter how hard she tried, Abigail was unable to summon the dream into daylight. What sprung to mind instead was the test she'd orchestrated with the oil pail in the lighthouse.

"One of your more inventive ideas," she said wryly.

As with the dreams that plagued her, perhaps she was better off not knowing the outcome. She sat in bed, debating.

"The lighthouse isn't going anywhere. And there's a ton of painting to do. Oh, who are you kidding? You're a coward and can't face it."

That may have been true in the moment, but not in the broader sense. Abigail had had three different roommates while recuperat‐ ing at the hospital's intensive-care unit, each released sooner than she was, evidence of how severe her condition had been—and that referred only to her physical wounds. She had courage; however, her reserves were low. Too low for a trip to the lighthouse turret today.

After a bowl of cereal for breakfast, it was time to paint the kitchen. A thorough sanding of the walls would eradicate the last of the wallpaper adhesive. Only that was a taller order than Abigail had predicted. Within twenty minutes, her hands were cramped into claws, she was breathing heavily, and her shirt was a lighter shade from the dust.

The prep work, though painful, proved to be worthwhile. Smooth from the sandpaper, the walls took the yellow paint evenly. Since the spots behind the refrigerator and oven were hard to reach, she wasn't going to bother.

"Nobody can see back there anyway," Abigail insisted, with an indifferent sweep of the roller. After which she thought she heard a soft bump.

"Or I could get a brush and touch that up."

Compared to the walls, the wainscoting needed serious sanding. Her insubstantial sheets of sandpaper were no match for the fossilized dribbles of paint, so she whittled away the most egregious blobs with another butter knife and applied a fresh coat of white. The cabinetry was next. Using a screwdriver salvaged from the shed to remove the hardware, Abigail went from cupboard to cupboard and drawer to drawer with her roller and brush. The bright white paint was an immediate improvement. She considered springing for new doorknobs too.

"That is, if Merle hasn't put a moratorium on selling me remodeling supplies."

Abigail left the empty cabinetry open to dry. Once she'd eaten what had become her customary lunch—a cold sandwich devoured at speed—she carted her painting supplies upstairs. Given a choice between the study, the bathroom, or the bedroom, the bathroom was her least favorite, for reasons she didn't want to revisit. The study was running neck and neck.

"The bedroom it is."

She pushed the heavy headboard and dresser away from the

walls, then moved the rocker and nightstand into the middle of the room, as she had done downstairs. In a cleared corner lay the newspaper article.

"Hey, there you are." Abigail picked up the clipping and began to read the article aloud. "*Last night the freight vessel,* the Bishop's Mistress, *was*—"

A shrill ringing interrupted her, nearly shaking her out of her skin. It took a second ring for Abigail to realize that it was the telephone. She shoved the article in her pocket and hurried downstairs.

"Hello?"

"Abby? Abby, you there?"

"Lottie? Is that you?"

"Yes, dear, it's me." A burst of static sizzled the line, drowning her voice.

"Lottie, where have you been? I've—"

"What's that, dear? I can't hear you. This darned cell phone my husband gave me isn't worth the plastic it's made with."

"Where. Have. You. Been." Abigail voiced each word loudly.

"I'm in Hatteras at the ER. My cousin broke her hip. Slipped and fell getting into her girdle. Been here since yesterday morning taking care of her."

Knowing that Lottie wasn't intentionally avoiding her assuaged a fraction of Abigail's irritation. But just a fraction.

"I wanted to check in with you, dear. How's it going?"

"I'm—"

A wave of static scorched the line.

"What was that?" Lottie shouted. "I couldn't understand you."

"I'm—"

"Say again."

This is your chance. Leave. Tell Lottie you've already done the cleaning she should have paid for. Tell her she might have mentioned the minor detail about a supposed ghost. Tell her you want out of this rental contract.

Abigail took a deep breath. "I'm fine, Lottie. Everything here is fine."

"Terrific. Well, gotta run. I think the battery on this cell phone is about to—"

The line went dead. Abigail hung up and looked around. The furniture was jumbled in the center of the living room, dishware was scattered across the floor, and half her groceries were waiting to be put away, yet the house was indubitably different.

"Maybe everything is fine."

❖   ❖   ❖

Painting the bedroom didn't seem like labor to Abigail, what with the radio playing and the ocean air gusting through the windows. She slid the cream polyester drapes off their rods, then repurposed them as drop cloths. Soon the new pale-blue paint, mimicking the sky, blotted out the stale green.

The call-in show Abigail had listened to the day before was on again. Dr. Walter was discussing modern romance and the new rules of courtship. At issue was first-date etiquette.

A guy on the phone was ranting, "I understand what women want. It's none of this sweet, sensitive crap. They need a man who knows what's what and knows how to take care of business. Holding doors and talking about your feelings ain't going to get you nowhere 'cept home alone on a Saturday night."

"Listen, Casanova," Dr. Walter quipped. "I have a sneaking suspicion you couldn't get a date with a woman unless she was drunk, stupid, or paid for, so why don't you try standing up straight, because I can hear your knuckles knocking on the ground as we speak, you dumb Cro-Magnon."

The tough-talking doctor disconnected before the guy could reply.

"You tell 'em, Dr. Walter," Abigail cheered.

"Do you have a dating horror story? Are you an incurable romantic? Is chivalry dead? The phone lines are open."

Caller upon caller recounted tales of blind-date catastrophes as well as perfect matches that resulted in marriage. Meanwhile, Abigail turned her attention from the walls, where the paint was drying, to the bedroom furniture. She propped the rocker on a drapery panel and took a brush to it, slathering on a coat of white. Next came the nightstand, which was stubby and bland. The paint certainly enlivened it. The same went for the dull dresser, which took the white well after some sanding. Pausing between drawers, Abigail stole a glance at the ceiling in the direction of the lamp room, to make sure what she was doing was okay. The only noise was from Dr. Walter. So she kept painting.

"This jerk stood me up," a female caller sniffled. "Don't you think that's cruel to do to someone when they've put on their prettiest dress and done their nails? To me, it's mean."

The usually salty doctor turned sensitive. "Don't cry, my lovely. I'm certain you looked beautiful that night. I'm also certain there's a special level in hell reserved for men who stand women up. Common courtesy," he sighed, "where has it gone? Show your fellow humans some respect and the world will show you some back."

Was she being thoughtless, Abigail wondered, painting a place that wasn't hers and furniture that didn't belong to her? In a certain respect, she was. In another, she saw herself as bettering the long-neglected home. Whatever the case, the point was moot because the painting was finished. If it was an insult rather than assistance, she felt as certain as Dr. Walter that she would find out shortly.

There was one last thing Abigail wanted to try. The old drapes she'd put under each piece of furniture to protect the floor also made the items easy to move. Abigail pushed the bed into the corner at an angle, switched the placement of the nightstand and the rocker, then resituated the dresser between the windows. The new layout was cozier, taking advantage of the space. The bedroom went from looking like a cheap beach motel to cottage chic.

"Some blinds. A new lamp shade. Could be cute in here after all."

Admiring the arrangement, Abigail had a flash of moving into her old house with Paul the year before Justin was born, each room an open expanse of potential. Paul had been making more money with his firm, and their new house was three times the size of their former home. They didn't have even remotely enough furniture to fill it, but Paul's attitude was: "If we don't have it, we can buy it." He'd given Abigail carte blanche on the décor. The style of the home was colonial, a favorite of hers. High ceilings, inlaid floors, marquetry cabinets, and intricate crown molding in every room, it was traditional to a T. Although she'd delighted in the process of selecting historically correct paint colors and ordering custom furniture, she prized that moment when the house was still empty and replete with possibilities. Tears welled in her eyes.

"No," Abigail said. "I don't want to do this. I am *not* going to do this."

She refused to allow what she'd accomplished that afternoon to be overshadowed, to be lost so fast. Abigail rushed down the stairs, barreled through the front door, and doubled over in the high grass, unsure if she would faint.

"Breathe," she told herself. "Breathe."

Abigail unsteadily made her way to the station wagon. She was conjugating Latin verbs as she sped away from the lighthouse, desperate to be anywhere but there.

◆　◆　◆

Rows of boats were bunched along the pier, masts listing against the darkening sky. Pickup trucks lined the town square. This was the most crowded Abigail had seen it since she'd arrived. By chance, her usual parking space outside the Kozy Kettle was vacant. That was as provident a reason as any for her to stop.

"You're hungry. You'll feel better once you've eaten."

Haggard and covered in paint, Abigail pushed the door to the café open and immediately had to resist the urge to pull it closed again. The place was packed. Each stool at the counter was taken, and there wasn't a booth to be had. All eyes—including Janine Wertz's—shifted toward her as she entered. Janine was having coffee and a cigarette with one of the women Abigail had seen her with at bingo.

From the boiling pot to the frying pan.

"Fancy seeing you here, Abby," someone called out.

It was Denny. She should have known. He was at her side in a second flat.

"Ruth didn't save you a seat this time. Want to sit with us? We got room."

"Sure," Abigail replied, passing Janine, who exhaled a belligerent stream of smoke right at her. "Thanks for the invitation."

Denny led her to the table he was sharing with his father and proffered a seat with a gentlemanly flourish of his hand. Janine and her cohort were two tables away. Across the aisle Abigail recognized Nat Rhone from the night before. He was with three other men, each wearing a flannel shirt, canvas jacket, cap, and heavy boots— the unofficial fisherman's uniform. Most of the patrons had coffee cups but no plates. Either Abigail had missed the meal rush or no one was eating. The Kozy Kettle seemed to be an island hangout rather than a dinner destination. Without food to occupy them, everyone in the café abandoned their conversations to take in the scene that was about to unfold.

"Hey, Pop, this is that lady we brought over from the mainland the other day. Her name's Abby."

Denny's father grunted his greeting and fiddled with his coffee cup. He appeared as painfully aware of the attention as Abigail was.

"You been painting?" Denny inquired.

"Yes, and I made quite a mess of myself," she admitted self-effacingly.

"No harm done," he said. It was the truest thing Abigail had heard in a while. "You hungry? I can grab you a menu."

"No, no, I can—"

Denny was already on his feet. "I got it."

"Hey, Denny. Is that your girlfriend?" Nat Rhone asked from the opposite side of the aisle.

"Uh, no," Denny said, flustered. "I was—"

"Ain't much of a first date, taking her out to eat with your dad."

The other men at the table snickered. Denny's father sipped his coffee without a word.

"If you need any lessons on how to treat a lady, I can give you some pointers. Free of charge."

"Hey, Casanova," Abigail snapped. "My guess is you couldn't get a date with a woman unless she was drunk, stupid, or paid for, so why don't you mind your own business."

The quote from Dr. Walter's show rolled off Abigail's tongue effortlessly, and the insult hung in the air like the smell of a firecracker that had gone off. Everyone had heard her. The sting of her remark reddened Nat's face.

Denny clapped. "Ooh-wee, she told you."

Nat sprang from his seat. In an instant, he had Denny by the throat with one hand and was pummeling him in the stomach with the other. Both men's caps went flying from their heads. Denny was squirming and no one intervened, including his father. Abigail jumped to her feet but could only stand outside the fray, shouting at the men to stop while others egged them on. Then Merle Braithwaite walked into the café. In two strides he was between Nat and Denny. He put a massive hand on Nat's shoulder and yanked them apart, but Nat broke free from his grasp to get in his last punch. Denny scrambled backward to avoid the blow. Lunging for Nat, Merle twisted awkwardly and went careening to the ground, overturning chairs in his wake. The sound of Merle hitting the floor silenced the entire restaurant.

Ruth rushed from the kitchen to Merle's side. "Everybody out. Café's closed. And you," she said to Nat Rhone. "Don't come back."

He snatched his fallen cap and strode away. His buddies followed, along with the rest of the patrons, some groaning as they left behind freshly poured cups of coffee with the money for their meals. Janine shot Abigail a nasty glance when she walked by. Others stared. In a single swoop, Abigail had started a fight and injured three men. She hurried to Merle.

"Are you okay?"

"If being on the floor is okay, then, yeah, I'm dandy."

"Let me help you."

"Not unless you've got a forklift in your pocketbook."

"I've gotcha." Bert Van Dorst, the man from the laundromat, was shuffling over from the counter. "Saw you fall, Merle. That hurt?"

"You could say so."

"How's your laundry?" he asked Abigail.

"Bert, maybe now's not the time," Merle advised.

"Just making conversation."

Ruth shut the door to the café and locked it as the bell overhead ceased to ring. "Denny, you and your father get on one side of Merle. Bert, you get on the other."

Together the three of them hoisted Merle into a chair. Abigail tried to make eye contact with Denny's father. He refused to meet her gaze. Her first thought was that he was mad at her for sparking the fight. Then it dawned on her that he was embarrassed, by Denny and by the fact that he didn't have his own son's back.

"Let me get a look at that ankle, Merle." He winced as Ruth removed his boot. "It's swelling already. Think you can put weight on it?"

Merle set his foot on the floor, testing. "Not for long."

"It's not broken."

"How do you know?" Denny was squatting to have a look for himself.

"Because if it was, he'd want to toss his cookies when he stood on it. In the early days, people'd strike a tuning fork to tell if a bone was broke. The vibration would make the bone shake. The toss-your-cookies test will have to do."

"Got plenty of forks here. I can get you some."

"No, hon," Ruth told him, patting Denny's shoulder. "I think it's only a bad sprain."

"Shouldn't we get him to a doctor?" Abigail asked. "To be safe?"

Ruth shook her head. "I'm not going to trouble the gals at the UC."

"We got an urgent-care unit on the island," Bert explained. "Two nurses and a doctor on call. People try not to bother 'em unless it's an emergency."

"Ruth's right," Merle said. "It's a sprain, not a stroke, for Pete's sake."

Abigail was still processing the fact that there was virtually no medical care available on the island. "You're saying there's no hospital here and only one doctor on Chapel Isle?"

"During the off season, yeah," Ruth informed her flatly.

"But we've got Ruth," Denny chimed. "She's practically a doctor herself."

"Really?" Abigail said.

Bypassing the topic, Ruth instructed Denny and his father to take Merle home. "Bert, you go with them. They'll need the extra set of hands. See that he gets into bed and puts an ice pack on that ankle. I'll stop by in the morning to check on him."

"Ruth, there's no need to bother—"

"Don't fuss at me, Merle Braithwaite, or that sprain will be the least of your injuries."

He gave in, then the men steadied him on their shoulders, helping him limp out of the café. All Abigail could do was hold the door for them.

"I'm sorry, Merle."

"You've got nothing to be sorry for, Abby."

In actuality, she had a profusion of things to be sorry for, herself included. What Abigail wanted to hear was that Merle didn't blame her. She blamed herself for too much already.

From the window of the café, she and Ruth watched as the men got Merle into his truck.

This is your fault, Abigail thought.

"It's not your fault," Ruth told her.

"Gee, the voice in my head must be getting loud if other people can hear it."

"Don't beat yourself up. Money says Nat was pining for a fight before you shot him that zinger."

"You heard that?"

"Did I!" Ruth nudged Abigail's arm, congratulating her. "Dr. Walter couldn't have said it better himself."

"Do you think anybody else knew I was plagiarizing a radio personality?"

"Naw. They probably figure you're a badass."

"A badass? That might be a stretch."

"Who's to say? Boston's a tough town." Ruth had known Abigail was a widow instinctively but had likely heard she was from Boston through Lottie. News certainly did travel fast on the island.

"Not as tough as Chapel Isle."

"You got that right, hon. Come on and fix these chairs with me, will ya? Give a tired broad a hand."

Abigail cleared the mess from the fight while Ruth collected the leftover dishes. Though the café was closed, the smell of hot coffee and the warmth of people's bodies lingered. Abigail had been rattling around the lighthouse on her own like a marble in a jar. She'd forgotten how it felt to be in a space that wasn't always vacant. She gathered the plates Ruth couldn't carry and trailed her into the kitchen.

"This here's Zeke."

Ruth introduced her to a sinewy man in an apron with an anchor tattooed on his forearm, the blue ink so dark it seemed like a bruise. He was vigorously scraping the grill with a metal spatula. A day's worth of grease oozed from the burner, making Abigail glad she hadn't had the chance to eat.

"We got the dishes for you," Ruth told him, and he nodded.

"He cooks and does the dishes?"

"Says it clears his mind."

"Clears the mind," Zeke repeated, tapping his temple.

"If you ever want to clear your mind at my house, you're welcome anytime."

Zeke didn't respond. Then the comment sunk in and he chuckled. "Funny," he said.

"Yeah, this gal's a riot. Lemme tell you," Ruth said sarcastically. "Don't get her riled or heads will roll. The Boston Bruiser, we'll call ya."

"Please don't."

"Bye, Bruiser," Zeke said, as Ruth guided her out of the kitchen.

"Great. Another nickname."

"I've got to cash out the till. You don't have to stay," Ruth said. "You've done enough."

"No argument there. I don't have much else to do, though."

"Can you count change?"

◆　◆　◆

While Ruth tallied the day's take, Abigail sat at the counter sorting coins.

"I feel awful about Merle getting hurt."

"Don't. He would've tried to break up the fight even if you weren't involved."

"Me? Why would that matter?"

"He knows you're alone here on the island. Plus, I told him you were a widow, so I think he was looking after you."

"A widow? How did you—"

"Darlin', it takes one to know one."

"Was it because I'm not wearing a wedding ring?"

"Pssh. Nope." Ruth set a stack of cash on the counter. "Put it like this. You can tell I'm from North Carolina by how I talk. I can tell you lost your husband by what you *don't* say."

Abigail had no idea she could be giving herself away when she wasn't even speaking.

"I met my husband, Jerome, on the mainland, but he was born on Chapel Isle," Ruth told her. "Army'd put him through medical school after the Korean War, and he wanted to give back to his hometown. For years he was the only permanent doctor on the island. We'd get phone calls in the middle of the night. Sore throats, broken wrists, toddlers with earaches, women going into labor." Ruth marveled at what she'd endured. "I'd go with him. Got my honorary medical degree along the way."

Abigail now understood what Denny had been talking about earlier.

"So you're not a native?"

"Been here long enough that I kinda am."

"You must love it here if you've stayed."

"Didn't at first, believe you me. When the ferry would break down in the winters, we'd wonder if the market was going to have food. Had to ration what milk and eggs you had. With our three kids to take care of, that was no joyride. There was only one proper plumber on the island for half a decade, so if your toilet broke, you got real close with nature. Can't say they were all bad times. But they weren't all rosy. Island's like a resort compared to how it was. Take a gander," she said, pointing at the outmoded coffeemaker and wear-beaten furnishings. "That's saying something. My grandkids, they visit from Florida and think it's old-fashioned here. I tell 'em, 'This isn't old-fashioned. This is new-fashioned.' I may not have loved Chapel Isle in the beginning. Thing was, I loved Jerome. He's been gone eleven years. Not a day goes by that—well, you understand."

Ruth closed the register, shutting the drawer hard enough to make the metal clang.

"Is it that obvious?" Abigail asked. "About me being . . ."

"I doubt anybody is wise to it 'cept me. And Merle," Ruth added apologetically.

Abigail had become part of an unspoken league, one nobody wanted to join, because there was no resigning. She'd already met Chapel Isle's charter members, Ruth and Hank. She was the newest inductee.

"So how's it going at the lighthouse?"

"It's fine. Everything's fine." Abigail could tell Ruth was trying to see if she'd heard about the ghost.

"Uh-huh," she answered, unconvinced. "Remember, if you need anything, Merle can swing over—"

"I doubt Merle will be 'swinging' anywhere for a while. I'll be okay."

"I know you will, hon. I know you will." Ruth meant it in every possible way.

"Can I go with you to see him tomorrow?"

"'Course you can. Meet me at his house at eight-thirty." She jotted Merle's address on her order pad. "Morning rush'll be done. Should be quiet enough for me to sneak away."

"Remind me again: When exactly is this morning rush?"

"About five a.m. The men have to be on the water by five-thirty."

"What a hard life." The hours, the conditions, the labor—Abigail thought it had to be a demanding way to earn a wage.

"Maybe," Ruth said. "But what I've learned living on this island is that life is only as hard as you make it."

Abigail had chosen to pick up and move to Chapel Isle, chosen to leave her family and friends behind, and chosen to live at the lighthouse alone. Was *she* making her life harder than it had to be?

lum•pen (lum´pən), *adj.* **1.** of or pertaining to disfranchised and uprooted individuals or groups, esp. those who have lost status: *the lumpen bourgeoise.* —*n.* **2.** a lumpen individual or group. [1945–50; extracted LUMPENPROLETARIAT]

◆ ◆ ◆

The early-morning air was brisk. Standing outside Merle's house waiting for Ruth, Abigail wished she'd worn a sweater. She felt so terrible about what had happened at the Kozy Kettle that she was impatient to make amends.

Merle lived on the north end of the island. His property sloped into the bay. A lone motorboat was tethered to his private dock. Floral drapes hung in the windows of his gray-shingled cottage, and there were tulips embossed on the welcome mat, roses stenciled on the mailbox, and a plastic daisy wreath gracing the entry.

"Flowers would have been thoughtful," Abigail told herself as she paced the sidewalk, feeling guilty for arriving empty-handed. "If Merle's front door is any indication, he does seem to like them."

As she was eyeing the neighbor's bed of marigolds, contemplating stealing some to improvise a bouquet, Ruth arrived.

"Why didn't you head in, hon?"

"Merle wasn't expecting me, and I wasn't sure if he was, well, miffed about yesterday."

"When Merle Braithwaite is miffed, trust me, you'll know."

Ruth let herself in the front door, hollering, "I brought you a visitor."

The home's interior was furnished in feminine antiques and reams of mauve chintz. Abigail tried to imagine a man as large as Merle getting comfortable on the small tufted sofa or setting a beer on the diminutive maple coffee table. The swirled legs of the arm-chairs seemed as if they would splinter if he looked at them too intently.

"You-know-who's a bit of a bull in a china shop here," Ruth whispered. "His ex-wife loved this girly stuff, so he won't change a lick of it."

"Ex-wife?"

"He married a gal who visited the island one summer. This was back, oh, years and years ago. After a few months, she couldn't stand it here. The isolation drove her nuts. Couldn't hack it, so she divorced Merle. Only she didn't tell him she was pregnant. He found out through an in-law and volunteered to leave Chapel Isle, to move to California to be with her and the baby boy. She told him not to. She'd already shacked up with another fella."

"My God, that's horrible—" Abigail began. Then she heard Merle clomping toward the living room.

"I'm coming, I'm coming. Oh, hey there, Abby," he said, pleased to see her. Merle was using an umbrella as a cane and wearing a special vest with pockets for lures. The vest was wet.

Ruth folded her arms. "Jesus, Mary, and Joseph, were you fishing?"

"Maybe." Merle hung his head.

"You could've killed yourself in that little boat of yours with a sprained ankle. I have half a mind to put you under house arrest until you've healed. Get off your feet this instant." She badgered him toward the kitchen table and started making coffee.

Abigail joined him. "How are you feeling?"

"My leg hurts some."

"Not enough to prevent you from fishing."

"I'd have to be in a full-body cast not to fish. Even then I'd float myself on the water and put a line in my mouth."

"That would be a sight."

"You won't have to wait if he doesn't stay off that ankle," Ruth threatened, setting out two cups for them.

"Aren't you having any?" Abigail asked.

"Since our patient is obviously doing fine, I've got to get back to the Kettle. Give a jingle if you need me, Merle." She scooped up her purse and went for the door as the coffee continued to perk. "Too-dles."

"How are the renovations coming?" Merle inquired once Ruth was gone.

"You say that like I'm putting a new wing on the house."

"Are you?"

"Don't tempt me."

"I've witnessed you in action. I wouldn't dare."

"I'm making progress. I'd planned on stopping by your store today to buy some new drawer pulls for the kitchen. Scratch that."

"You can go and get what you want. Back's always open."

"You don't lock your doors? What about the robberies?"

"If those burglars want to steal a dozen boxes of threepenny nails and some WD-40, they can have at it."

"This from the mouth of the man in charge of Lottie's security."

"Speaking of which, I have a favor to ask."

"Whatever I can do, consider me at your service. Groceries, cooking, cleaning, you name it."

"No, no, nothing like that. I can't drive because of my ankle. If I can't drive, I can't check on the rental properties for Franklin."

"You're saying you want me to take over your night watchman post? Merle, no offense, but you're humongous. I have trouble opening jars when the lids are too tight. There's no comparison."

"Abby, my brain may be a quart short o' full, but my vision's top notch. I realize you're a . . . delicate flower. This isn't a job where sizes matters."

"What about Bert?"

"He doesn't drive."

"Doesn't drive? How does he get around?"

"Walks. Chapel Isle isn't what you'd call a sprawling metropolis."

"Then how about Denny?"

"Don't get me wrong, he's a sweet kid. Not the sharpest tool in the kit."

"What if something happens? What if I see the robbers?"

"Go straight to the sheriff's station. All you have to do is make sure the cottages haven't already been broken into and that the doors and windows are locked. Easy-peasy."

"You mean I have to get out of the car?"

"Unless you've got a real long reach."

As much as she would have liked to, Abigail couldn't turn Merle down. She owed him.

"I can't pay you, so you can have whatever supplies you want from the store."

"Some offer. You were prepared to let the burglars take you for everything you own."

"Okay, how about this? Make my rounds for a week while I heal up and I'll get an electrician to recheck the wiring for you at the lighthouse. Deal?"

Merle took a map from his back pocket. Lottie's properties were circled in red. Abigail reluctantly accepted it from him.

"Deal."

◆ ◆ ◆

The morning fog had cleared, revealing a bald blue sky. Somehow the total absence of clouds kept Abigail from feeling as though she had just agreed to a ludicrously bad idea.

"Nothing could be that awful on a day this beautiful."

That's what you think, bemoaned the voice in her head.

A cardboard box was waiting for Abigail on the front steps when she returned to the lighthouse. *Enjoy,* read the attached note, with Lottie's signature in script at the bottom.

The box held dozens of paperback romance novels. Every cover was emblazoned with buxom women, cleavage heaving from their corsets, as muscled men with chiseled features embraced them lustily. Some were soldiers, some princes, some cowboys, some cops. No matter their stripe, each wore an outfit strategically torn to reveal rippling muscles.

"Can't wait to dive into these."

Abigail added the carton to the others in the study—the next room to be painted. Piled as it was with books, it took more time to empty the tiny space than it did to tape around the crown moldings and baseboards. Before popping open a new can of yellow paint, she plugged in the radio. Dr. Walter was on the air.

Today's topic was a proposed two percent tax hike to fund programs for schools. A man phoned in criticizing the increase. "I pay a king's ransom in taxes as is. School was fine for me. Should be fine for kids today. We don't need no changes."

Dr. Walter didn't hold back. "Given your less-than-exemplary grammar, sir, you've made a concrete case for upping the school tax a full two hundred percent. Next caller."

Abigail applauded. "Bravo, Doc."

What she appreciated most about the show was that Dr. Walter said what was on his mind. He shot from the hip and didn't sugarcoat his opinions. That took gumption, an attribute Abigail considered herself sorely lacking.

Paul had the same type of spirit. He spoke from his heart and was practically incapable of telling a lie. To him, lying was like bad math. It would be wrong in the end regardless. Honest to a fault, Paul lectured the telemarketers who would call during mealtimes, calmly taking them to task on how they could consider themselves upstanding citizens if they purposefully phoned at inappropriate hours. It amused Abigail to hear him harangue them, presenting his argument to the dumbfounded salespeople, who could either listen patiently or disconnect. She wanted to believe that some measure of Paul's zeal had rubbed off on her during their years of marriage. She often doubted it had.

"Give me a break," Dr. Walter was bellowing. "Call back when you grow a brain."

The sound of him cutting the connection was followed by a dial tone that whined across the airwaves.

"You did stick it to Nat Rhone," Abigail told herself. "Even if it was Dr. Walter's line, you have to start somewhere."

◆　◆　◆

The study had been the watch room for a reason. It had the best view in the house, which Abigail realized while touching up the window trim. The position provided a broad vantage of the Atlantic, a panorama that spread for miles. A large part of the lighthouse keeper's days would have been spent in this room, gazing through these very panes of glass. Abigail imagined him watching passing ships, the changing weather, the coming and going of the tides. She stood at the window, thinking she was seeing the very same sprawl of ocean Mr. Jasper must have looked at every single day.

When she was done painting, Abigail moved the final piece of furniture—the shelf—in from the hall, then started on her books.

"You're really going to put them away. No reading. No dawdling."

Each book had its own personal story—where she'd bought it, how many times she'd read it, why it held a place in her soul—but seeing her books stacked on a thrift-store shelf in the small study wasn't where she'd envisioned them. It was like putting a sentimental family photo in a cheap plastic frame. With the bookcase filled, there was no space left to spare for Lottie's paperbacks, except on the top ledge.

"What, have you become a book snob? Romance novels aren't of regal-enough caliber to sit next to literature and history? They can't be *that* dreadful."

Abigail crouched on the floor, cracked one of the bodice rippers, and read the first paragraph. The writing was decent, albeit melodramatic, and she was soon turning page after page. A period romance, the tale traced the love affair between a ravishing heiress and a pirate captain. The lovers were separated by twists of fate and a conspiracy to keep them apart, orchestrated by the girl's suitor, a villainous count. A chapter in, Abigail was hooked, so much so that she forgot she was squatting until her thighs started to burn. She was about to move onto the cot to continue reading when a rumble reverberated from below, making her flinch. Her backside hit the floor with enough force that the impact shook her shoulders.

"Fabulous. Another bruise."

Abigail kneaded her tailbone as she got to her feet. The noise hadn't come from the living room or the kitchen. This sound seemed deeper.

"I bet it's your favorite. The basement."

She stalked across the study, summoning her valor.

"You're going to go see what it is. There's nothing to be afraid of. This is all in your head."

Before she could lose her nerve, Abigail flew downstairs and threw open the basement door. Common sense intervened.

"The flashlight might help."

Because the one Merle had given her was new, as were the batteries, it should have come as no surprise that the flashlight worked. Nonetheless, Abigail was disappointed.

"No backing out now."

The stairs squeaked as she tried to tiptoe into the basement.

"At least nobody can sneak up on me here."

Though the overhead light didn't make much of a dent in the darkness, especially in the far corners, the flashlight did. Crates were stacked high around the basement's perimeter. Among them were the silhouettes of what she guessed were chairs covered in sheets.

In a burst of bravery, Abigail yanked them off. As she suspected, underneath was a set of dining chairs, an inlaid side table, and a formal, wood-trimmed settee. Beneath another sheet awaited a dining table with scrolled legs and a handsome writing desk. The pieces were antiques, high quality at that.

"This furniture puts the hodgepodge upstairs to shame."

Another rumble suddenly radiated through the basement. Abigail gripped the flashlight tightly.

"Who's there?"

She was trembling, causing the beam from the flashlight to tremble too.

"If there's somebody here, come out. Come out or else. . . ."

Except she didn't have an *or else*.

Edging toward the cistern, Abigail caught a whiff of the same scent she'd smelled before, mildew with a trace of pipe smoke. That frightened her as much as the noises.

"I said show yourself."

Abigail shined the flashlight into the cistern's mouth. The cavern was empty. However, a puddle of water had bubbled in from a drain, bobbling the metal grate so the sound was amplified by the cistern's stone walls.

"It's only the water in the drain," she sighed. Then she turned to head upstairs and crashed into a pile of crates.

Were they there before?

She couldn't recall.

If they were, wouldn't you have tripped on them?

One crate's lid had come loose. Inside were volumes of leather-bound ledgers. They piqued Abigail's curiosity, tempting her to stay in the basement despite the darkness and her apprehension. Such journals would have been expensive, even on the modern market. The thick leather bindings were still supple to the touch, and the spines were in immaculate condition. When Abigail opened one of the ledgers to the first page, the name *Wesley Jasper* was printed in a steady hand at the top.

She shoved aside her anxiety and began to flip through the pages. Each entry documented the sunrise and sunset, the weather, the tides, and the hours the lighthouse was operating. She marveled at the meticulousness. There were no cross-outs or scribbled corrections. The lettering was painstakingly precise. Abigail combed through the entire box, and every ledger was equally well preserved.

"For as old as you are, you guys look great."

The other crates held more ledgers. Abigail was fascinated by the entries, the details of everything from thunder and rainstorms to hot spells and heat lightning. She was as absorbed by Mr. Jasper's writings as she'd been by Lottie's romance novel.

When Abigail checked her watch, it was after seven. She was supposed to be doing Merle's rounds. She didn't want to stop reading, but she had to.

After gingerly repacking the crates, she went upstairs and threw some food into a grocery bag to take with her. As she walked out the door, flashlight in hand, a thought occurred to her.

What if you run into the burglars? Maybe you should bring something to defend yourself.

She scrounged through the kitchen drawers for an implement with which to fend somebody off. The sharpest item she could find was a butter knife, a sibling of the one she'd used to scrape down the wallpaper.

"This is about as menacing as a spork."

She remembered seeing a hammer in the shed. With the flashlight as her guide, Abigail delved into the night. The shed door, which she'd left unlocked, was shimmying in the breeze. She deliberated over locking it, just to be safe.

"First things first. I need a weapon."

A rusted claw hammer with a chunky wooden handle lay in a bucket on the floor of the shed.

"Now, this has a little more presence. Hopefully, you won't have to make your *presence* known."

◆　◆　◆

Finding the houses marked on Merle's map was easier said than done. The interior of the island was oppressively dark, blacker than the night sky, because of the overhanging trees. Again and again, Abigail drove past road signs and had to double back.

"I could do with a streetlight or two."

The first stop along her route was on the southwest end of the island, where she was stunned to discover a slew of modern homes built on stilts.

"Must be a flood plain."

Contemporary in style, the houses were accented with sweeping decks, angular rooflines, and spurts of block glass. Their mammoth size was meant to convey wealth and grandeur. The result was a parade of gaudy monsters that looked out of scale and out of place in their surroundings.

"A flood might actually be an improvement."

Abigail squinted at the house numbers until she found the one that matched her map, a white stucco whale with a carport beneath the house.

"This is it." She steadied herself, breathing slowly and deliberately. "Don't forget your hammer."

Due to the stilts, the first floor was more than a story off the ground. There was no access to the back door on the deck from the exterior. The front door would be a thief's safest point of entry.

"Less for me to do."

Weapon in one hand, flashlight in the other, Abigail had no hands left to check and see if the door was locked, her primary responsibility. She had to wedge the flashlight under her armpit so she could still wield the hammer.

"Now *I* look like the burglar."

When she tried the knob, it held tight.

"One down, thirteen to go."

The next few rental units were also on stilts, making her job a cinch.

"This isn't so bad," Abigail said, munching on a banana as she drove to a different section of the island. Then she pulled up to a rambling cottage surrounded by heavy brush and low-slung trees that shrouded the house on every side. The place was the epitome of spooky.

"That's what I get for speaking too soon."

Scraggly tree limbs cloaked the front door, and the windows were barely visible behind the bushes. Someone could easily sneak up to the house and be hidden in the foliage.

"If I had to rob a house, I'd rob this one."

Abigail needed a plan.

Make noise. That will scare them off. Presuming there is a them.

"Cross your fingers there's not a *them,*" she told herself.

Abigail exited the car, humming theatrically. "Gosh, what a long day," she shouted. "Man, oh, man, am I glad to be home."

Hammer at the ready, she tried the front door. It was locked. There was still the back door to attend to as well as the windows. She cut around to the rear of the cottage along an overgrown stone path. Briars caught on her clothes, scratching her forearms.

"How delightful. More scrapes and bruises."

Fortunately for her, the back door to the cottage was locked too. The windows were closed tight.

"Done," Abigail declared, just as a rustling rose from the bushes to her left. She raised the hammer and raked the yard with the flashlight. The din of the crickets was deafening.

"Who's there?" Her attempt at a demand came out as a murmur.

She trained the flashlight on the bushes, bathing them in its intense beam. The leaves shone a glossy black, frightening because of what they might conceal. Abigail took a step forward. Suddenly, a bird burst from the foliage and flew into the night, wings flapping in tandem with her pounding heart.

"Thanks a lot, bird."

Stressed yet unscathed, Abigail finished the rest of Merle's rounds that evening without event. As she navigated back to the lighthouse, reality hit her square in the conscience.

"You're a Ph.D., an educated woman, and you've basically become a night watchman."

Her former life no longer applied. It had gone up in flames with her home. On Chapel Isle, she wasn't Abigail the lexicographer, the mother, the wife. She was the lighthouse caretaker, the security guard, the lady who talked to herself and started fights and was covered with injuries from head to foot. Abigail would have to redefine herself with a new vocabulary while mastering the language of Chapel Isle.

mun•di•fy (mun´də fī´), *v.t.,* **-fied, -fy•ing. 1.** to cleanse; deterge: *to mundify a wound.* **2.** to purge or purify: *to mundify a person of past sins.* [1375–1425; late ME < LL *mundificāre,* equiv. to L *mundi-,* s. of *mund(us)* clean + *-ficāre* -FY]

◆ ◆ ◆

October was half over, though the leaves had yet to fall or hint at changing color. The island refused to conform to the season, stubbornly clinging to the departed summer. Mornings were cool, but with every hour that passed, the sun beat away the chill. Abigail hadn't used the fireplace in days. Not that she minded.

She hauled her last can of paint into the bathroom, more of the same buttery shade that was in the kitchen, living room, and study. The minuscule space would be a snap to paint. Or so she believed.

From the middle of the wall up, rolling on the cool blue paint was easy. From there down, it was a total inconvenience. Abigail had to lie on the floor and contort herself to reach around the toilet, then squirm into a corner to get at the walls behind the tub. Eroded enamel flaked off the underbelly of the bathtub as she painted.

"What this needs is some sealer to stop the corrosion. The floor could stand to be regrouted too. A medicine cabinet wouldn't hurt either."

Over the symphony coming from the CD player, Abigail heard a muffled *bump,* timed as a reply to her comment.

"Seriously? This mirror's nothing special, and the grout is, to be blunt, gross. Anyway, I don't have anyplace to put my toothpaste."

Logic began to nag at her.

Who are you talking to? This is preposterous. These are random noises, not communications from the beyond.

A worrisome notion slipped into Abigail's brain like a note being slid through a mail slot. What if she truly was going crazy?

"People who are going crazy don't have the presence to ask themselves if they're going crazy."

Or do they?

Abigail put her paintbrush aside. "That's enough of that. I'm going to town."

◆   ◆   ◆

The parking place she'd come to think of as hers was ready and waiting. Abigail headed over to the hardware store and went around to the rear, as had become her custom. When she reached the door, she had a flush of misgiving. She wouldn't normally walk into a store and leave with merchandise she hadn't paid for.

"Merle did tell you to take whatever you wanted. He gave you permission," Abigail said, talking herself into opening the back door.

Inside, the shades were drawn, the rooms dark. She patted the kitchen walls for a light switch but couldn't find it. While plodding blindly into the main part of the store, she bumped into the counter, which guided her to the shelves where she'd seen containers of grout the day she came for the paint.

"Hello, Abby."

Startled, she bounded backward, knocking into a display of wrench sets.

"Who's there?" It was a phrase Abigail had been saying more often than she cared to admit.

Bertram Van Dorst peeked around the aisle. "Didn't mean to scare you. I heard you at the back door and I called to you. Thought ya heard me."

"Why are you in here with the lights off, Bert?"

"Don't need 'em. I memorized what's on every shelf. Why waste the electricity?"

"Okay. Can I ask what you're doing here?"

"Washer number seven's been acting touchy. Rotator belt's about to go. I came to see what Merle might have to fix it so I wouldn't have to order a new part."

"Bert, are you the manager of the laundromat?"

"Me? No."

"And you said you weren't the owner. Then . . . ?" Abigail couldn't think of a courteous way to ask him why he spent so much time there.

"Must seem kind of strange."

"No, no, it's—"

"I like it there. It's quiet. No distractions. I can keep an eye on the place for Lottie, make sure the machines are running right."

"Lottie owns the laundromat too?"

"Well, her and her husband. They own most of Chapel Isle, really. Since his accident, Franklin hasn't been able to do much with the businesses, which is why Lottie runs them."

"Accident?"

"Car crash. Three years ago, one of the summer people was driving drunk. Hit Franklin's car and flipped him into a ditch. Broke his spine in three places. He won't ever walk again. Got big bucks in the settlement, but Franklin didn't need money. He had that in spades." The story was a sore spot for Bert.

"I retooled his electric wheelchair for him. Adjusted the wheels for an improved turning radius and rerouted the wiring so he could get more power. Franklin says it runs like a Porsche. Zero to sixty in six seconds."

Abigail had dropped her chin and let her shoulders fold, sympathy melting her stance into the posture of compassion. She'd seen people slide into it after they learned of her husband's and son's deaths. As she stood there in the darkened hardware store with Bert, Abigail knew what she was about to say. The words were already forming in spite of how she hated hearing them herself.

"I'm sorry to hear about your friend."

"He's a decent guy. Done a lot for this town. Everyone does what they can."

An unspoken bond existed between the residents of Chapel Isle. The island was the same as the nets its fishermen cast at sea, a tight lattice of people tied by lives lived closely, knotted by friendship. Being here meant Abigail could become a part of that net as well, which was a bit intimidating. The responsibility may have been more than she could be entrusted with.

"So how's it going at the lighthouse?"

"Fine. Everything's fine." As often as Abigail said it, that didn't make it true.

"Nothing out of the ordinary?"

"Oh, Bert, not you too? You're a man of science. You can't possibly have bought into this ghost story."

"Had to ask. Most people around here have heard about him. Some believe. Some don't. Either way, Mr. Jasper took care of this island and its sailors for years. Guess he has the right to be here still."

Be it a right, a privilege, a curse, or contrivance, Wesley Jasper had become Abigail's problem. She was lying that everything was fine while painting the caretaker's cottage top to bottom and trying to appease a spirit she wasn't convinced existed. If Abigail couldn't shake the shroud of his presence—real, imagined, or mythologized—she would become known as the woman who lived in the haunted house. She wasn't even okay being known as "Abby." She couldn't let this go any further.

◆　◆　◆

When Abigail got home, the cottage was brutally quiet. She couldn't concentrate and craved a mindless activity to give her wits a rest. After wandering aimlessly around the living room, she stopped and stood at the window, staring at the ocean while waiting for inspiration to arrive. Minutes passed. She grew impatient. Her eyes drifted across the lawn to the station wagon. The grass was as high as the car's headlights.

"Lottie did mention a lawn mower."

A tarnished manual hand mower leaned in the corner of the shed, with a ragged-edged rake propped against it.

"Couldn't hurt to see if it works."

Abigail dragged the mower out for inspection. The blades were matte gray, so dull they refused to reflect the sunlight. She pulled the mower along the grass to test if the blades would cut. Much to her amazement, they did. The newly sheared patch of grass was a drastic improvement, incentive to forge onward.

Progress was slow, each pass a struggle, but Abigail didn't stop. The exertion drained her mind and burned off the angst that had clung to her since running into Bert at the hardware store. The smell of the fresh-clipped grass was a welcome distraction.

Over the course of the afternoon, she worked her way across the yard, pausing occasionally to wipe her forehead with her sleeve. Her hair was soaked with sweat, as was her shirt. The sun was setting once she was through.

The time had come to do Merle's rounds. A bath would have to wait. Abigail packed a sandwich for dinner. There was one piece of bread left, besides the heel of the loaf. Her sandwich was a sad statement about how she'd been living. She used to love to cook. When she and Paul were newlyweds and low on cash, Abigail had embraced the challenge of concocting lavish meals on their shoestring budget, defying their circumstances with some ingenuity and well-chosen spices. She missed cooking, not so much the act, but the purpose—feeding her family and providing them with what they needed.

Abigail stowed her dinner in the empty bread bag and took it to the car.

Tonight the moon was high, making the street signs legible—that was if they weren't obscured by branches or leaves. Abigail was still getting the hang of how the island was laid out, reading Merle's map by her dashboard lights. The roads didn't run on a grid pattern;

quite the opposite. Each curvy lane unraveled of its own accord, un-repentantly irregular, like the rest of Chapel Isle.

The first few properties were unchanged since the previous evening, not a hinge or windowpane disturbed. Abigail was thankful for that. Midway through her route, she took a break to gobble down her dinner. As she sat in the station wagon eating, headlights appeared, glowing in the distance. Then the lights began to flash. It was a police patrol car.

"Uh-oh."

In her side mirror, Abigail saw Sheriff Larner climbing from the cruiser.

"Evening, Abby."

"This must seem a little suspicious, me sitting in my car on a dark road, eating a sandwich by flashlight with a hammer in my lap."

"Not what I expected. Care to tell me what you're doing?"

"It's kind of a long story."

"No such thing as a short story around here."

"I'm checking on Lottie's rental properties for Merle because . . . uh, because I owed him a favor." Abigail intentionally avoided the specifics of how she came into that particular debt.

"Oh, right, the infamous fight at the Kettle."

"It's *infamous*?"

"Only to the people who've heard about it."

"Wonderful."

"So Merle sent you to . . . ?" Larner expected her to fill in the blanks.

"Test the doors and windows. See if any of the units have been broken into."

The sheriff cocked his brow. "Guard duty?"

"Merle can barely walk and it's basically my fault. It's just for a week, until he's better."

"A week, huh?"

"I know, I know. I'm turning into a nuisance, what with starting that fight and the changes I've made to the caretaker's house."

Her comment visibly caught the sheriff's attention. Abigail presumed that whatever she did, whether buying a paintbrush or washing her laundry, somebody had already reported on it to everyone else. Wasn't that how the grapevine worked? And wasn't Larner the person who'd warned her about it?

"What sorts of changes are we talking about?" he inquired coyly.

Abigail's defenses went up. She chose her answer prudently. "A little paint. That's all."

"Paint never did anybody any harm."

"Let's hope not," Abigail said under her breath.

"You almost finished with your security detail?"

"I have some more houses to visit, then I'll be off the streets," she joked.

"Be careful. We haven't caught the guys responsible for those break-ins. Watch yourself with that hammer, 'kay? Lucky for you it's not considered a concealed weapon."

"Okay. I mean, yes, sir."

With that, the sheriff rode away in his patrol car.

Aside from the police cruiser, Abigail hadn't seen anybody else drive by in the past two nights. There had been dozens of people at the bingo game. Where were they, she wondered.

At home, she surmised. *With their families.*

The children would be in bed. Their parents were probably watching television or washing the dinner dishes, getting ready to call it a night. Abigail envied them. She couldn't see them, didn't know who they were or where they lived, yet those nameless, faceless people had what she longed for. They would wake up the next morning and their lives would be the same.

◆ ◆ ◆

The last house on Merle's map was a white bungalow with flowers blooming out front. Yawning, Abigail circled the building. She glanced at the windows and halfheartedly shook the doors until a set of headlights brightened the road.

"Don't let it be the sheriff again. I can only take so much humiliation per night."

The approaching vehicle was a truck rather than a car. Abigail stopped where she stood. She'd left the hammer in her station wagon. The lights grew closer. Whoever was driving would be able to see her shortly.

It could be anybody. Including the thieves.

Abigail hid. Kneeling behind the bushes, she peeked between the leaves. The twang of country music was coming from the truck, along with a woman's giddy laughter. Two silhouettes hovered in the truck's cab. The driver pulled to the side of the road, preparing to park a few yards behind her Volvo.

"No, not there. Keep going. Keep going," she whispered.

The truck's engine shuddered to a halt, the lights dimmed, and the giggling ceased as the two shadows melded into one.

"Oh, jeez. I could be here all night."

She considered her options, most of which were mortifying. A woman wandering from the bushes of a deserted house was going to seem odd, and even if she could get to her station wagon without the two lovers in the truck noticing, they would hear her start the car.

"Why do you care? Remember, you're a badass. You're *infamous*. You scoff in the face of adversity. You also talk to yourself too much."

Abigail emerged from the brush, intent on strolling to her station wagon in a composed fashion. Except her legs moved faster and faster until she broke into a trot.

"Stop. I hear something," the woman in the truck said.

Two bewildered faces stared at Abigail from behind the steamed windshield. Mid-stride, she locked glances with the female passenger, a woman with wavy hair and wide, plaintive eyes. Abigail recognized her as one of the "hens" sitting with Janine Wertz at the bingo game. Behind the wheel of the truck was Clint Wertz, his arm slung over the woman's shoulder, her blouse unbuttoned. Abigail jumped into her car and peeled out. She couldn't tell who was more embarrassed. Her or them.

◆ ◆ ◆

Even in the dark, the caretaker's cottage looked better with the grass cut. Abigail sat in the station wagon with the headlights illuminating the front yard to soak in her accomplishment while trying to forget about her awkward run-in with Clint Wertz. Ruth had been right about him. He was bad news, news Abigail would have preferred not to have firsthand.

She got out of the station wagon and heard a crunch. Abigail scanned the ground and the car seat. There was nothing there. When she shifted her weight, the crunching came again. She dug in her pocket. It was the newspaper article from under the bed.

"Sorry, sorry, sorry," she said, feeling guilty for having crumpled that fragile slip of paper.

She went inside, smoothed the clipping on the dining-room table, and reread its heading: BISHOP'S MISTRESS SINKS.

The article was dated 1909. It was about a trade ship from Boston bound for Charleston that was caught in a hurricane that blasted the southern coastline. The storm wreaked havoc from Florida to Delaware. The ship met its end by smashing into a shoal in the Ship's Graveyard, east of Chapel Isle. Fifty-nine men were lost. No bodies were recovered. The last portion of the article insinuated that the *Bishop's Mistress* had gotten trapped in the graveyard because the lighthouse beacon hadn't been visible to guide it safely into harbor. The final sentence read: *A tragedy has befallen the* Bishop's Mistress, *perhaps one that was avoidable.*

The question the last line raised lodged in Abigail's mind. A sunken ship, drowned sailors, a spectral lighthouse keeper—the pieces were falling together in an eerie way. She fought the impulse to return to the basement and sort through the ledgers for an answer. Wesley Jasper had kept such precise notes, she was certain there would be some annotation of that night, some clue to the events that occurred.

"Are you really in the mood to go snooping around down there in the middle of the night?" Abigail asked herself. She had grass stains on her clothes from mowing the lawn, scratches on her arms from doing Merle's security route, and a battered ego from becoming "infamous" in town.

"I didn't think so."

no•va•tion (nō vā´shən), *n.* **1.** *Law,* the substitution of a new obligation for an old one, usually by the substitution of a new debtor or of a new creditor. **2.** the introduction of something new; innovation. [1525–35; < L *novātiōn-* (s. of *novātiō*) a renewing, equiv. to *novāi(us)* (ptp. of *novāre* to renew, deriv. of *novus* NEW) + *-ion-* -ION]

◆ ◆ ◆

Like it or not, Abigail had to go into town that day for food and supplies.

"Make a list this time," she reminded herself as she sat at the dining-room table eating a bowl of mushy cereal. The dilemma was, she still didn't have any paper, except for the crinkled article, which she'd covered with a cast-iron skillet to flatten the creases.

"I'd put *paper* on the list if I had something to write it on."

She remembered she had the receipt from her first foray to Weller's Market. On the underside of it, she wrote the items she needed from Merle's shop as well as those she wanted to ask him to order, including a new medicine cabinet. She hoped he'd have drawer pulls in stock. The house remained in disarray because she hadn't reattached the originals or put the dishes and dry goods in the cupboards.

"This is definitely a work in progress."

Part of that progress would be to swap the current living-room furniture for the antiques in the basement, a transition she couldn't make on her own. She doubted Merle could help her, which left Denny or Bert, neither of whom she wanted to spend hours on end with. No matter who gave her a hand, having the carved desk from the basement in the study upstairs was worth looking forward to. She hadn't looked forward to much in recent months, so that made the desk, as well as the other furniture, a big deal to Abigail.

◆　◆　◆

The back door to Merle's store was wide open, and he was standing at the sink washing out a bait bucket, his umbrella-cum-cane hooked on the lip of the counter.

Abigail rapped on the door in an effort not to scare him again. "Up and about, I see."

"I'm definitely up. It's the 'about' part I gotta practice." He was favoring his good foot and leaning into the sink for support. "Glad you're okay," he said. "I was worried when I heard."

"Heard what?"

"Another house got broken into."

"When? Where?"

"Last night. Wasn't Lottie's. Privately owned. Six doors away from her cottage on Timber Lane."

"I was on Timber Lane. I didn't see anything. . . . Wait. I did see something. I saw a couple—a man and woman—in a truck." Abigail decided not to say specifically whom she'd encountered.

"A couple? What were they doing there?"

"What couples do alone together in parked cars."

"Oh, my. Well, you should tell Caleb Larner that. Might be . . . noteworthy."

Informing the sheriff was the right thing to do. However, Abigail had absolutely no desire to get involved in the Wertzes' private life. She'd started one fistfight already.

"Maybe I should have somebody else take the rounds tonight," Merle suggested.

"Why? Because I'm a woman? You think I can't handle it?"

Merle chewed his bottom lip, proving that was exactly what he was thinking.

Infuriated, Abigail said, "I'll do the rounds. End of discussion. Here." She handed him her list.

"This is a receipt for groceries. You do realize this is a hardware store."

"The *other* side."

"Oh, right. I got most of this stuff. I'll have to order you the mirror, though. Take three or four weeks."

"No problem. It's not like I'm going anywhere."

"You sure about this, Abby? Sometimes change isn't everything it's cracked up to be."

Abigail folded her arms, sticking to her guns.

"Okay. Okay." Merle pretended to zip his lips shut and directed her to a shelf with a small assortment of knobs, then hobbled off to retrieve the items from her list that he had in stock.

Given the limited selection, Abigail picked a simply styled round drawer pull with a pewter finish and counted out the number she needed. While Merle packed her purchases into bags, Abigail spotted him putting a new screwdriver in with the rest.

"I don't need that, Merle. I found a screwdriver in the shed."

"That thing's half broken," he told her, making it a present, his form of an apology.

"Would you like me to pay my tab?"

"What for? You'll be back tomorrow with another list."

"True."

"Be careful tonight, will ya, Abby? I'm not being sexist. I'd say it to anyone. In fact, I'd say it to myself."

Be careful. It was the same advice Sheriff Larner had given her. None of Abigail's recent decisions had been made with much care, an atypical departure from her typically logical self. She wasn't being *careful* when she painted the house or when she agreed to do Merle's rounds or even when she decided to come to Chapel Isle. She had thrown caution to the wind and gotten carried away like a kite in a gale. Abigail was still waiting to see where she'd land.

◆　◆　◆

Weller's Market was Abigail's next destination. She was not looking forward to it. Head low, she quickly pushed a cart through the store, grabbing an extra loaf of bread among other things because she'd gone through the first so fast. Abigail thought she might escape without running into Janine. That was until she rounded the produce aisle and nearly wheeled straight into her.

Janine's face hardened the instant she saw Abigail.

"Sorry," Abigail mumbled.

Janine went on unloading heads of lettuce from a crate as if she hadn't heard her.

No one was manning the registers when Abigail was ready to pay, but she wasn't about to ask Janine.

"Coming," a female voice called from somewhere in the store.

A woman with her hair in a ponytail jogged to the register. Abigail immediately recognized her as the one in the truck with Clint Wertz. The recognition was mutual. The woman hastily rang up Abigail's groceries, jamming them into bags.

"That'll be twenty-one forty-five."

When Abigail gave her the money, the woman's face was awash with shame. She held out the change, her hand quivering. Rage pooled in Abigail's chest. This woman knew that what she was doing was wrong. She knew she was hurting her friend. Abigail's anger deflated into empathy as she realized that she saw a similar pallor of guilt in her own face every morning. Surviving the fire was a constant burden, a shadow she couldn't outrun or leave behind. Abigail wouldn't wish it on anybody. Not even this woman, who deserved to feel guilty for what she'd done.

◆　◆　◆

Afternoon sunlight was flooding into the caretaker's house. Since the property was so secluded, there was no need for what little privacy the ashen drapes had provided. That left Abigail in limbo between liberation and loneliness.

"You have new doorknobs. That's something."

Insignificant as they were, the knobs were the high point of her day. Before installing them and reassembling the kitchen, she went through the hordes of crockery on the dining table and sifted out what was worth saving. Among the rejects were blackened pans, more ladles than anyone could ever need, and a cracked mug with a cartoon of a fish wearing a sailor's cap.

"Seems a waste to throw these in the trash. Maybe I could give them away. Though I'm not sure who'd want them."

All the less-than-desirable dishware went into grocery bags, then Abigail put everything else back in the cabinets. Anxious to install the drawer pulls, she was glad to have the screwdriver Merle gave her. She pitched the other one into the garbage. With the cupboards repainted, the knobs replaced, Abigail reviewed the completed kitchen and said, "*Better Homes and Gardens,* here we come."

Finishing the grass and tackling the grout were her next chores. But Abigail had been running a debt with her body, the balance of which was constant soreness. Pushing and pulling the lawn mower might bankrupt her altogether.

"Grout it is."

It was two o'clock, time for Dr. Walter's show. She brought the radio and the ungainly tub of grout up to the bathroom. Abigail tuned in as Dr. Walter was announcing that day's topic.

"For those of you just joining us, we're talking about how to discipline your children. Our first call is from Sue. She says her five-year-old son refuses to sleep in his own bed."

"That's right," Sue interjected. "He wants to sleep with me and my husband. Every night without fail he comes in crying, begging to stay with us."

"And you're wondering if you should continue to allow him to sleep with you or if you should—"

"Put my foot down. Make him sleep in his own room. It's hard. He says he can't fall asleep if he's not with us, and if I tell him no, he cries and cries. I feel awful." Dr. Walter couldn't get a word in. The woman was spilling over with desperation. "I'm not a bad mother. At least, I don't think I'm a bad mother. I don't want to be a bad mother."

"You're *not* a bad mother, Sue."

The doctor's voice was calm, convincing, comforting. He could have said anything in that voice and Abigail would have trusted him.

"The lines are burning up with listeners who want to speak to this issue. We'll hear what they have to say after this commercial."

During the break, Abigail read the instructions on the grout container.

"This doesn't seem too hard."

Using the trowel Merle had supplied, she slopped a dollop of grout into the far corner of the bathroom, slathering it into the crevices between the tiles. White and thick as cake icing, it was an immense improvement over the dingy grout.

"We're back," Dr. Walter said, "and the switchboard is on fire."

Phone calls were streaming in from mothers who sympathized with Sue. They, too, found themselves unable to turn their children away from their beds at night. Each was more racked with worry than the woman who preceded her.

A fearful mother asked, "Am I ruining my kid for life by letting her sleep with me?"

"There are hundreds of ways you can ruin your child for life," Dr. Walter assured the woman. "Letting her sleep with you on occasion isn't one of them."

He went on to give suggestions about how to wean children into their own beds and instructed the women to be gentle yet firm. Abigail nodded in agreement as she continued to grout, edging toward the door.

"Hold on, we have a listener who has a differing opinion. Go ahead, Charlene, you're on the air."

"I think your callers are sick," she began. "Children have night-mares. Comes with the territory. As soon as you let them start sleeping with you in *your* bed with *your* husband, you've crossed a line. A very sick line. I have five kids, and I never let them sleep with me and my husband. They're grown and there isn't a thing wrong with them."

"I'm sure they're right as rain," Dr. Walter said.

The woman continued her tirade, unaware that she was being made fun of. "And that's because I didn't let them share my bed. I can't understand these mothers today. They let their kids run wild in the stores, mouth off, scream in restaurants—behavior that shouldn't be tolerated."

Abigail stopped grouting. She was growing more and more ag-itated by the woman's arrogance, her insensitivity. She envisioned her as the type who threatened to get a switch if her kids didn't do as they were told.

"You want my advice?" Charlene boomed.

"I'm all ears," Dr. Walter replied.

"Women today need to be stronger. Children want discipline. They need it. If they don't have it, they run right over you."

Unlike the rest of the women who had phoned in, Abigail wouldn't get the chance for her child to crawl into bed with her again. She'd never get the chance to cuddle with him after he had a nightmare or feel him sleep against her in the shelter of her body. A spike of sorrow shot through her.

Charlene was winding up for another diatribe when Dr. Walter put her on mute. "If anyone is interested in responding to these statements, please feel free to call in."

"Interested?" Abigail said. "Let me at her."

She threw aside the trowel and went for the stairs as Dr. Walter relayed an 800 number. Her hands were shaking so violently, she couldn't get her finger into the rotary slots. The harder Abigail tried, the more frustrated she became. Incapable of dialing, she slammed down the receiver.

"Is this 'Abby'? Is this who you are now?"

Abigail had to conjugate in Latin to regain her composure.

Invenio, invenire, inveni, inventum.

Operor, operari, operatus sum.

Beside the telephone lay the newspaper article about the *Bishop's Mistress*. She'd moved it while clearing the table. Sadly, the weight of the skillet hadn't removed the wrinkles.

"I'm going to make it up to you," she told the clipping.

Grabbing the flashlight, which she'd left beside the phone along with the hammer, Abigail made for the basement door, set on learning more about the ship's demise. She dragged the crates into an open area of the basement and searched their contents for a reference to the *Bishop's Mistress*. Eventually she found a ledger that corresponded to the year the ship sank, 1909. It was shoved at the bottom of one of the crates, out of order from the rest. The first portion of the ledger was reminiscent of the others. Details of the tides and the weather were scrupulously penned in a rigid script that was plumb with the margins. Then came the date of the sinking of the *Bishop's Mistress*.

The page appeared to be written in an entirely different hand. Notes about the morning tide and wind were at the top in a wavering scrawl. From there, the writing turned illegible. Abigail held the flashlight close to the page, trying to decipher it. A single sentence mentioned the *Bishop's Mistress,* something she was able to deduce only because she recognized how Wesley Jasper formed his *S*'s. The rest of the words were too mangled to decode, except for a pair toward the end: *oil* and *pail*.

The entry ceased cryptically. Abigail flipped the page. The ledger returned to normal. The penmanship was clear and upright and didn't meander outside the lines.

"Three weeks are missing between these entries."

As she spoke, the flashlight flickered. She rapped it against a crate. "But these are brand-new batteries."

Exactly. They are brand-new batteries.

Clutching the ledger, Abigail ran to the first floor and flung the basement door shut. She contemplated locking it. That was what Lottie would have done.

"For the record, I'm not going to lock the door the way *some* people would. Nope. No need to lock the door."

Lottie was scared of the basement. Abigail didn't want to be. Still, she tested the handle to make sure the door was closed tight.

◆　◆　◆

The day the *Bishop's Mistress* sank was etched into the soul of the ledger. The entry made the perfection of the others pale, and that page felt thinner than the rest. Abigail spent hours poring over every inch of it, mindful not to touch the paper. From her work with antique dictionaries, she knew that the oil from human hands could seep into the paper fibers, causing deterioration. Under normal circumstances, Abigail would have worn cotton conservator's gloves. Her rubber dish gloves would have to do.

Unable to puzzle out most of the words in the entry, Abigail studied the drastic change in penmanship. The acute slant of the script indicated the speed at which it was written, while the low pitch of letters and the hasty slashes that topped the *I*'s and *T*'s confirmed her theory. The entry had been dashed off, the author distracted.

From the article, Abigail had gleaned a general sense of what happened. A vicious storm had blown in, assailing the *Bishop's Mistress* and sealing her fate. Yet there had to be more. Whatever truly transpired that night had affected the lighthouse keeper to the point of altering his handwriting. Abigail knew that only tragedy was powerful enough to transform a person that thoroughly.

Night had swept in, and she'd been scrutinizing the ledger entry for so long her eyes hurt. Abigail would soon have to leave to do Merle's rounds.

"Oh, no. The grout!"

Upstairs, the radio was playing and the trowel was lying on the tile where she'd discarded it. The layer of grout had dried into a meringue-y mess. In her fervor over trying to call Dr. Walter, Abigail had completely forgotten to wipe the excess grout with a damp cloth, as the directions dictated. However, her watch said it was time to go.

"I'll deal with you later," she told the floor.

❖   ❖   ❖

That evening's route began with the modern houses on the southwest end of the island. They were a warm-up, as they were closer to the lighthouse than the others, easier to inspect, and far less foreboding. Because the homes were new, the foliage hadn't grown in, meaning fewer places for anyone who didn't belong there to hide. It was the older homes Abigail hated. She imagined they must be lovely during the day, the trees swagged with Spanish moss, flowering shrubs nestled in close. That beauty turned ominous come nightfall.

Abigail sped through her rounds until she got to Timber Lane, the road where the burglary had occurred the night before.

"They wouldn't come to the same place," she reasoned.

Would they?

Lottie's cottage on Timber Lane was the quintessence of charm. Roses dripped from trellises and a hammock swayed from an elm tree in the backyard. Abigail could imagine Lottie describing it to potential renters as an adorable love nest, the perfect setting for a romantic getaway.

"And prime for a thief's picking."

After a quick whirl around the cottage, Abigail deemed the property untouched and hurried to the next unit three lanes over. She checked the windows and gave the back door a shake, then her flashlight faltered.

"Not now. Please not now."

Tapping the head of the flashlight against her palm, she attempted to resuscitate it. The bulb dimmed, leaving Abigail in the dark. The crickets seemed to grow louder in the absence of light.

"Thanks for the faulty merchandise, Merle," she griped. "Just get to the car and you'll be okay."

As Abigail pushed through the shrubs into the front yard, arms held out as antennae, she heard the steady sound of footsteps. Between the shadows of the trees ahead, she glimpsed movement. It was the figure of a man walking in the street.

Abigail accidentally stepped on a branch, and the man stopped. *Did he hear you? Can he see you? Don't scream. Don't move. Don't breathe.*

Seconds later, the figure strode onward while Abigail stood, holding her breath, less than twenty feet away. If the flashlight had been working, she would have been seen. Abigail was thankful the batteries had died on her.

Once the footsteps faded, she sprinted to her station wagon, locked the doors, and switched on her high beams. There was no sign of the man. Her whole body was quaking, more with adrenaline than fear.

"Where did he go?"

Since the man could effortlessly have slipped into the woods and been hidden from sight, he might still be in the vicinity, so Abigail took off for town and came to a skidding halt outside the sheriff's station, which was in a corner of the square. The fluorescent lights were on inside the shingled one-story building, but the glass door was locked. A Post-it on the pane read, *Back in five minutes.*

"You've got to be kidding me."

Every store in the square was closed except for the bar across the street, the Wailin' Whale. A far cry from a haunt for Captain Ahab, the exterior looked more like a Wild West saloon. All that was missing were the swinging half doors.

Bars weren't the sort of places Abigail frequented. The gloomy lighting, sticky tabletops, and cigarette smoke depressed her. However, there was a chance that was where Sheriff Larner would be. If not, maybe someone would know where he was. Abigail was willing to give it a shot.

While she ratcheted up her nerve, the front door to the Wailin' Whale burst open. Hank Scokes lurched out, with Nat Rhone hard on his heels. Nat caught Hank by the shoulders before he could lose his balance.

"Let's get you home," Nat said in a gentle voice.

"I don't want to," Hank slurred. "You can't make me."

Going home meant having to endure the emptiness of his own house, the void left by his wife's death. Abigail felt sorry for him. She also envied him. At least Hank had a home to go to. Sure, she had the caretaker's cottage, but that wasn't her real home.

"You're tired, buddy. You're ready for bed."

The tenderness in Nat's tone didn't jibe with the image Abigail had of him brawling with Denny at the Kozy Kettle.

"I'm not tired. I swear I'm not," Hank whined.

Nat helped him into the passenger seat of a gray truck, saying, "Upsy-daisy."

Rounding to the driver's side, Nat noticed Abigail across the street. Hank spied her too. Abigail stood motionless, ready to make a beeline for her car.

"You," Hank said, brightening. "You know my boys. You seen 'em. In that picture. Remember? She knows my sons," he told Nat excitedly. "Tell him what you said."

After Hank had yelled at her at the bingo game, Abigail was afraid to utter a syllable.

"Tell him. You said they were handsome. She's a nice lady," Hank insisted. "Isn't she a nice lady?"

Nat stared at her without blinking, a wordless warning not to speak of what she'd witnessed, then climbed into the truck's cab and drove away.

"Wow. After that, I could actually use a drink. Guess I'm going to the right place."

She shook her head and ventured into the Wailin' Whale.

◆　◆　◆

Honky-tonk music played while pool balls cracked. The blue glow from the jukebox gave the bar the aura of an aquarium. Abigail definitely felt as if she was on display. The patrons, most of them men, turned to look when she entered. Some went back to their conversations or their drinks. A large part of the crowd continued to stare.

Hold it together, she told herself.

"Is Sheriff Larner here?" she inquired at the bar. "He's not at the station."

"Doubt it," the bartender replied. He was heavyset and sporting suspenders. Abigail thought he looked familiar.

"Are you the one who was calling the bingo game?"

"That's me," he answered, refilling a shot glass for the guy three seats over.

"You work here too?"

"A fella has to wear many hats in this town to get by."

"Understood." Abigail had been wearing a lot of hats since she'd arrived. None of them seemed to fit or be flattering.

"Caleb might've gone home for a bite to eat."

"What about the deputy?"

"Teddy? Probably his night off. Why? You got an emergency?"

Those who weren't already staring began to pay attention when he said that.

"Um, no. A question. I have a question for him."

"You can wait here if you want."

"No. Thanks, I mean. This is a great place. Don't get me wrong. It's fantastic. Really, um, fun. I, uh, have to get going, though."

The bartender waited patiently until Abigail was able to shut herself up, then asked, "You managing okay at the lighthouse on your own?"

She suddenly felt exposed. He'd told a roomful of men where she lived and that she lived there alone. But if the bartender knew, everybody else did too.

"Yeah. I'm fine. Everything's fine."

"If Caleb comes by, I'll mention you were looking for him."

"Thanks. Oh, I'm Abigail. Or Abby. So you can tell him who was asking."

The bartender nodded. "I know."

Apparently, infamy had its privileges. Abigail walked to her car, realizing that she didn't even need to introduce herself to people anymore. Nickname or not, she was known.

The caretaker's cottage was freezing when she returned. She was too exhausted to vie with the fireplace. She was getting accustomed to being cold. Perhaps it a was sign that she was acclimating to her new surroundings. Then again, it might just be her body catching up with her heart.

op•er•ose (op´ə rōs´), *adj.* **1.** industrious, as a person. **2.** done with or involving much labor. [1660–70; < L *operōsus* busy, active, equiv. to *oper*– (s. of *opus*) work + –*ōsus* –OSE¹ —**op´er•ose´ly,** *adv.* —**op´er•ose´•ness,** *n.*

◆ ◆ ◆

Daybreak brought a haze to the windowpanes. Instead of an early October frost, a humid film of condensation clung to the glass. Abigail opened a window, and the air was unusually balmy. It would be an ideal day to finish the grass. However, there was another project that required her immediate attention. The bathroom.

Ridges of hardened grout jabbed through her socks. On tiptoe, Abigail brushed her teeth and got one contact in. Then she heard pounding.

"It's too early in the morning for this."

Except the noise hadn't emanated from the lamp room or the basement. Someone was knocking at her front door. When she ran downstairs to open it, Nat Rhone was standing on the stoop with a toolbox in hand.

"Merle sent me to check your wiring," he said gruffly.

Thanks a lot, Merle.

"Uh, come in." Abigail crossed her arms to cover her layers of pajamas.

"Basement?"

She put on the light for him. "Do you need a flashlight? I have one if—"

"I got a flashlight," he told her, descending the steps.

While Nat was in the basement, Abigail tore up to her bedroom, wriggled into yesterday's clothes, and put in her other contact. Dressed, she went back down to the living room and waited at the basement door.

"I'd offer you some coffee," she hollered to him, "but I don't have any. I don't have a coffeepot. I have some milk. And water."

"No thanks," Nat answered, his inflection flat.

"If there's anything I can—"

A thud reverberated from below. Nat cursed loudly. Abigail rushed into the basement and found him dusting himself off. He'd slammed his shin into the crates she'd been digging through.

"Are you all right?"

Nat limped a step. "I'm fine."

"Sorry, I should have warned you. I've done that myself. Have the bruises to prove it."

She was babbling, and Nat could not have been less interested.

"Where's your breaker box?"

"I think it's over here. Watch the furniture," she warned, as they moved toward the row of antiques along the far wall. Chair arms and table legs protruded here and there, ready to impale or trip any hapless passersby. She noticed Nat do a double take at the desk.

"It's nice, isn't it? *Nice* isn't the right word. Too general. Unique, maybe. Or striking. Or . . ."

Abigail couldn't believe she'd admitted to not using a precise enough adjective. That was how nervous having Nat in the house made her.

"I'm planning to bring the desk into the study and the other pieces into the living room. Problem is, they're too heavy for me. It would be such an improvement compared to what's there. Did you get a load of that stuff? How dismal."

Nat looked at her. "The breaker box?"

"Right. Over here." She pointed it out, sensing that Nat was waiting for her to leave. "I'll be, um, upstairs if you need me."

"Uh-huh."

Abigail retreated to the kitchen, muttering to herself, "Who does he think he is? This is my house. Or it's sort of my house. What was Merle thinking, sending him here? Him of all people."

"I owed him for some supplies from his store." Nat was standing at the kitchen door. "I couldn't pay him, so he told me he'd clear my debt if I'd take a look at your wiring."

Embarrassed at being overheard, Abigail took a second to respond. "I had no idea you were an electrician."

"I'm not. Anymore, that is. I was. Before."

Nat shifted on his heels. Discussing any aspect of his personal life made him as uncomfortable as it made Abigail.

"Merle mentioned something about the bathroom light, that you were having trouble with it."

"You could say that."

She led him to the bathroom. "You'll have to ignore the grout situation."

"Forgot to wipe it, huh?"

"Yup."

"It's not hard to fix. What you do is get it damp again, remove the excess, reapply the grout, and wipe it fast. Like this."

Nat wet a bath towel and started scrubbing the rigid swirls that were caked on the tiles. Then he began to respread the grout around the tub. He was deft with the trowel.

"I take it you've done this before."

"I've done a lot of things before."

Abigail understood how it felt to have a *before* and how distant it could seem compared to the present.

"I'm sorry about what happened at the Kozy Kettle. I think you and I got off on the wrong foot."

Nat glanced at her as if to say, *That's the understatement of the year, lady.*

"And I didn't mean to stare last night when you were with Hank—"

He cut her short. "Don't worry about it."

Yet that was what Abigail thought she ought to do. Worry. Hank Scokes was evidently in pain and drinking to numb it. He had lost his spouse like she had. However, Abigail had her own worries.

"You mind?"

Because the bathroom was barely big enough for one person, Nat had to back out in order to finish. Abigail was blocking his path.

"Sorry." She'd been peering over his shoulder, so she stepped into the hall, giving him a wider berth. "Listen, I really want to move that furniture up from the basement and I can't do it alone. Maybe I could pay you to help me."

He shook his head firmly. "Couldn't take money for that."

"Why not?"

"Just can't."

"Then we could trade, like you and Merle did."

"What are you going to swap me for?" Nat said, incredulous.

Cooking was out. Cleaning too. He wouldn't believe she was decent at either, based on the current state of the house. Abigail was stumped.

"You still thinking?"

"Uh-huh."

"Well, what did you do before you came here?"

For a moment, Abigail genuinely couldn't remember.

"I was a lexicographer. That's a—"

"I know what it is."

"I didn't mean to—"

"I don't see how writing dictionaries is going to do me any good."

Abigail had been forced to burrow into her memory to retrieve her old life, only to be told it had no value. Nat's remark smarted.

In the past, when she'd met someone new and they asked what she did for a living, she would have to explain the parameters and politely defend hers as a real job. Most people didn't even realize lexicography was a profession. There was no dedicated training program, no section in the classifieds for open positions. One time, after clarifying the details of her occupation to another mother in Justin's playground, the woman deemed Abigail "a word cop." It wasn't Abigail's optimal description, but it wasn't entirely inaccurate. At her last consulting job, she'd assessed existing foreign-language-dictionary entries and searched for evidence to consider possible new entries. Like police work, the task involved logic, information gathering, and sound judgment. Now, however, Abigail didn't feel like an off-duty cop or an unemployed lexicographer. She just felt unemployed.

"You seem pretty handy with a paintbrush." Nat motioned at the roller and paint cans at the end of the hall. "I owe Duncan Thadlow for some mechanical repairs he did on the boat. Have to paint his house. I've done most of the prep. Could use a hand to finish."

"The outside of the house? I haven't done that before."

"Ain't much of a difference. You want in or not?"

"In exchange for moving the furniture? Yes, definitely."

"We'll start tomorrow." Nat stood and stretched his legs. The grout was complete, the job immaculate. "Let it dry for an hour. It'll be like new."

"Thanks. You didn't have to——"

Nat was already partway down the stairs. "I'll pick you up in the afternoon once I get back."

"Back?"

"From work. Fishing? Tomorrow's Wednesday. I was off today only because Hank's boat is still being repaired."

The days had bled together for Abigail. She hadn't seen a calendar since she left Boston.

"Right. Of course," she sputtered as Nat headed toward the front door. "Hey. What about the electricity and the light switch in the bathroom? Was there a short in the wiring?"

"Nothing wrong with them." He set his toolbox in the flatbed of his truck, saying, "See you tomorrow."

"Yeah. See you tomorrow," she replied, lost in thought.

Abigail had convinced herself the light was broken and that confirmation of the defective wiring would make her feel better. Except the wiring wasn't broken. Though the bathroom bulb hadn't come on mysteriously in days, the chance that it might happen again was an unpleasant preoccupation that had built into dread.

Dread was only one syllable. However, when spoken, the sound stretched, elongating like the feeling it defined. Dread wasn't about *if*. It was about *when*. And *when* was always somewhere on the horizon, impending and preordained. *When* was merely a matter of time.

◆   ◆   ◆

Abigail liked surprises about as much as migraine headaches. Nat Rhone's early-morning visit was just such a surprise. A warning would have been nice. She was knocking on Merle's front door to give him a refresher course on common courtesy, but he didn't appear to be home.

"Maybe it's the same as his store. You have to go around back to get service."

Merle's deck overlooked the bay. A grill filled with months' worth of charcoal cinders stood next to a wooden table where many a fish had met its end. The wood glimmered with scales embedded in the grain.

"Thought I heard someone sneaking around out here," Merle said through the screen door. "Glad you're not a prowler. Guess it's too early in the morning for prowlers, huh?"

"A little. I've been pounding on your front door for five minutes."

"Figured it was somebody selling something."

"You get a lot of Avon ladies here on Chapel Isle?"

"No, but those Girl Scouts are relentless."

Abigail put her hands on her hips.

"All right, all right, if you've come to read me the riot act about Nat Rhone, let's get it over with." He leaned into the screen that was separating them and put his chin out, miming that he was ready to take the verbal blow. "Go on. Gimme your best shot."

"You could have at least told me you were sending him."

"Then would you have let me?"

"Point taken."

"Want a cup of coffee?"

"Can't. I'm on my way to see Sheriff Larner."

"Caleb? Why?" Merle opened the screen door and joined her on the deck, hobbling with his umbrella cane.

"I saw someone during the rounds last night. A man. He was on Timber Lane."

"Did you recognize the guy?"

"It was dark. All I could say for sure was that it was a 'him.'"

"This was last night?"

"I drove straight to the sheriff's station afterward. Larner wasn't there. He had this sign in the window—"

"*Back in five minutes.* That's always there. Even when Caleb's in the office."

"What is it with you people and not answering your doors?"

"If it's that important, it can wait."

"Ah, more Chapel Isle logic."

"Only kinda logic I got. Anyhow, I was meaning to give you a ring. You don't have to do my route anymore. Tonight can be your last night. I'm feeling better. I can do it myself."

"Are you sure? You're still walking with your umbrella."

"Yeah, yeah. I'm peachy. And I'm well prepared if it rains."

"Okay, but what about the man I saw? Do you think I should tell the sheriff?"

"Your call," Merle answered, indifferent.

"Don't you care that somebody's coming to the island, *your* island, and breaking into people's homes?"

"Yes, I care. Except those houses that are being robbed, they're for the tourists. They're not for us. I worry for Lottie's sake. If she's hit, she'll get the insurance money, then she'll have to pay to fix whatever damage the burglar did and her rates will skyrocket. That's a raw deal. Fact is, she sends me around only so she can keep track of which units have been broken into and which haven't. It's not prevention. It's treading water."

"What if it was your house? What then?"

"It won't be."

"How do you know?"

He wouldn't answer.

"Merle," Abigail pressed.

"Whoever's doing these burglaries, they never target islanders' homes. Don't even step foot on our side of town. Because as soon as they came to one of *our* houses, there'd be real hell to pay."

"Then who is it? Someone from the mainland who visits during the summer?"

Merle looked at his feet, as though his expression might give him away.

"You think it's somebody from Chapel Isle."

He frowned yet didn't disagree.

"Why would someone who lives here do that?"

Merle lowered himself onto a folding chair. What he was about to say appeared to pain him more than his injury.

"Wasn't the best summer this year. People were praying for better. Heck, they were counting on it. Fishing industry's gone soft. There are more boats in these waters than fish. People've gotten to depend on the summer money. Weak as this season was, it's not a shock someone's gotten desperate. Not a shock at all."

"Do you think the sheriff knows what's going on?"

"Dunno."

"What if he does?"

"Then he does."

That was how it was on Chapel Isle. A secret could be widely known but still be a secret. A crime could occur with an island full of witnesses and not be a crime.

◆　◆　◆

The road from Merle's house brought Abigail to an intersection. She could either turn right toward town or left to the lighthouse. She had a choice to make: whether to tell the sheriff what she'd seen or let it lie.

As her engine idled, a school bus pulled up on the opposite side of the road. Children were running from their houses to catch it and waiting in line to board. It was such a normal sight that it made Abigail feel normal simply watching it.

The school bus rode onward, passing her station wagon. She flipped her turn signal. She went left.

Abigail spent the rest of the day pushing and pulling the manual lawn mower across the backyard. The constant whirring of the blades drowned out thought. The steady motion anesthetized her mind. When she finished, the lighthouse appeared taller and the brick caretaker's house seemed less dilapidated.

Satisfied, she went inside, then drew herself a hot bath. Abigail had gone three days without bathing, a lapse that would have been unconscionable in the past.

"Your hygiene certainly has suffered since moving here. Welcome to the new Abby."

For a change, she was excited about being in the bathroom. The white grout made the tiles gleam. The pale yellow paint gave the cramped room an airier feel. While the bathwater ran, Abigail went to the study to grab something to read in the tub. She perused the shelves. None of the books struck her fancy. That was until her eyes fell on the romance novel she'd started the other day. She remembered that Janine had been reading a similar paperback the first time she'd locked horns with her at Weller's Market.

"The one thing we have in common is our choice in reading. How ironic."

After a few minutes in the steamy bathwater, Abigail's sore muscles ceased to ache as badly. The knot in her neck loosened. When she rejoined the winsome heiress and her rogue pirate captain, their romance had put both in jeopardy from her sinister suitor, who was setting the captain up to be captured and killed.

Despite the ridiculousness of the story, Abigail didn't put the paperback down until she was a hundred pages further into the tale, and then it was only because her stomach was rumbling.

"Hold that thought, heiress. I'm starving."

Believing she might finally conquer her fear of the oven after the fiasco with the pilot light, Abigail had purchased a frozen dinner at the market.

"Showdown time," she said, toweling off. "In this corner we have one wet, tired woman. In the other we have the challenger: turkey tetrazzini."

Abigail switched on the lights as she moved through the house. Having the place lit made it feel warmer. Shivering, her hair damp, she skimmed the cooking instructions on the frozen-dinner package.

"Preheat oven to three-fifty. I can do that. I can preheat."

She sidled over to the stove and turned the knob. The gas snapped on loudly. Abigail flinched.

"Relax, champ. It's only warming up."

Normally, preheating would take ten minutes. Considering the stove's age, it could take double that to reach the correct temperature.

"Are you going to stand here staring at the darn thing the whole time?"

The answer was *yes*. Abigail couldn't bring herself to leave the oven unattended. She was waiting for any sign of danger. After five minutes, she was slouching against the wainscoting. Bored, she opened the refrigerator. In spite of her recent trip to the grocery store, the fridge was disgracefully empty. A lone container of milk and a packet of sliced turkey sat on one tier. An untouched carton of eggs perched on another. The apples she'd set on the bottom shelf had rolled over to a loaf of bread, as though huddling next to it for warmth.

"Even your food is needy."

She unwrapped the turkey tetrazzini entree, held her breath, and prepared to open the stove door.

"Ready or not."

Eyes shut, Abigail jerked open the oven, anticipating an intense blast of heat. Instead, lukewarm air wafted out.

"Is that it?"

The instructions said the cooking time would be approximately twenty-five minutes. A half hour later, Abigail's dinner remained frozen solid. She stabbed at it with a fork and nearly broke the tines. Already running late for Merle's route, she switched off the stove and slapped together a sandwich to take with her on the road.

"I forfeit. Turkey tetrazzini wins. Time to hang up the gloves."

◆   ◆   ◆

While making the rounds, Abigail felt a ripple of disappointment. This would be her last night. Each evening she'd been either humiliated or petrified, yet Merle's route had given her something she'd been missing—a purpose. She was sorry to lose that.

"Now you *must* be going crazy."

The cottage on Timber Lane was her last stop. Abigail elected to believe the thief wouldn't return so soon, logic that hadn't leached down to her nerves. Her palms were sweating, making the flashlight and hammer hard to grip. She was wiping her hands on her pants when her customary lap around the house was interrupted by footsteps.

This can't be happening again. Not again.

She ducked behind a clump of shrubs. This hiding in the bushes was not the type of activity Abigail ever thought she'd be making a habit of.

A glimmer of light flashed in the dark. She recognized the figure of the man from the night before. Moonlight was glinting off his wristwatch, illuminating the arc of his arm swinging as he walked. He had a slow, lumbering gait, a pace suggesting he was an older man or overweight. Abigail tracked him until he turned at the end of the lane, then she scrambled to her car, intent on pursuit. The rational side of her brain advised against it.

What are you going to do if you catch him? Make a citizen's arrest?

Common sense lost the tug-of-war to curiosity. Abigail threw the station wagon into drive, panning from side to side along the rows of houses. The man was gone. Again.

"Relax. You are not in some scary B movie. You're on Chapel Isle in a town full of seafaring, bingo-loving people who are, for the most part, sane, and none of them will be jumping out of the bushes with an ax."

Or so she hoped. Since the man had vanished, Abigail was stuck with the same choice as yesterday. To tell or not to tell. She hadn't gotten a close enough look to describe him in detail, so the conclusion was simple.

"I'm going home."

The word *home* resonated in her ears like the hum of a tuning fork. Had the lighthouse become her home? Her house in Boston, the place she'd truly considered home, was gone, leveled, the land sold off. The new owner would rebuild. It hurt Abigail to picture a new house replacing hers.

She and Paul had fallen in love with the property on sight. The Classical Revival home was the picture of elegant refinement, with its white stucco façade, dental molding, and black shutters. What made the house all the more appealing was that it had been modeled after The Mount, Edith Wharton's estate in Lenox, Massachusetts. Abigail couldn't have asked for more than to live in a lovely home resembling that of one of her favorite authors. But soon a new house would be constructed where hers once stood. No one would remember the detail about Edith Wharton or that it was Abigail and her family who had lived there. The facts that would endure were that the former house had burned down and that two people had lost their lives to the fire.

Abigail was getting into bed when the day's exertion finally caught up to her. She'd forgotten to buy any pain reliever at the market, and the achiness threatened to keep her awake. She would have to cope with being sore the way she coped with everything else: by ignoring it as best she could.

Thinking a book might put her to sleep, Abigail went downstairs to look for Lottie's romance novel, which wasn't in the bathroom, where she thought she'd left it. In the living room, she passed Mr. Jasper's ledger on the table.

"You could read that instead."

Cradling the ledger, she went back upstairs and settled in under the quilt, with the book propped on her knees. A page in, her eyelids began to droop, then she drifted to sleep with the ledger lying by her side.

per•si•flage (pûr´sə fläzh´, pâr´–), n. **1.** light, bantering talk or writing. **2.** a frivolous or flippant style of treating a subject. [1750–60; < F, deriv. of *persifler* to banter, equiv. to *per-* PER- 1 *siffler* to whistle, hiss < LL *sifilāre,* for L *sībilāre; see* SIBILANT, -AGE] **—syn. 1.** banter, badinage, jesting.

❖ ❖ ❖

Abigail awoke with a start to the sound of the ledger falling to the floor.

"Good morning to you too."

Groggy, she picked up the ledger, dusted it off, and got dressed, donning the painting togs she'd worn the week before; a pale plaid shirt and a pair of now-spattered khakis. She hunted around for Lottie's romance novel, found it in the study, then settled in at the dining-room table, thinking she'd read over breakfast before undertaking more household chores.

The story of the heiress and her pirate captain continued, each chapter ending in a crescendo of betrayal, a sword fight, or a chase on the high seas. As a battle ensued between the armada commanded by the dastardly count and the pirate's band of sea dogs, Abigail felt a pain in her stomach. It was long past lunch. A whole chunk of the day had vanished. The predictable romance novel had become unpredictably entertaining.

Abigail ate a yogurt as the story hurtled onward at a swift clip, laden with soppy adjectives and fervent verbs. The count was about to have the heiress's beloved pirate captain murdered in a secluded cove when a horn honked outside. Through the front window, Abigail could see Nat's truck in the drive.

"Right at the cliffhanger."

She closed the paperback and stood up too fast, making her head spin. She'd been sitting for so many hours that her legs were falling asleep. Abigail slapped her thighs and hopped on the balls of her feet, forcing the blood through her legs. The horn honked again.

"I'll be right there," she shouted out the window. Legs tingling, Abigail shuffled down the front stairs a step at a time.

Nat stared at her from the cab of his truck. "You hurt yourself?"

"It's a reading-related injury."

He didn't understand and didn't seem as if he wanted to. "You bringing any food?"

"Why?"

"This'll take a while. You might get hungry."

Abigail awkwardly walked back into the house, grumbling, "How was I supposed to know I needed to bring food?"

She threw together her usual sandwich and took an apple. The only bag she had to pack them in was a jumbo paper sack from Merle's store.

Nat raised his brows at the bag as she slid into the truck. "You must have some appetite."

They rode in silence as they crossed the island. Aside from the scuffed leather seats and sandy floors, the truck's interior was surprisingly tidy. A paper evergreen tree dangled from the rearview mirror.

"What?" Nat said. "You assumed it'd stink of fish in here."

"Kind of," Abigail confessed.

"You know what they say about assumptions. They're usually wrong."

Abigail would have readily admitted to being incorrect about several matters regarding Nat Rhone, except one. His attitude.

"Usually," she added.

The northwest end of the island was flat as a tabletop and blanketed by scrub brush. Nat pulled onto a bumpy, unmarked road. A quarter mile in, the single-lane path drained into a clearing. Scattered throughout the glade were a variety of boats in various states of repair. A handful of outboards were mounted on cinder blocks, while a damaged rowboat acted as a catchall for miscellaneous parts. Grass refused to grow in the clearing. The weeds were more persistent, though, poking their heads up through a gigantic anchor that had come to rest next to a gutted dinghy.

Between the clearing and the bay beyond was a clapboard cottage with a shake roof. The paint had been scraped away, yet traces of the former color—a ruddy beige—remained, giving the house a crusty appearance. Nat had mentioned prepping the place himself, which would easily have cost a couple hundred dollars. It must have taken days. Abigail wondered how much he owed this Duncan Thadlow.

The deal she'd struck with Nat was starting to seem unfair. All he had to do was move a few pieces of furniture, while she had indentured herself to a far more grandiose task.

"Don't wait for an invitation," he told her, getting out of the truck. Abigail followed.

Standing at the door to the cottage was a man with a thick brown beard so long it touched his chest. "Afternoon, Nat. Here to finish painting?"

"It'll get done." The man's innocent question had rubbed Nat the wrong way. Repaying a debt in labor rather than cash wasn't something he appeared proud of.

"Who's your assistant?" Duncan asked.

"Oh, yeah, this is—"

"I'm Abigail. Or Abby. Whichever."

She didn't want to hear Nat Rhone say her name. That would make their arrangement too personal, as if they were friends instead of convenient acquaintances.

"Happy to meet you. Holler if you need anything. Besides help, that is," Duncan deadpanned as he retired inside.

Not wasting a second, Nat said, "Get a ladder. We'll start high and paint down."

"Whatever you say."

Abigail carried over one of a pair of ladders from the truck's flatbed, as Nat hauled the cans of primer.

"Sorry. Forgot." He took the ladder from her, propping it against the side of the house.

"Forgot what?"

"That ladder's heavy."

"Weren't you just talking about assumptions?"

"Thought you might still be woozy from that 'reading-related injury.' Far be it from me to act like a gentleman." Nat removed the tops from two gallon-size containers of primer and gave her a brush.

"Any tips?" Abigail asked.

"Tips?"

"On how to do this."

"Put the brush in your hand and go like this." He started priming.

"Always a pleasure to learn from a pro," she said, trying to get in the last blow.

He ignored her. She did the same. It was going to be a long afternoon.

◆ ◆ ◆

The sunny, windless day worked in their favor. The primer went on easily and dried rapidly. Abigail wished she'd brought her radio. Silence while she was alone was manageable. Silence with Nat Rhone was uncomfortable.

When the quiet became too much for her, Abigail volleyed a question. "What about the back of the house?"

"Duncan took down the shingles. Had termites."

"Is he going to replace them? Winter will be here soon and—"

"You'd have to ask him," Nat snapped.

Jerk.

Both returned to priming, inching inward along the side of the house so they would meet in the center. Once they did, Abigail checked her watch. An hour had gone by.

"That went pretty fast," she said, more to herself than to him.

"Two hands are better than one."

"Don't you mean four?"

"Don't know about you, but I can paint with only one hand at a time." He took his ladder and his can of primer and went to the other end of the house.

Jerk.

They completed that side equally quick.

"Do you want to do the front before we break to eat or after?"

"Before. I'm not really hungry yet, if that's what you're asking," Abigail replied.

"That wasn't what I was asking, but fine."

Jerk.

Each started at the far end of the front of the house, maintaining their distance. Finishing turned into a race between them, the goal being to get to the door. Abigail kept tabs on Nat out of the corner of her eye. She could tell he was doing the same. He had the advantage of stronger arms, while she had speed. Soon they were mere feet from the front door. Abigail got there first.

"Finished?" she inquired smugly.

"I am now," he huffed. "Let's eat."

Abigail got her giant paper sack from Nat's truck. He slid behind the wheel and opened a cooler.

"Are you going to eat in there?"

"Why not?" he answered.

"It might be more pleasant to eat outside."

"I've been outside since sunrise."

"Well, I'm going to eat out here."

"Suit yourself."

Jerk.

She took a seat on the steps of Duncan's house and dumped the contents of the sack. Despite its size, the skimpy sandwich had gotten crushed somehow, and she'd forgotten to wash the apple. Abigail had also forgotten to bring a drink, and she was incredibly thirsty.

"Not much food for such a big bag," Nat called through the passenger side window. "Didn't you bring a drink?"

"Normally when I go to paint people's houses, I remember to pack a thermos. It must have slipped my mind."

Rudeness was a rarity for Abigail. Nat Rhone brought out the worst in her.

"I got an extra soda."

Abigail went to the truck and took the can from him. "Thanks," she said curtly, then returned to Duncan's front stoop.

They ate without another word to each other. Nat gazed at the water. She stared at the ground. Her sandwich, though squashed, was delicious. Intense hunger transformed the plain turkey and bread into a feast.

"This is how you can tell you're famished," she mused.

"How's that?"

"When even a mangled sandwich tastes amazing."

"How could you *not* realize you were hungry?"

He was angling for a quarrel. Abigail could feel it.

"You can sense something without being completely cognizant of it," she countered.

"Doubtful."

"Haven't you ever been exhausted and soldiered on because you loved what you were doing too much to stop?"

"Not the same," he replied between bites.

Nat was baiting her. Abigail refused to fall for it, choosing to change the subject to something he might be less inclined to haggle over.

"Duncan must have made quite a lot of repairs if you have to pay him back by painting his house."

Nat took a gulp of his soda. "Had to get Hank's rig fixed after the accident."

"Accident? At the dock? I thought he was drunk."

"It was an accident," he corrected her sharply.

"That's not what I heard."

"You heard wrong."

"It's not your boat, it's Hank's. So why——"

"Why is none of your business. You just got to Chapel Isle. You think you have it figured out? You haven't got a clue about this place or these people. And you don't have a clue about me."

"Hmm, let me hazard a guess. This tough-guy act is a cover for the sensitive, heartbroken kid who lurks beneath the surface of the notorious Nat Rhone. Please, spare me. Because you don't know a thing about me either, and all I know about you is that you're a real asshole." Abigail threw aside the rest of her sandwich. "Where's the paint? I want to get this over with."

She snatched a can of taupe exterior paint from the flatbed and marched to one side of the house to start painting. The truck door opened. She heard Nat moving his ladder to the opposite side of the house. Her hands were shaking so badly it made opening the paint can impossible. Abigail almost started to cry.

You only have to make it through to the end of the day. A few more hours.

Then she remembered the other half of their bargain. Nat was going to move the furniture with her. It would be worth it to leave the antiques in the basement if it meant not having to spend an extra second with him.

They met at the front of the house, each toting their respective ladders, briefly making eye contact before getting to work. This time it wasn't a race between them as much as a race to finish.

Later, Nat put on the final stroke of paint, saying, "I'll clean the brushes at home. You can load your gear in the truck and we can go."

"I can clean them."

"I said I'd take care of it."

"You're the boss."

Duncan came outside as Nat was capping the last can. "Is this a present for me?" He motioned wit the toe of his boot to the apple Abigail had left on the steps. Beside it was her half-eaten sandwich, lying on the paper bag. She scrambled to clean the mess.

"No worries. You can leave me food anytime," he proclaimed, patting his belly.

"Excellent job," Duncan said, walking from end to end of the house. "Only now the missus will be on me to straighten up the yard. Say, you guys make a good team. Maybe you should go into business together."

Abigail and Nat exchanged glances. He pulled his hat lower on his head, hiding under it instead of answering.

"I've really got to be getting back to the lighthouse."

"'Course. Glad to have met you, Abby." Duncan offered his hand. She shook it, though her fingers burned from gripping a paintbrush for hours on end.

"This squares you with me," he told Nat. "You and Hank, that is."

Nat thanked him and got into the truck. Abigail did the same, then they drove across the island as they had come, not speaking. He pulled up to the lighthouse and Abigail hurried out.

"What about the furniture?" Nat asked.

"Forget about it."

"What? No. I'm not welching on my end of the deal."

"Whatever. I'm too tired to do it today."

"Okay, I'll come tomorrow. Hank's been under the weather. Doesn't want to take the rig out. I can be here in the morning."

"Like I said, whatever."

Abigail went inside and slammed the door harder than she had intended, making it shiver on the hinges. Then she slid down to the floor and cried, also harder than she had intended.

quoth•a (kwōˊthə), *interj. Archaic.* indeed! (used ironically or contemptuously in quoting another.) [1510–20; from *quoth a* quoth he]

Q

◆   ◆   ◆

The house was quiet. The solid stillness was so dense that it filled the living room and pressed against Abigail as she sat on the floor with her back against the door. When she lifted herself to her feet, her knees cracked. The pain in her arms was intense enough to make her ears ring. She was too tired to sleep, too hungry to eat. On reflex, she drove to Merle's house and sat outside in the station wagon, baffled as to what had brought her there.

"You're here. Might as well go in."

Abigail headed around to the deck, where she could see in through the sliding glass door. The lights were on. She could hear a football game being broadcast. She tapped on the slider and heard Merle ambling toward the door. He noticed she had been crying. Abigail made no effort to conceal it.

"Something wrong?"

"No."

"Something break?"

"No."

"Did the lighthouse collapse?"

"No."

"You want to come in?"

"Please."

"You eaten?"

"Not much."

"Got some leftover tuna casserole."

"Sounds delicious."

While he reheated the food in the microwave, Abigail took a seat. The kitchen table was covered in hooks and thread for fashioning lures. A miniature plastic beetle was affixed to a stand.

"Used to buy my lures," Merle said, "but I thought I could make 'em more lifelike myself."

"You've got talent. They look real."

"Knock on wood the fish concur." He set a mug of coffee before her. "Had a bad day, huh? I've had my share of those. I prefer the good ones."

"It's Nat Rhone. He's so . . ."

"Arrogant? Obnoxious? Infuriating?"

"Yeah, that."

"The guy's not easy to get along with. Never has been. Never will be. He's had a hard life."

"Who hasn't?"

The microwave beeped, giving Merle an out. He spooned a large serving of casserole onto a plate for her. "It's hot. Don't need to burn your tongue again."

Ignoring the warning, Abigail dug into the meal. It tasted wonderful. She devoured forkful after forkful, cleaning her plate. She didn't dare confess to Merle that it was the first warm meal she'd had since she arrived.

"For such a skinny person, you can really put it away. You're not one of those, what do you call it, narcoleptics, are you?"

Abigail laughed, nearly choking on her food. "You mean bulimics? No, I'm not."

She suspected that Merle made the slip on purpose to squeeze a laugh out of her. She appreciated that as much as the food.

"Want to talk about it?" he asked.

ht=

"It doesn't matter. Nat's got a chip on his shoulder. That's that. Whatever happened to him, he must deserve to be angry."

"Being that angry usually means somebody's been hurt. Hurt something fierce," Merle said, insinuating that he had a full story on the notorious Nat Rhone.

Abigail put up her hands, as if to physically stop him. "You don't have to tell me. It's none of my business. And Nat would go ballistic if you did."

"Probably."

"You're going to tell me anyway?"

Merle's expression was impassive. He was going to tell her anyway.

"If you'd confide Nat's secrets to me, who's to say you won't spill mine to him? Or anybody else?"

"S'pose you'll have to trust me."

Trust was a tricky concept for Abigail. In the wake of the fire, she couldn't always trust her senses or herself. Putting her faith in someone else was asking a lot.

"I'll trade you a little trust for another plate of that tuna casserole."

"Coming right up."

❖　❖　❖

The fishing lures and the racket from the football game were the lone strands of masculinity in Merle's house. An ivy wallpaper border lined the kitchen, the magnets on the fridge were in the shape of watering cans, and the pot holders hanging from the oven had a floral motif. Merle, the strapping embodiment of manhood, was immersed in the girliness of his ex-wife's possessions. At first, Abigail wondered why he held on to them after what she had done, jilting him and taking his child. Then she realized that if her house hadn't been destroyed, she would have continued to live in it after the fire. She would have given anything to be reminded of the special times imbued in every wall, banister, and floorboard, willing to look past the sadness that was incised in them as well.

"Is this the kind of story that'll make me cry? Because I've already done my share of that today."

Merle set the refilled plate of casserole on the table for her. "Depends on what you cry at."

"Okay, okay. If you're going to tell me, tell me already."

"Nat didn't relay this to me himself, not personally."

"Is that a preface to the saga?"

"It's not—what do you call it—hearsay. But it's not from the horse's mouth neither."

"Whose mouth is it from?"

"Hank Scokes."

Abigail was hazy on the island's lines of alliance. She was unaware of who was close with whom and who wasn't. "I didn't realize you and Hank were friends."

"Friends in as much as I've known him most of my life."

"Sorry. Go on."

"A while after Hank'd taken Nat on as his mate, they got to drinking together. Liquor doing what it does, Nat opened up to Hank. Nobody else knew hide nor hair about the guy. Hardly the chitchat type. He'd already been fired by three other captains. Not because he couldn't handle himself on a rig, but because of his temper. That got rumors swimming."

"Rumors about what?"

"That Nat was some parolee or an escaped convict or that he'd broken out of a mental hospital with only the clothes he had on him."

"Was that all he came to the island with?"

"Maybe less."

"But that's not what really happened, is it?"

Merle had a seat at the table with her. "Hank said one night after he and Nat drank a few beers—too many, knowing Hank—Nat told him he'd come here from South Carolina. Before that he'd been in Florida. He'd lived in a dozen places on the southern seaboard, taking any job he could get. From menial stuff to things he should've had a license for: electrical work, plumbing, engineering, you name it."

"Wait. You sent someone who's not a real electrician to check my wiring?"

Caught, Merle's cheeks went pink. "He *is* the best electrician on Chapel Isle. Having the proper credentials is, um, a technicality."

"Thanks for explaining. I feel much better."

"As I was saying, Nat told Hank about how much he moved around, taking the bus if he had the money. Hopping trains if he didn't. Then Hank asked Nat about his family. Well, Nat got real quiet. Didn't answer. Thankfully, Hank, drunk as he was, had the sense to keep his trap shut and let the boy speak. Nat told Hank he didn't have any family. None living, that is. Parents died in a car crash when he was a toddler, both of 'em killed instantaneously. He was strapped into his car seat, made it through the crash without a scratch on him."

Hearing that, Abigail could have cried. Except she didn't want to. What she wanted to do was wring Merle's account from her head. She resented having to pity Nat Rhone, hated having something so personal in common with him. But she did. He'd lost his family and so had she. Abigail wondered if the tale touched a chord with Merle as well. Nat didn't get the chance to know his parents, while Merle had a son he hadn't met. She would have liked to ask Merle about it. However, this was Nat's history he was volunteering, not his own.

"He was sent to live with a relative, an aunt," Merle went on. "As Nat got older, his temper got worse. The aunt couldn't get him to mind her and there was no one else, so he was sent to a foster home, then got kicked out and bounced from place to place. Since nobody could control him, nobody would have him. Nat started stealing, getting on the wrong side of the law. Mentioned jail to Hank. Not prison, though. Broke into a car to take the change from the ashtray and got busted. That was when he was seventeen. He drifted from there on."

"Why are you telling me this, Merle? So I'll feel sorry for Nat and that'll absolve his terrible behavior? A bad life isn't a defense for bad manners or a bad attitude."

"No, I'm only telling you so you'll know."

"How does that change anything?"

"There's a wide gap between knowing something and not knowing something."

Abigail pushed her plate aside. "I can't take many more of these oblique maxims that sound like they came out of fortune cookies. They don't make any sense."

"Sure they do. You're a smart lady. You get the picture."

She did and she didn't. Merle took her plate to the sink and washed it, while Abigail sat drumming her fingers. "What do I do when Nat shows up on my doorstep tomorrow to help me move the furniture from the basement?"

"Do what?" Merle nearly dropped the plate.

"We made an agreement. I'd paint Duncan Thadlow's house with him if he'd move the antiques in the basement upstairs for me. It seemed such a shame to leave them down there. I'm no expert on wood, as you've already observed, but the dampness couldn't be doing the furniture any favors, right?"

Merle was processing what she'd told him. The faucet was running on high. He appeared not to hear it.

"Merle. The water."

"Oh. Yeah." He shut off the tap, preoccupied.

"Are you all right?"

"Uh-huh. Hunky-dory."

Abigail thought otherwise. "I've troubled you enough this evening," she said, standing.

"Not in the least. You want me to pack you what's left of the casserole?"

Stuffed, she rubbed her stomach. "I may not eat another bite for a week."

"Don't go getting narcoleptic on me."

"Thanks, Merle. Really," she added on a serious note. "I mean it."

"You're welcome. Really."

◆　◆　◆

Once Abigail was home, she remembered what she had intended to ask Merle. It wasn't about Nat Rhone. It was about the ledger entry regarding the *Bishop's Mistress*.

"One sad story per night is my limit."

While brushing her teeth in the bathroom, she admired the grout work Nat had done for her, though she was too irritated to give him credit.

"Just because he's handy doesn't make him any less of a jerk."

She shut off the light switch. If Nat was the top electrician on the island and he claimed there weren't any issues with the wiring, she should believe him. But could she?

Downstairs, the phone rang, startling Abigail. It was past nine. She worried it might be her parents and rushed to answer.

"Abby, is that you?" The reception was spitting static.

"Lottie?"

"Yes, dear. It's *moi*. Wanted to make sure you got my gift."

"The romance novels. Yes, I found them. Thanks. They're . . ." Abigail scrolled through a range of descriptive phrases, selecting the least disparaging. "A quick read. Say, there are a few things I'd like to discuss with you about the house."

No time like the present to come clean about the changes she'd made.

"Wish I could chew the fat, dear, but my cousin is still recuperating from her girdle thing, and I have to wait on her hand and foot. Such a princess."

"Then maybe I could come by the office to talk. When will you be back?"

"Say again, Abby?" Lottie's cell phone hissed. "I can't hear you over this noise. Sounds like frying bacon. Mercy, I need to put that on my grocery list. Wouldn't a BLT be delish about now? Gotta go, Abby. You have my mouth watering with all this gabbing about food."

"Hold on. Lottie?"

The line dissolved into a dial tone.

"From books to bacon. A quantum leap. She must have thought

you were going to yell at her about the caretaker's cottage. Can't say you didn't try to tell her."

Upstairs, the ledger was lying on the unmade bed. Abigail moved it to the nightstand, then reconsidered. She had slept soundly the night before, which she hadn't done in months.

It worked yesterday. It might work again.

Slipping under the quilt, Abigail placed the ledger at her side and waited patiently for sleep to find her.

ruc•tion (ruk´shən), *n.* a disturbance, quarrel, or row. [1815–25; orig. uncert.]

R

♦　♦　♦

Pain rather than sunlight roused Abigail. The ledger was digging into her shoulder blade. Her watch read a quarter past seven, the same time she'd risen the day before.

She moved the ledger onto the nightstand. "You're as trusty as an alarm clock."

If only her body were as dependable. Painting Duncan's house yesterday had thrust Abigail past her physical limit. Stiff, she slowly rooted through the dresser for something to wear. She was running out of clean clothes. The garbage bag she was using as a hamper was full. A trip to the laundromat would be in order shortly, as would a stop at the market for some aspirin.

Abigail wanted to assess the situation in the basement before Nat arrived. Sheets off, she counted fourteen pieces of furniture. The dining chairs were light, and Abigail could manage them herself. However, navigating the narrow, rickety stairway was going to be a challenge.

As she crested the stairs, lugging a chair, there came a knock at the front door. Nat was on the other side.

"We doing this?" he asked.

"Yes," Abigail sighed. "We are." She waved him in.

"Do you need to change?"

"My clothes? Why?"

"They look too fancy to be moving furniture in."

Abigail couldn't see how a sweater and a pair of trousers could be construed as overdressed. "It's not like I'm wearing a ball gown and pearls."

"Okay."

"I didn't have anything else that was clean," she admitted.

"Okay."

"I have to go to the laundromat. I'm going tomorrow."

"Okay."

"I shouldn't have to explain myself."

"Okay."

"Now you're placating me."

"I'm trying."

"Stop."

Nat motioned at the dining chair she'd brought up. "You started without me?"

"It was a trial run. The basement stairwell is fairly tight, and the one to the second floor is even tighter."

"We can manage."

His optimism surprised her. The normally surly Nat was undaunted, while she was ready to throw in the towel. Abigail hoped he wasn't underestimating the project the way she'd underestimated him.

They descended into the basement, where he appraised the stairs from the bottom. "Small, but somebody got the pieces down here. Which means we can get them back up. They're actually in decent shape," he remarked, studying the writing desk.

"You're familiar with antiques?" Abigail asked, careful not to act shocked. She didn't want to let what she'd learned about Nat slip, yet she wasn't inclined to be excessively kind to him either.

"A bit."

"I can't understand why somebody left them here, in a musty, dank basement."

"People hide things for a whole bunch of reasons."

"Who said the furniture was hidden?"

"Hiding it, storing it, whatever." Nat got on the other side of the desk. "We should do the heavy pieces first. You ready?"

Abigail was stuck on the notion that the furniture had been hidden intentionally.

"You've heard about the, um . . . How should I put this?"

"Ghost? Yeah. And? You didn't fall for that story, did you? That's just the local yokels trying to pull one over on ya."

"Right. Of course."

His dismissal made Abigail feel less apprehensive about what they were going to do, although only marginally.

"Ready?" Nat repeated. "Push that wingback chair over and we'll angle the desk toward the stairs."

While he removed the drawers, Abigail shimmied the wingback out of their path. Together they moved the desk to the foot of the steps.

"Turn it the opposite way," he instructed.

"Which direction?"

"In line with the stairs, not perpendicular to them."

Hearing Nat say *perpendicular* struck her. Abigail could tell that level of language suited him more than his regular style of speaking. What she respected about language was that it was like a puzzle— crossword rather than jigsaw. It provided a frame and lots of clues for understanding people. There was a distinct possibility Nat was dumbing himself down in order to fit in with the Chapel Isle men he socialized and worked with.

"What?"

Abigail was staring at him, waiting to hear him speak again and confirm her theory.

"Nothing, nothing," she said, covering.

"Let's switch places. You go high. I'll go low. You'll have to walk backward, but I'll take most of the weight. This desk isn't light, so tell me if you need to rest."

For a change, Nat wasn't insulting her. He was being honest.

She got into position and they lifted the writing desk in unison. Nat grabbed the legs to steady the load, while Abigail gripped the lip of the desktop. They had three stairs to go when Abigail's fingers started to slip.

"I'm losing it."

"We can make it." He inched the desk higher against his chest, rebalancing.

"It's going to fall."

"No, it won't."

In a final push, Nat forced the desk over the threshold, safely onto the floor.

"See," he said, breathing hard. "You didn't drop it."

"*Almost* didn't drop it."

"Where's this going?"

"The study."

"After you." He gestured for her to lead the way.

Upstairs, Nat got out his measuring tape. "Some of this furniture will have go in order for the desk to fit."

"I won't need the smaller desk or the chair. And I certainly don't need that cot."

"You say that like you don't plan on having any visitors."

Abigail felt Nat searching her face. The scrutiny was too intense for her, so she sidestepped him, saying, "This chair is light. I'll take it down to the living room."

He followed behind, hauling the wafer-thin mattress from the cot under his arm. "If you aren't going to use it . . ."

"It's all yours."

"I'll consider it a loan. Even though the cot isn't really yours to lend. You are renting this place. You forget?"

She had. "Then loan it is."

"Might need a hand to get the frame onto my truck."

They made their second trip to the study and began to disassemble the bed. The legs folded in, making it easy to maneuver through the stairwell. Nat went first, Abigail trailing. Since he had his back to her, she could finally blot the sweat from her forehead.

"At least this isn't heavy," she remarked, pretending she wasn't short of breath. "What are you going to do with it?"

"Sleep on it."

"What about your bed?"

"You're carrying it."

Abigail was astounded. The man literally had no place to sleep. Had he been bunking on somebody's couch or, worse, the floor? They slid the frame into the rear of his truck and he shut the tailgate.

"Need any other furniture? Seriously. What else am I supposed to do with it?"

"Dunno about that." Her generosity made him antsy.

Nat was retreating into the house when Abigail said: "I won't tell if you won't."

He turned and hunted for intention in her eyes. This time, Abigail held her ground.

"You're on."

◆ ◆ ◆

Piece by piece, they emptied the basement. For every chair that came up, another went onto Nat's truck. Soon the living room was full of antiques and his flatbed was piled high. By noon, Abigail was spent. She plopped onto the front steps of the house.

Nat wiped his face with a handkerchief. "You hungry yet?"

"Yet?"

"You don't seem to eat much."

"I eat. I eat plenty."

"Uh-huh."

Nat headed into the house. Abigail found him in the kitchen inspecting the contents of her refrigerator.

"This is a sorry sight."

"It's not very polite to—"

"Go through people's medicine cabinets. This is your fridge."

"Laugh it up. I don't have any food. Ha-ha-ha."

"This a start," he said of the frozen dinners in the freezer. "At least you can throw these in the oven and. . . ." He mimed the gesture, inadvertently exposing the half-baked turkey tetrazzini from two nights ago. "Saving this for later?"

Face burning, Abigail stormed out of the kitchen. She sulked on the stoop. Nat appeared minutes later with a sandwich on a plate.

"This must be your favorite, because it's all you got."

Abigail took the plate. The sandwich was so artfully presented that her mouth began to water.

"You should've made one for yourself. Or I could make you one," she offered lamely.

"Don't worry. I brought my own." Nat unpacked a delectable-looking overstuffed sandwich from his cooler. He saw Abigail eyeing it. "You want some?"

"No, I couldn't."

Nat put half of his sandwich on her plate, then took the other half of hers. Abigail had a bite. His sandwich was perfection.

"That's what a couple months as a short-order cook will teach you."

"Is there a job you haven't done?"

"Other than president?"

"Yes, besides being the leader of the free world, what occupation haven't you taken a stab at?"

"Can't think of any," he said. "Except lexicography, of course."

The topic had become too intimate for Nat, too personal. He began to fidget with the cap of the soda he'd brought. Abigail changed the subject. It was the least she could do after he'd made her the sandwich.

"What's your take on these robberies? Weird, huh?"

The second the words tumbled from her lips, she recalled that

Nat had been arrested for breaking into a car as a teen and regretted raising the issue. Abigail expected him to get tense or fly off the handle. Instead, he chewed his food, pondering his answer.

"Mostly, people steal because they're desperate. Because they have to. It's a rare few who steal for the fun of it."

Until she posed the question, Abigail hadn't considered that Nat might be the thief. Even after Merle explained his past, she didn't make the connection, and she now had reason to be glad. If she'd suspected him, Abigail was positive Nat would have intuited it.

"Hope it stops soon, though," he said. "Folks are getting nervous."

"I thought nobody cared as long as it wasn't their house."

"There are only so many rental units on the island."

It was a logical inference, a conclusion Abigail had been avoiding. What if the thief started targeting the places where people lived?

"Didn't mean to scare you."

"I'm not scared."

"I'm sure you're safe here."

"Me too." But Abigail wasn't that certain.

It was Nat's turn to change the subject. "I've had a lot of jobs. Never as an interior decorator. I can stick around and 'arrange.' Isn't that the woman's favorite part?"

"Pardon me?" The edge in Abigail's voice was unmistakable.

He put his arms up defensively. "All I'm saying is I'm here."

"Now *you're* on," she replied, echoing his earlier statement. "Better finish that sandwich. You're going to need your strength. This *is* the 'woman's favorite part.'"

◆   ◆   ◆

Rearranging the furniture was almost as taxing as moving it, yet far more fun for Abigail. Though she wasn't going to tell Nat that. They tried positioning the settee at countless angles and turning the dining table again and again. They relocated the pair of wingbacks in every conceivable spot. Once they got the layout set, they finished by replacing the wobbly table that held the telephone with a sturdy, carved console.

"Looks good."

Abigail agreed. With the new paint and furnishings, the living and dining area had the homey atmosphere of an inn. She couldn't resist smiling.

"That's a big fireplace. Brick's original. You must get a lot of use out of it."

Nat's mention of the fireplace caused her smile to sink.

"Would you mind helping me in the study? I want to get the desk in the right spot, and I won't be able to lift it on my own."

Her shift in tone obviously confused him. "Uh, all right. No problem."

With the desk centered under the bank of windows, Nat proffered the matching chair. "Want to take it for a test drive?"

"I can do that later."

"Come on," he urged, dusting the seat.

Reticently, Abigail sat down. The chair cupped her firmly. The height of the desk was a tailored fit.

"Looks like it was built for you."

The desk and chair, she presumed, had belonged to Wesley Jasper. Abigail could picture a man sitting there gazing through the windows and making notes in the ledgers. She thought of the night the *Bishop's Mistress* sank and how Mr. Jasper must have felt.

"What's wrong? You seem . . . sad."

"Nothing, nothing." Abigail hurried for the stairs as Nat pursued her. "I, um, remembered I wanted to show you something."

From the kitchen, Abigail produced the bags of plates and pots she'd culled from the cupboards. "It's not bone china and Waterford crystal. But it's not broken."

Nat peeked in at dishes. "Hell, I'll take 'em."

"Super-duper. I'll bring these bags to your truck." Abigail couldn't get out of the caretaker's cottage fast enough. She was suddenly brimming with worry. Had she made a mistake bringing Mr. Jasper's possessions up from the basement?

Bewildered, Nat grabbed a bag himself, saying, "Super-duper? That's quite the word, Ms. Dictionary."

Outside, the day was darkening. The clouds threatened rain. Wind was flogging the trees.

"You heard about the storm?" Nat asked, putting the dishes on the passenger seat of the truck.

"What storm?"

"It's hurricane season. Since you don't have a TV, you should always listen to the radio for weather reports," he cautioned. "It's been on the news. They're predicting the storm will swing east, out to sea. Except a hurricane can turn tail in a heartbeat. You got candles and flashlights and water and such?"

"Most of it."

"If I were you, I'd get to the market by tomorrow morning. Stock up. Better safe than sorry."

It was a sliver of friendly advice, yet Abigail felt awkward getting it from Nat. She swiveled the conversation in a different direction, away from herself. "So are you going to have room for this bountiful cornucopia at your place?"

"Didn't have much to start with. When Hank rented the apartment to me, it was empty. Loaned me an air mattress, a hot plate, a folding card table. That was it."

"I didn't realize you lived with him."

"Not with him. Over his garage. This is his truck."

At last, Abigail understood why Nat took such care of Hank, why he guarded him and protected him. Hank had not only given Nat a job, he'd opened his home to him. It may have been more than anyone else ever did.

"Well . . ." he said, signaling his departure.

"Thanks."

"Deal's a deal. Bet you thought it wasn't going to be a fair trade."

That was exactly what Abigail thought. Given the amount of labor, Nat had done more for her than she had for him.

"I had my reservations."

Nat smirked at her and got into Hank's truck. "Don't forget about those supplies."

"I won't. Thanks again."

During the two days they'd spent together, she and Nat had exchanged a few dozen words at most. Though they had worked tirelessly, side by side, they'd hardly spoken. It wasn't the absence of discourse that troubled Abigail—she could do without pointless chatter. Rather, it was the implication. On Chapel Isle, language—her primary currency—held a lesser value. The exchange rate was not in her favor. That left Abigail feeling like her proverbial pockets had been picked.

◆　◆　◆

The early-evening hours ebbed away. Abigail didn't notice. She was busy admiring the new appointments to the house. She sat in each chair, cozied up in both wingbacks, snuggled on the settee, and rested her feet atop the coffee table. This was how the caretaker's cottage should have been from the beginning. Curtains would add the finishing touch. She didn't think any of the stores on the island carried drapes, so the windows would have to wait until she made a trip to the mainland or could order some from a catalog. What could no longer wait was her hunger.

Abigail tore open a frozen dinner, turned on the oven, and summarily threw the decaying dinner into the garbage.

"Turkey tetrazzini will not beat me."

Heat ticking, the stove slowly came to life. Abigail stood watch as it preheated, then put the entrée in to cook. She tried turning her back on the oven but kept stealing glances over her shoulder. She finally made herself leave but got only as far as the door between the kitchen and living room.

Adjectives clicked through her head: *timid, pusillanimous, spineless, lily-livered.* She settled on the most juvenile.

"Chicken."

The house was miserably icy. Abigail needed to start a fire. Using the stove and the fireplace simultaneously would be a tall order.

"I'm going to get some firewood, and you're going to stay here and not do anything out of the ordinary, right?" she asked, addressing the oven.

You've gone from trying to reason with a ghost to negotiating with an inanimate object. Talk about a downward spiral.

Outside, the ocean was crashing against the seawall. The sky was striated with orange clouds. Abigail felt lucky that she could open her front door and see a sight this sublime. She also felt categorically unlucky. She wouldn't have been looking at this sunset if it weren't for the fire. With the oven on, Abigail didn't have a moment to waste, either on the view of the landscape or the view of what her life had become. There would be plenty of time for both later.

She lugged in some wood from the shed and prepared the fireplace, ripping apart the container from her frozen dinner and sticking the cardboard pieces between the logs. Once the fire took, she had to decide whether to stay or go guard the stove. An ember popped in the fireplace, sending her back a pace.

"What we need is a screen."

We was a term she hadn't uttered in a while. For Abigail, there was no more *we*. To her, *we* meant her family, her husband and son. Her main frame of reference was as *we: We bought a new house. We're having a baby. We're going out to eat.* Now all that remained was *I.* It was the second of only two one-letter words in the entire dictionary, the first being *A.* Each was defiantly singular. The language would be nothing without them. Abigail felt she was nothing without *we.* She missed *we.*

"At least now you can make a list," she said, careful to say *you* instead. She got a pen from her purse and wrote *fireplace screen* on what was left of the box the frozen dinner came in.

"What about kerosene for the lamps in the shed? Maybe a second flashlight. Some more batteries. Jugs of water. Canned food."

She continued until she smelled something. The aroma of food.

The scent drew her into the kitchen. Through the oven window, she could see the entrée bubbling. Hungry as she was, the aluminum tray of food looked scrumptious. Abigail set herself a place at the dining-room table, spooned the contents of her frozen dinner onto a plate, and poured herself a glass of milk. The meal was miles from gourmet, but with it and the new paint and furnishings, she was as near content as she could be.

◆ ◆ ◆

After dinner, Abigail's plate was clean, her glass empty, and her stomach full—too full, truth be told. Her stomach ached, not because of the quality of the meal but because of the speed at which she ate it. Bushed, she could have fallen asleep where she sat. She had to force herself to wash the dishes and wipe the crumbs from the table, which reminded her that she wanted to buy wood soap. Abigail had dusted each piece of furniture after she and Nat hauled it up from the basement, but she intended to give the antiques a thorough cleaning.

"Wood soap. Another thing to put on the list."

As she spoke, a rattling *whap* reverberated from the side of the house. Her heart began to pound. The noise wasn't coming from the basement or the lighthouse. It was outdoors. Abigail glanced at the phone.

What are you going to do? Call the sheriff and tell him you think the ghost is mad at you for moving his furniture?

Beside the phone were her keys. She readied herself to make a break for the car. The rattling sounded again, reminiscent of a door bashing into a frame.

The shed.

"Either you go see if you left the door open or it'll bang away all night long and you won't get a minute's peace."

The flashlight cut a wide arc into the night. Abigail wished it were wider. The vista she'd been admiring hours earlier was obliterated by darkness. She quickened her pace as she rounded the lighthouse, as if running off a diving board instead of walking. There in the glare of the flashlight was the shed. The door hung open, wavering in the wind. The shadowy figure she'd seen on Timber Lane traipsed into her mind. If there was someone inside the shed, her best chance was to lock him in there.

With one big breath, Abigail sprinted across the lawn, slammed the shed door, and snapped the padlock.

"I'm calling the police. Do you hear me? I'm calling the police."

There was no reply. There was no one inside. Relief hit her as the first raindrop landed on her arm. Then came a deluge. Abigail dashed into the house, laying the flashlight and keys beside the telephone.

Who could you have called if there had been someone in the shed?

Abigail would have been too embarrassed to call Nat or Denny or Bert, even if she did have their numbers. She couldn't count on Lottie and wouldn't have wanted to bother Ruth. The only person left was Merle. He'd give her a hard time about it, but she was confident he would come. Having one person she could rely on was better than none. That was enough to see Abigail through the night.

sed•u•lous (sej´ə ləs), *adj.* **1.** diligent in application or attention; persevering; assiduous. **2.** persistently or carefully maintained: *sedulous flattery.* [1530–40; < L *sēdulus,* adj. deriv. of the phrase *sē dolō* diligently, lit., without guile; r. *sedulious* (see SEDULITY, -OUS)] —**sed´•u•lous•ly,** *adv.* —**sed´u•lous•ness,** *n.*
—**Syn. 1.** constant, untiring, tireless.

◆　◆　◆

*The list Abigail began the day before had grown. The scrap of card-*board was overrun with additions squeezed in wherever there was room, items ranging from crucial necessities to nonessential indulgences. Be it candles or hand lotion, canned food or wood soap, Abigail needed far more than she originally thought and wanted more than she'd been willing to give herself.

She took a different road into town, assuming it would lead to the square. Instead, the lane let out into a cul-de-sac dominated by Chapel Isle's grade school, a boxy brick structure flanked by a playground. Abigail had been on the island for more than a week and still hadn't gotten the lay of the land.

"You're not a tourist. You live here now. Start acting like it."

While she circled the cul-de-sac, the name on the building across from the school grabbed her attention. It read: *Chapel Isle Library.* A slate roof and stained-glass accents in the windows spiffed up the otherwise plain façade.

"You did say you wanted to act like you lived here."

Warm, quiet, and well lit, libraries were a favorite of Abigail's. She always felt at home in a place where books outnumbered people. A library was like a country club for reading enthusiasts, only everybody was welcome.

"You must be here about the loggerheads," a librarian said, greeting Abigail excitedly when she entered. The woman's gray hair was cropped short, as if having it any longer would have been a hassle.

"Loggerheads?"

"We have a microfiche machine," she said proudly. "It's in the back."

The small library was empty except for an elderly man in a wool jacket, reading the newspaper at a table. The fluorescent lighting made a low buzzing sound and tinged the entire room with a yellow glow. Even the round braided rug in the children's reading corner took on an amber cast.

"I think you have me confused with someone else," Abigail said.

"My apologies. A gal from the mainland phoned about doing some research on our loggerhead-turtle population. We don't get a lot of out-of-towners in, so I thought you were she. What can I do for you?"

The island's loggerhead turtle population gave Abigail an idea.

"I'm glad you asked. What can you tell me about the lighthouse here on the island?"

"What sort of information are you looking for?" Suspicion starched the woman's reply.

"General information, historical data, that sort of thing."

"Well, we have a book on the lighthouses of the Outer Banks, which has details of each of the lighthouses in the area."

"Do you have anything more *specific*?"

"No, we don't. As you can see, we're a modest library."

The woman was giving Abigail the runaround. Saying she was the new caretaker might open a door. Or close it tighter.

"It's such an interesting old lighthouse. I'm surprised nobody has written a book about it."

"Yes," the librarian agreed. "It's a mystery."

❖ ❖ ❖

Unlike at the library, Abigail could get what she was after at the hardware store. She could see Merle through the window in the back door. He had his head buried in the refrigerator.

"Morning," she said, entering. Startled, Merle jammed the refrigerator door into a pile of fishing rods, which cascaded to the floor.

"Morning, Abby," he said begrudgingly.

"Sorry. Let me get those. I wouldn't want you to strain yourself."

"Where would the fun in that be?"

"No more umbrella cane, I see."

"It was cramping my style."

"Perish the thought." Abigail collected the rods and replaced them in the corner.

"You just here to make my life flash before my eyes or do you have some other home improvements you're undertaking? Bear in mind, I don't carry wrecking balls."

"Here." Abigail handed him the piece of cardboard with her list on it.

Merle flipped it over, revealing a picture of turkey tetrazzini. "I can already tell you've left two integral items off o' this list. Paper and a cookbook."

"And you said you weren't funny."

"Candles, duct tape, water. Take it you heard about the hurricane. Amelia or Amanda or . . ."

"Don't say it. It's not?"

"Nope, it's not Abigail. Dodged a bullet there."

"Did I ever."

"I have a hunch Lottie didn't tell you diddly about what to do in case we get hit by this hurricane."

"Not a peep."

"Then I'll skip to the important parts. If there's enough warning,

I'll board up the windows at the lighthouse. That's what I did in '96. Wasn't a scratch on the place. You can ride the storm out as long as you got food and water. Keep your radio close. If the island has to be evacuated, you'll hear it on there first. Town has an air siren. They tend not to use it. Too apocalyptic. If we do have to evacuate, you get to the dock and take the ferry to the mainland. The police will direct you to a shelter."

"What about you? Won't you be going to the shelter?"

Merle tapped the cardboard list against his palm, disinclined to respond.

"What? You're too macho for a shelter? Or you're too macho to leave?"

"Not macho—stubborn. Some might say stupid. State's tried to evacuate Chapel Isle more than ten times in my life. Haven't left once. If I'm gonna kick the bucket, it's going to be right here."

Abigail admired his conviction. It made perfect sense.

"Can I ask you something?"

"Fire away."

"What happened to the original lighthouse keeper?"

Merle solemnly took a jug of kerosene off a shelf and brought it to the register. "I only know what I've heard since I was a kid."

"And I only know what I've read."

"Meaning?"

"I found a newspaper clipping about the *Bishop's Mistress* under the mattress in the caretaker's house. The article said there was a storm, that the ship sank because there was no light to guide it in."

"That might be the headline. It's not the whole story."

"There's an unabridged version?"

Merle rested against the counter, taking weight off his healing ankle. "Everyone said Mr. Jasper was diligent, faithful. The lighthouse was his life. This was back at the turn of the century, when Chapel Isle was a one-horse town, an outpost for sailors, fishermen, and their families. Supposedly, one day Mr. Jasper went to the lamp room to put the oil in for the night. On the way down, he slipped, hit his head, and fell; rolled clear to the bottom. Should have killed him. He must have lain there for hours, nobody to help him. By nightfall, the storm had swept in. When people realized there was no beacon for the sailors, somebody went to the lighthouse and found him. It was too late for the *Mistress*. But not for Mr. Jasper. He was alive. Barely."

"You're saying he was hurt and couldn't have operated the beacon. Then what happened to the *Bishop's Mistress* wasn't his fault."

"I don't think that's how Mr. Jasper saw it."

On occasions too numerous to recall, Abigail had wished she'd died along with her husband and son. She was ashamed for being able to breathe and speak and smile when they couldn't. She wore that shame like tight-fitting clothes she couldn't remove. The ever-present pinch of grief was taut across the shoulders; bereavement laced around the chest, sorrow cinched at the waist, while her anguish was snug at the neck, despair restricting each movement, regret cramping each memory. There was no unbuttoning her heartache. While the fire wasn't her fault, that didn't make her loss any easier to wear.

"What happened to Mr. Jasper afterward?"

"Story goes that he healed up, kept tending the lighthouse. Stayed there until he died almost twenty years later."

"There were a lot of ledgers, so it makes sense."

"Ledgers?"

"Mr. Jasper wrote a daily record of the goings-on at the lighthouse, like a diary. The ledgers were in the basement."

Merle did not look pleased.

"What? You figured because Lottie doesn't go down there, I wouldn't either? I was in the basement moving furniture for hours yesterday."

"Abby, who else knows you moved that furniture?"

"Nat. But he won't tell Lottie, if that's what you're thinking."

"Lottie's not who I'm concerned about."

Before she could ask what was upsetting Merle, Bert Van Dorst came pounding on the back door of the hardware store, panting as if he'd run a hundred-yard dash.

"Good Lord, Bert." Merle let him inside. "Come in before you faint."

"I ran here," he said, gulping air.

"You *ran?*" Merle asked skeptically.

"Do you want some water?" Abigail offered.

He shook his head no, still catching his breath.

"Bert, it is a concrete fact that a man of your age and proportions should not be running anywhere," Merle told him. "Have a seat. Tell us what the fuss is about."

"Can't. No time," he blurted between breaths. "Hank Scokes is dead. The sheriff's got Nat Rhone in the lockup for killing him."

◆ ◆ ◆

If there was a storm coming, Abigail couldn't have predicted it. The sky was cloudless, the sun radiant, as she, Merle, and Bert stood outside the sheriff's station, rapping repeatedly on the door.

"Come on, Caleb," Merle called. "We're not paparazzi."

The door opened a hair and Sheriff Larner let the three of them slip inside. The front office was outfitted with metal desks and linoleum tile. At the far end was an opening, beyond which Abigail spied a set of cells. The thirteen-inch television sitting on a filing cabinet showed a newsman pointing to a colossal swirl of clouds on a weather map. Meanwhile, a radio was relaying news of the storm simultaneously, the reporters' voices overlapping like those of an arguing couple.

"You're the first ones here, and you'll be the only ones if I can keep a lid on this until the hurricane's blown over," Sheriff Larner confided in a hushed tone. "How'd you find out?"

Merle and Abigail looked to Bert, who turned bashful. "I saw you taking Nat in, then I listened at that open window."

"Now you see why I'm being so careful." He shut the window.

"What happened?" Merle asked.

"Best I can tell, Rhone pushed Hank over the side of his rig."

"There's no way he would hurt Hank." Abigail was adamant.

Whatever her feelings about Nat, she knew he revered Hank as if he were his father. "There's got to be some misunderstanding."

"Scokes is gone. There's no misunderstanding that. That man hasn't left this island in years except to fish, so if he's not at home, not on his boat, and I can't raise him on his phone, something's wrong."

Abigail crossed her arms tightly over her chest. "What if he's passed out somewhere? Had too much to drink and is sleeping it off?"

"I checked," Larner assured her. "He's not at the Wailin' Whale either. Nobody's seen him. Duncan Thadlow stopped by, said he'd been looking for Hank to talk over the repairs on his boat. Couldn't find him and was worried. Which is why I went looking myself. When I did, all I found was Nat. Then he told me there'd been an accident. But if it was an accident, why didn't he report it sooner?"

"You arrested him for *not* reporting an accident?" Abigail said. "Is that legal?"

"No Hank. No body. And only Nat's word. Suspicion is all I need to hold him."

Merle released a long breath. "What did Nat say happened?"

"Rhone claims he went over with the net."

The men shuddered at the mere mention. Abigail didn't understand. "Went over with the net?"

"The fishing nets on trawlers are massive," Merle explained. "When you release them, there's a danger of getting caught and dragged down. With the current and the weight of the net, you'd drown without a doubt. Doesn't happen much, but it's happened."

Larner sniffed. "That's a neat alibi, because conveniently there's no evidence. I don't buy Rhone's story. Not for a second."

"You think Nat killed Hank on purpose? What reason could he have?" Abigail demanded. The men were silent. "What? What aren't you telling me?"

Bert spelled it out for her. "Hank's sons wouldn't want the boat, so it would be auctioned here on the island. It's customary for the crew to have first dibs. His rig was in iffy shape after he hit the dock. Even with repairs, the bids would start low."

Merle finished the thought. "Low enough that even somebody without much money, like Nat, would have a shot."

Abigail was stunned to see Merle entertaining the idea that Nat was responsible for Hank's death.

"Except Nat just paid Duncan Thadlow to have the boat fixed for Hank."

That added fuel to Larner's fire. "Did he, now?"

She cursed herself for mentioning it. "What if Nat's telling the truth? What if Hank did get caught in the net?"

Merle was somber. "Hank'd been sailing his whole life. He wouldn't have made that mistake."

"You said it could happen. What if Hank was drunk? Every time I've seen him, he's been three sheets to the wind. He could have fallen if he'd been under the influence."

"Abby," Merle cautioned.

"I'm sorry to speak ill of the dead, but I can't believe what I'm hearing."

"All we have is Nat's word," Bert stressed.

"Which doesn't count for much." Larner waved a sheet of paper. "I looked into Rhone's priors. He's got two aggravated assaults. He was also suspected in a couple of breaking and entering charges."

"Breaking and entering?" Abigail exclaimed. Merle and Bert were equally surprised. "You're assuming he killed the closest friend he had *and* he's been robbing houses on the island too?"

"Wouldn't be a stretch."

"No, I have proof it wasn't Nat who robbed those houses."

"Proof?" Larner said.

"I saw him, the person, the man," Abigail stammered. "I saw him walking in the dark on Timber Lane the night that house was robbed. Then I saw him again the night after that."

"Why didn't you report it?"

She glanced at Merle as she crafted an appropriate lie. "I'm new on the island. I wasn't sure you'd believe me."

"Can you describe the man you saw?" Larner pressed. "Did you see his face?"

"It was dark. I could tell he wasn't that tall. Not as tall as Nat. And he was heavyset. He moved slowly, how an older man would."

Bert cleared his throat over the din of the television and radio.

"You have something you want to add?" Larner snapped.

"Um, that was me that night."

Merle put his hand on Bert's arm. "You broke into those houses?"

"No, no, I meant it was me who Abby saw."

"You?" Abigail asked.

"I don't live too far from there. Timber Lane's a shortcut to the laundromat. I'd left a book there and wanted to get it. When I recognized your car, I was going to say hello, only you got so frightened when I said hi at Merle's store the day before that I didn't want to scare you again, so I stayed quiet. Then I saw you the next night and did the same."

"You were skulking around in the dark when you knew somebody was robbing people's houses?" Abigail didn't see the logic. "If I mistook you for the thief, someone else might have too. You could have gotten hurt. Or worse."

"Not much choice in the matter," Bert said. "I don't have a car."

"And whoever's robbing those houses has gotta have one," Larner interjected. "Too many heavy high-ticket items. No chance somebody could carry them around and not be seen. They'd need a car. Or, better yet, a truck. Like Nat's."

"This is stupid," Abigail insisted. "You can't make me believe he's a thief and a murderer."

"I don't have to make you do anything, Ms. Harker. In fact, it is by the grace of my kindly nature that I'm allowing you to remain in this office. I've got a killer in my cell and a hurricane on my doorstep, so I have neither the time nor the inclination to convince you of a goddamn thing."

Larner's outburst caught Abigail off guard, pitching her backward on her heels to avert the verbal strike.

"Nothing's personal here, Caleb," Merle said, stepping in.

"This island is too small for it not to be personal," Larner whispered to him tartly.

Bert motioned at the television. "Wait. Listen."

A female news anchor had interrupted the broadcast. "It's been announced that the space shuttle is being moved into its hangar at Cape Canaveral, and the Kennedy Space Center is being evacuated."

"They haven't done that since Hurricane Andrew," Larner said.

Merle's shoulders sank. "And that was a Category Five."

"Officials are reassessing this once-innocent storm system and deeming it 'unpredictable at best.'"

The female anchor's voice was dueling with that of the male reporter on the radio, who was saying, "This hurricane began as a tropical-wave disturbance that produced thunderstorms off the western coast of Africa. The combination of light upper-level winds with warm ocean water allowed the storm to develop. Tropical Storm Amelia officially became a hurricane about 2,500 miles outside of Miami when NOAA's Hurricane Hunter airplane was deployed and clocked over 75-mile-per-hour winds. Officials are scrambling to chart Amelia's course. However, they're quick to remind us that even the best satellites can't predict a hurricane's precise path. Please stay tuned to this station for the latest weather and evacuation updates."

Bert lowered the volume. "If it's a Category Three, they'll let us stay."

"If it's more . . ." Merle's voice trailed away.

"We'll have to evacuate?" Abigail didn't think it would come to that.

Sheriff Larner went for the phone. "I have to get on the horn with the mainland. Before I do, let's get one thing straight. Right now, it's only the four of us, plus my deputy, who know what's happened. It has to stay that way. If word gets around, the hurricane will be the least of my problems."

"Why?" Abigail had to ask.

Merle looked to her, then toward the rear of the station, where Nat Rhone was being held. "People find out what happened to Hank, that boy's going to be grateful he's got bars between him and them."

tour•bil•lion (tŏŏr bil´yən), *n.* **1.** a whirlwind or something resembling a whirlwind. **2.** a firework that rises
spirally. **3.** *Horol.* a frame for the escapement of a timepice,
esp. a watch, geared to the going train in such a way as to
rotate the escapement about once a minute in order to
minimize positional error. Cf. **karrusel.** [1470–80; earlier
turbilloun < MF *to(u)rbillon* < VL **turbiliōnem,* dissimi-
lated var. of **turbiniōnem,* acc. of *turbiniō whirlwind. See
TURBINE, -ION]

❖   ❖   ❖

Abigail half-expected an angry mob to be waiting outside the sheriff's
station. The only crowd was in front of Island Hardware.

"Where you been, Merle?" one man hollered. "We got us a
storm comin'."

"Hurry up," another shouted. "Haven't got all day to wait on
you."

Abigail was confident that if any of them had heard the news
about Hank Scokes, it would have been the first thing out of their
mouths, trumping the hurricane.

"Keep your caps on, boys."

Merle unlocked the store and the group piled in behind him.

"Why didn't they go around back?" Abigail asked Bert.

"Just because it's common knowledge the other door's unlocked doesn't mean Merle lets everybody go in that way."

Abigail felt a swell of honor. Among the islanders, the natives,
Merle had afforded her a special distinction, a mark of his trust,
even after knowing her for such a short time. If Merle was, indeed,
an excellent judge of character, then that raised another issue. He

was as dubious of Nat Rhone's story as was Sheriff Larner, which made Abigail second-guess herself. She had come to rely on Merle. Since he had qualms, maybe she should too. She'd spent two days with Nat, enough to form an opinion but little else. But instinct was the one sense the fire hadn't fully stripped from her. Regardless of the incriminations and recriminations, her instincts told her Nat Rhone was innocent.

"Can you guys pitch in?" Merle was limping around the store, assisting customers. "I got to go to the storage shed for more sheets of plywood. Bert, you see to those ladies there. Abby, you ever worked a register?"

"No."

"It's a piece of cake. If you can use a calculator, you can use a register. Heck, this clunker's more like an abacus." Merle gave her a speedy tutorial on how to operate the antiquated machine.

"What if I mess up?"

"Then it's coming out of your pay," he said with a wink.

People were waiting, so Abigail hurried to punch in the prices and tally the tax and totals. Five customers in, she had the swing of it. The flashlights were flying off the shelves, along with the batteries.

"You best get to the market soon yourself, dear," an older woman suggested. "Another hour and there'll be no more bottled water."

"If we're going to be evacuated, why would you need bottled water?"

"It's not written in stone they'll do that. Storm's coming whether we're here or not."

At that moment, it crystallized for Abigail that there truly was a hurricane heading for Chapel Isle. She'd experienced run-of-the-mill weather changes back in Boston, such as snowstorms and humid summers, but nothing with the intensity of a hurricane.

Storm's coming whether we're here or not. And whether we're ready or not.

Once the store eventually cleared out, Abigail and Bert found Merle hefting sheets of plywood onto the flatbed of a truck parked in front of the shop. Another car with boards strapped to the roof was pulling away. Merle laid the last piece of wood on the flatbed and hobbled onto the sidewalk as he bid the driver goodbye.

"The upside to a hurricane is extra revenue."

"Then you've got a lot of upside," Abigail informed him. "I was making change for people with nickels and dimes instead of dollars."

"You should have told me." Bert produced a slew of quarters from his pocket.

"See, Bert's ready for the hurricane," Merle joked. "He's got himself weighted."

The comment was meant in fun, yet Abigail had to wonder, could anyone ever really be ready for a hurricane?

"Hey, y'all. Hey, Abby," Denny called, coasting up to store in a green truck.

"Denny, my friend, you're just the man I was looking for," Merle told him.

"Really?"

"Abby here has to be prepped for the hurricane. There are sheets of plywood in the basement of the caretaker's house. I ripped 'em down to fit the windows years ago. What I need you to do is get them nailed in."

Denny jumped at the opportunity to impress her. "I'm on it."

"Bert, you go with them."

"Righto," Bert replied.

Denny and Bert, Abigail thought. *Talk about a dream team.*

"Thanks, guys," she said, trying to sound enthusiastic. It took effort.

News of the hurricane had shaken loose the townsfolk of Chapel Isle. The square was bustling the way Abigail imagined it did during the summer season. Drivers were cruising for parking spots, and pedestrians were rushing from place to place, weaving through the stopped cars, carrying grocery bags. Abigail didn't mind leaving the chaos behind for the calm of the lighthouse.

◆ ◆ ◆

Denny and Bert followed her home in Denny's truck. When they arrived, the two men were staring at the lawn as though it were a mirage.

"How'd you cut all this grass?" Denny asked her in awe.

"With a lawn mower."

"The whole place?" Bert said. "By yourself?"

The men were flabbergasted. It was as if Abigail had moved a mountain with a shovel.

"I knew Merle'd been meaning to get around to cutting it himself," Bert told her. "It was the getting-around-to-it part that gummed him up."

"Guys, I didn't cut the lawn with a pair of scissors. It's only grass."

"But it's a *ton* of grass," Denny exclaimed. "Where'd you get the new mower?"

"New? I used the hand mower from the shed."

Bert *tsk-tsk*ed. "The blades on that thing wouldn't cut butter."

The sprawling property was larger than she'd realized. Abigail hadn't been aware of how much grass she'd cut. Upon closer examination, it was a considerable amount. What bothered her was that, according to her science expert, the mower shouldn't have been able to cut the lawn at all. Then why had it worked?

"Makes the lighthouse look a lot nicer," Denny acknowledged.

"Could do with some new paint," Bert added.

"Fix the shutters."

"Front steps are a wreck. Maybe get 'em relaid."

"Put in a new handrail."

"Guys," Abigail butted in. "There's *a lot* wrong with this lighthouse. What we need to focus on is what we can make right before the hurricane hits."

She led them inside, and both men stopped dead at the threshold.

"This is amazing," Denny gushed. "It's like a magazine."

"When'd you do this?" Bert asked. "Does Lottie know?"

"I don't want to let Lottie in on the refurbishments quite yet. Catch my drift, fellas?"

"I won't say a word."

"Bert?"

"Me too. I won't tell."

"Good. Then let's find the plywood Merle was talking about."

They toted the boards up from the basement. Abigail was grateful they were light. Her knees cracked as she climbed the stairs.

You're getting as creaky as this house.

One flight of steps and she had to take a break. Bert needed one as well. He took a box from his pocket and showed it to Abigail. "Merle gave me some nails."

"Bert, what *don't* you have in those pockets of yours?"

"Let's see, I—"

Foreseeing the list might be lengthy, she said, "Why don't you tell me while we install the plywood."

The sheets had been cut to slot into the window frames because nails couldn't be driven into the brick exterior. Bert handed the nails to Abigail, who passed them to Denny, who knocked them into the casings using Abigail's hammer. Without a ladder, they could reach only the lower windows.

Bert pulled at his lip. "The second floor has to be covered too. If any of the glass breaks, the wind will change the pressure inside the house and blow out the rest of the windows, boarded or not."

"We definitely wouldn't want that." There was that *we* again. Abigail quickly corrected herself. "I mean, Lottie and me. Lottie wouldn't want that either."

"I'll go get a ladder from my place. Be right back." Denny drove off before Abigail could argue, leaving her alone with Bert.

"Want to hear what's in my pockets now?"

On the scale of things she didn't want to do, that fell someplace in the middle. "Why not?"

Fatigued, Abigail rested on the front steps. The news of Hank's death, Nat's arrest, and the pending hurricane were taking a toll. Bert joined her on the stoop and systematically emptied his pockets.

"There's quarters, of course. And my wallet. And my keys. And some mints. And there's my pocket watch." He displayed a gold watch with ornate engraving and a roped fob.

"Bert, this is beautiful. Where did you get it?"

"My father. It was my grandfather's. See? That's his name there on the inside. Elias Van Dorst. It was his, then it was my father's, and now it's mine," he said, as if the order was paramount.

Bert's story tugged at her. The pocket watch had been handed down from generation to generation, a gift of history, of family. Abigail hadn't had anything similar to pass on to Justin, even if he were alive. After she and Paul had taken him for his first haircut, Abigail considered saving a lock of Justin's hair. He had curls like his father's, only lighter, closer to her color. He'd cried as he sat in the barber's booster seat with the hairstylist gently nipping the scissors around his head. Justin held his arms out to her, begging to be rescued; she and Paul had tried to soothe him, Abigail insisting he was safe and Paul assuring him the hair would grow back. She'd thought her son was frightened of the scissors and the experience. But what if Paul was right? What if Justin was frightened that cutting his hair meant it was gone forever? Even a toddler could fear loss. That was how hardwired the feeling was. Maybe, Abigail thought, it was because the heart knew what the mind couldn't: that loss was the inverse of love and that it was especially hard to get over.

Sadly, Abigail had no mementos of her family, save the scant trinkets left at her parents' house—a broken piece of a plastic toy and Paul's ratchet set he'd let her father borrow. Nothing precious. Nothing sentimental. She regretted not being more sentimental, not stashing more keepsakes. There were so many criticisms Abigail could have heaped upon herself. She should have been a better wife, a better mother, a better person. At the bottom of that mound of *should haves* was the reality that no matter what she should have done, she did the best she could.

"Bert, can I ask you a question?"

" 'Course."

"You're a man of science, a man of logic—why do you believe in . . . ?" She motioned toward the lamp room.

He thought for a second. "Even though the atom was first proposed by a Greek philosopher in 500 B.C., it wasn't until 1857 that a scientist identified what he called a 'negative corpuscle,' an electron, the first atomic particle. That's a fancy way of getting to the point, which is that there are a lot of things we can't see, but they're there. So many things we can't taste or touch or hear, but they're there. Since I was a kid, folks have claimed they've seen the ghost of Mr. Jasper. I don't know anybody personally who has. Can't say for certain anybody does. That's how a story becomes a story. People talking about something until what may be fiction becomes fact. Even if nobody ever does see Mr. Jasper, that doesn't mean he isn't here."

"I did something," Abigail admitted. "I moved the oil pail in the lamp room. It was a test to determine if it would move back by itself. Not very scientific, huh?"

"Did it move?"

"I've been too nervous to look."

"Would you feel better if the pail was in the same place?"

"I'm not sure. I wanted some sort of corroboration, I suppose."

"Will you feel better if you find out one way or the other?"

"I'm not sure about that either."

"Want me to check for you?"

"Would you?"

Bert nodded, happy to oblige.

"You won't be scared?"

"What scares me is that." He pointed to the ocean and the horizon beyond.

"The hurricane?"

"I don't understand much in this world. I do understand physics. A hurricane is a force of nature. Nothing else that can compare."

"You're afraid of this hurricane."

"You can be afraid of the known or the unknown," Bert replied. "Me, I pick the known. Then again, if I'm choosing, I'd pick not to be afraid at all."

"Me too, Bert. Me too."

u•su•fruct (yōō′zōō frukt′, -sōō-, yōōz′yōō-, yōōs′-),
n. Roman and Civil Law. the right of enjoying all the advan-
tages derivable from the use of something that belongs to
another, as far as is compatible with the substance of the
thing not being destroyed or injured. [1620–30; < LL
ūsūfrūctus, equiv. to L *ūsū,* abl. of *ūsus* (see USE (n.)) +
frūctus (see FRUIT)]

◆ ◆ ◆

The caretaker's house looked like a condemned building. With the
plywood covering the windows and the chipping paint, a casual ob-
server would have guessed it was uninhabited. Abigail had to remind herself she lived there.

"That's that," Denny declared, hammering in the final nail.
"You're as ready as you can be."

"Only I won't be able to see the storm coming."

"You won't have to see it," Bert told her. "You'll be able to
hear it."

"That's the worst," Denny agreed. "Sounds like the whole
world's crashing down on you."

"Not helping, guys."

"Sorry."

"We should get going," Bert hinted to Denny, who was reluc-
tant to leave.

"You got everything you need?" Denny asked. "Nothing else we
can do? Nothing?"

"I think I'm set."

Then Abigail realized she didn't actually have *any* of the things she needed. She'd left Merle's store without getting supplies for herself. She'd also forgotten to go to the market for food and water.

"Um, maybe not."

"I'm heading through town."

Denny opened the passenger door to the truck as if he were her personal valet. He wasn't taking no for an answer. So the three of them squeezed into the front seat, with Abigail wedged in the middle.

"Where do you want me to drop you, Abby?"

"At Merle's, please."

Bert clucked his tongue, the way he did at the laundromat. "Might want to hit Weller's first. They'll be running out of essentials shortly. If they haven't already."

"I'll be at the Kettle when you're through," Denny told her as they clambered from of the truck. "You can come get me and I'll take you home. Door-to-door service," he said with a grin.

"Are you going with him, Bert?"

"Not much else to do. Laundry's closed on account of the hurricane. Why?"

"No, no, I was just asking."

Bert appeared to appreciate her interest. "Okay, then. See you later." He gave her a nod and toddled off.

A dangerous hurricane was barreling toward Chapel Isle, yet to Denny and Bert, it was another ordinary day. Either they were resigned to the storm or they were putting on a convincing show. Feigning bravery was fine for stoic island men. Abigail had lived through the extraordinary and couldn't pretend to be anything except anxious.

◆ ◆ ◆

Most of the shelves at the market had been stripped bare. It wouldn't be a choice of what Abigail wanted but rather what was left. She loaded her cart with the remaining bottled water, fruit, milk and cereal. The last loaf of bread was pumpernickel, which she didn't care for much. She took it anyway.

Across the aisle, a mother with two little girls was tossing packs of juice boxes into her cart. One of her daughters pleaded for candy.

"We have candy at home." The mother was firm. "We're not here for candy. Not today."

Not today. That says it all.

Abigail was grabbing rolls of toilet paper when she heard a familiar voice in the next aisle.

"Lordy me, this hurricane. What a pain in my posterior. So much to do. Franklin hates to evacuate. Such a hardship for him. And me, I haven't left this island since . . . well, since Jesus was a boy."

Franklin, Abigail thought. Wasn't that Lottie's husband's name?

She pushed her cart around the corner and discovered her landlord gabbing with another woman.

"Haven't been off the island since Jesus was a boy?" Abigail demanded. "What about your cousin's 'girdle incident'? Were you lying this whole time, Lottie?"

The other woman made a hasty exit, leaving Lottie to fend for herself against an irate Abigail.

"Abby, dear. What a surprise to bump into you. My, you're looking well. Slender as a rail. How do you keep your figure? You have to tell me your secret."

Abigail wanted to smack herself for not putting two and two together sooner. Lottie couldn't have left her wheelchair-bound husband alone for that long. The trip-to-the-mainland story was a ruse, an avoidance tactic. Sheriff Larner's comment, that Lottie was "making herself scarce," sprang to mind. Abigail felt like a fool. Everybody around town was wise to what Lottie was doing except her.

"Lottie, stop. Be honest for a change. Why would you lie about something so . . . ridiculous?"

The short woman appeared to grow shorter as she rallied an answer.

"I'm sorry, Abby. Sincerely, I am. From the minute you called me when you were in Boston, I knew you were desperate for the lighthouse to be what you pictured, what you dreamed. And I knew it wouldn't be. I just didn't want you to be sad."

The truth siphoned all of the bubbliness from Lottie. She wrung her hands, waiting for Abigail to pass judgment.

Though Lottie had tricked her and lied to her and dodged her, Abigail was grateful for the intention. Abigail didn't want to be sad either.

"It's all right, Lottie."

Her face instantly brightened. She belted out one of her signature laughs, relieved. "Gracious, I thought you were about to smack me. I heard what happened at the Kettle. Really, Abby, I wouldn't want to get on the wrong side o' you. Ever again, I mean," she said, amending the statement.

Abigail affected a tough stance. "Is that a promise?"

"Oh, yes. Yes. Cross my heart. Not my fingers."

As Lottie scurried off, Abigail had to admit the debacle at the Kozy Kettle was starting to work in her favor. There was a hidden benefit to being "the Boston Bruiser." She could intimidate her landlord.

"Maybe you are a badass," Abigail told herself. But it was a stretch to feel strong with a hurricane looming.

The lines at the registers were lengthy and comprised mainly of women. Janine was at one register. The woman Abigail had seen with Janine's husband was working the other. Abigail opted for the mistress rather than the wife. The ladies in line were reminiscing about hurricanes past.

"I lost my front windows in '96," one recounted. "Boy, was my husband pissed about having to replace 'em."

"I lost *every* window that year. Least I got brand new shutters out of that hurricane," remarked another.

"I had to put on a new roof after the storm in '92," one woman complained, caressing her daughter's hair. "Hope I won't have to do that again."

The consensus appeared to be that, though inconvenient, the hurricane would come and go. All that could be done was to hope for the best. Abigail hadn't had much hope lately. When she did, it was usually to exclusion: She hoped she wouldn't have nightmares, that she wouldn't start crying, that her memories wouldn't unravel her. Abigail wished she could absorb some of their hope for her own.

When she arrived at the register, the woman pretended not to recognize her. Abigail did the same. While she waited, a gray-haired lady with a walker in Janine's line accidentally dropped a bag of oranges, scattering them across the floor. Abigail went to gather the fallen fruit and came face-to-face with Janine as they both bent down.

"Thanks," Janine said to Abigail.

Though there was no irritation or irony in her voice, that was the most she was willing to give. Having a hurricane on the way left no time for animosity, justified or not. They were both in danger, which made them equals.

◆ ◆ ◆

A note was waiting for Abigail on the back door to Merle's store. It read: *Abby, Had to bring tools to a friend so he could board up his windows. Your stuff is next to the register.*

"Merle the mind reader."

She cut through the kitchen into the shop and ran smack into a heavyset man wearing suspenders.

"Hey there, Abby. Getting ready for Ms. Amelia's arrival?"

"Um, yes," she admitted warily. Then she remembered who he was—the bartender at the Wailin' Whale as well as the caller at the bingo game.

"Some people might start to wonder."

"About?"

"You get here, then lo and behold, along comes a big ol' hurricane. Some might say you're bringing Chapel Isle the wrong kind of luck."

The man was kidding. Nonetheless, Abigail felt a stitch of

personal responsibility. Had she dragged her misfortune with her from Boston, unable to leave it behind or outrun it?

"Aw, I'm joking. Some luck's better than no luck, right?"

"We'll have to wait until after the hurricane to decide."

"That we will," he replied, and went on his way.

The bartender wasn't alone in the store. Two other men were milling around, picking items from the shelves. Before leaving, they wrote what they took on a clipboard Merle had beside the register. Abigail was astonished at the amount of trust he put in people. He chose to believe they wouldn't steal from him, that they would be honest. As far as Abigail could tell, that was exactly what they did. Like hope, trust required a certain amount of willful ignorance. That was why she found it so difficult.

Her shopping complete, Abigail headed over to the Kozy Kettle to find Denny. The café was empty except for a handful of men, including Bert and Denny, who were sitting at the counter along with Sheriff Larner. A radio played, updating the latest on the hurricane.

"Hey, Abby." Denny waved her over, excited. "Get this. Last report said Hurricane Amelia's turning into a Category Five. That's, like, totally huge. We're going to have to evacuate."

"Got the final word from the state police," Larner added. "Denny, that means you and your dad are going to have to run straight shifts." He turned to Abby. "I suggest you catch an early one. The shelters fill up fast. Want to make sure you get a bed."

The enormity of what was happening had Abigail's head throbbing.

"You seem disappointed," Bert said.

"I just got here and now I have to leave."

"Chapel Isle isn't going anywhere, Abby."

She knew that was true. It helped to hear it, though.

"Yeah, the shelters aren't the greatest," Denny remarked. "At least you can come home to a nice house full of pretty furniture."

Bert elbowed Denny in the side.

"Oops."

As fast as rumors flew around town, Lottie would learn about the furniture by morning, which made Abigail rue having to decamp even more.

"My bad," Denny whispered to her, as Ruth came out of the kitchen holding a paper bag.

"Here you are, Caleb. One cheeseburger and one hamburger with pickles on the side. Hey, Abby. What's wrong? You look like you've seen a——" Ruth stopped herself.

Everyone was quiet save for the newscaster on the radio, who was citing 180-mile-per-hour winds and twenty-foot swells off the Florida coast.

Sheriff Larner handed Ruth a ten, took his food, and left, saying, "Keep the change."

Ruth watched him go. "Is it me or is Caleb grouchier than normal?"

"He must have a lot to do to prepare for the hurricane," Abigail said, while Bert stared at the floor.

"Must be."

"Guess I'll be seeing the three of you on the ferry tomorrow morning?" Abigail asked.

"You'll see me for sure," Denny chirped.

Neither Bert nor Ruth replied.

"Didn't the radio report say the evacuation was mandatory?"

"Mandatory schmandatory."

"Ditto," Bert added.

Abigail had been on Chapel Isle for only a short time, yet she hated the idea of leaving.

"If you guys aren't evacuating, why should I?"

"You've never been through this before," Ruth told her. "It's damn terrifying."

"If it's so terrifying, why do you stay?"

The answer was the same as Merle's. Ruth and Bert had lived most of their lives on Chapel Isle. If they were going to die, it was going to be here, in their home.

"Denny, you make certain Abby gets on the ferry with you tomorrow, hear me?" Ruth was insistent.

"Yes, ma'am."

"You ought to get a suitcase together, hon."

The thought of packing her bags again made Abigail's heart cramp.

"Can we go, Denny?"

"Sure thing."

"Don't forget there's the bingo tonight," Ruth mentioned. "The last hurrah, if you're interested. Get your mind off the hurricane."

Denny downed the rest of his soda. "Bert, you coming?"

"Nope, I can walk. Bye, Abby," he said with a wave.

ve•rid•i•cal (və rid′i kəl), *adj.* **1.** truthful; veracious. **2.** corresponding to facts; not illusory; real; actual; genuine. Also, **ve•rid′ic.** [1645–55; < L *vēridicus (vēr(us)* true + *-i-* -I- + *-dicus* speaking) + -AL¹] —ve•rid′i•cal′i•ty, *n.* —ve•rid′i•cal•ly, *adv.*

V

◆ ◆ ◆

Evening seemed to be welling up from between the juniper and wax myrtle rather than filtering down from the sky. The temperature had plummeted. Denny raised the truck's windows and cranked the heat.

"It'll take a minute to get warm."

"It's fine. I'm fine."

"If you don't mind me saying, you aren't acting fine."

Resentment was a stopper in her throat. The fire had stolen everything from her. Now the hurricane was dictating her life. Abigail's own desires felt insignificant.

"I'm a real good listener if you want to talk."

"There's nothing to talk about, Denny."

"I know you're new in town and we're kinda strangers—"

"No, I'm the stranger." Her voice began to climb. "This was an idiotic, impetuous idea. I shouldn't have come here."

Denny was quiet. "Maybe you're right. Maybe you shouldn't have."

"What?"

"If you don't like it, you shouldn't stay."

"I didn't say I didn't like it."

"Then why'd you say it was idiotic?"

Frustrated, Abigail pinched the bridge of her nose. "It's not that simple."

"Yes, it is. You want to be here or you don't."

"Denny, there are some things you can't understand."

Even in profile, eyes on the road, he looked wounded. "I might not be book smart the way some people are, but I'm smart enough to know that there are only two kinds of things in this world. Those you have a say in and those you don't. Being smart means you can tell the difference."

He pulled into the gravel drive and waited for Abigail to get out of the truck.

"Denny—"

"I gotta get home. Pop's waiting on me."

After Abigail gathered her bags from the flatbed, Denny drove off.

She watched his truck disappear around the bend. "Smooth move, *Abby*."

◆ ◆ ◆

In the dark, she could hear the ocean, though she couldn't see it because of the plywood on the windows. The waves were bashing against the rocks, drawing attention to how close the lighthouse was to the water. Like a maidenhead on the prow of a ship, the lighthouse would have to bear the brunt of whatever came its way.

"This lighthouse has been here for ages. This isn't the first hurricane it's withstood."

It was, however, Abigail's first hurricane. She had to try to be as steadfast as the lighthouse.

With the windows boarded shut, the house was especially dark. She turned on all the lights and tuned her radio in to the latest weather update. Amelia was churning along the coast, wreaking havoc on Miami. The reporter described horizontal rain and palm trees fanning to and fro. Meanwhile, Abigail unpacked a mini-arsenal of flashlights, spare batteries, and bottled water onto the dining-room table.

"Ready or not."

She switched off the radio. She'd heard enough. Abigail would pack her suitcase and depart on the morning ferry. The hurricane was one of those things she didn't have a say in. That made her feel trapped.

Not as trapped as Nat Rhone must feel.

She tried to put him out of her mind. She wouldn't have a say in what happened to Nat either.

Once she'd filled her duffel bag with a few days' worth of clothes, Abigail found herself meandering aimlessly through the house. She paced the bedroom and wandered to the study, memorizing the rooms in case she didn't see them again.

The romance novel she'd been reading was splayed open on the bookcase. Her pulse quickened. She hadn't put it there.

Then Abigail recalled that Nat had set the book on the shelf as they were moving the furniture. She thought of him in his cell and the parable of his life. His parents had died, leaving him alone and adrift, and what befell him seemed to be a tragedy of his own creation. Abigail had been left too. What were Nat Rhone's chances after such a start in life? What were hers?

She would be gone the next day and the lighthouse would weather the storm without her, yet she would always be weathering her own storm, the gales that her grief would bring, the tidal rushes of tears, the surge of memories, and the rain of everyday reality without her husband and son. It was a storm she would have to wait out no matter where she was. Where she wanted to be was Chapel Isle.

Abigail picked up the romance novel, sat at the desk, and let the book carry her away.

◆　◆　◆

Fiction, as a form, was not that different from the dictionary. Every feeling and fact, even the etymology of emotion, could be found between the letters of *A* and *Z*. Alphabetization acted as the plot, and each word was a character with its own personality. Despite the absence of rising action, a climax, or a denouement, the dictionary told an honest tale.

The same might not have been said about the romance novel Abigail was reading. She took pleasure in polishing it off nonetheless. The hero won his battle, the villain got his comeuppance, the star-crossed lovers had their stars uncrossed, and those who were intended to live happily ever after did. Though *happily ever after* wasn't in the dictionary, Abigail chose to believe the concept wasn't reserved solely for fiction.

"Congratulations, Heiress," she said, pushing back from the new desk. "Same to you, Captain. Have fun sailing the high seas together."

The house had grown so cold that Abigail could see her breath. She was starving but in no mood to start a fire. The bingo hall at the fire station would be warm, and Denny would be there. She needed to apologize to him.

"And they have hot dogs. Junk food is better than no food."

With the keys in the front door, the phone flashed in her peripheral vision. Abigail had been meaning to call her parents. They were probably beside themselves with worry. She felt terrible for putting them through that. It was selfish. But she hated being grilled about how she was faring. She wanted to be normal again, and if that wasn't going to happen, then she wanted to be left alone.

Her parents were relieved when she phoned them. They'd heard about the hurricane on the news and were concerned for her safety. Abigail spent the next half hour guaranteeing them that she wasn't in danger and that she was being evacuated to a shelter to wait out the storm. What she omitted from the conversation was the state of the lighthouse and its former—or not so former—occupant. Instead, she waxed on about the pristine beaches and the charm of the town.

She could tell that her parents would have preferred to have her home. Her mother questioned if she was eating well. Abigail lied and said she was. Her father made her promise to call more often. Abigail agreed, and that wasn't a lie. After hanging up, she had to admit the anticipation of the phone call was far worse than the call itself. She crossed her fingers that the same would be true of the hurricane.

◆ ◆ ◆

The fire station's hall was full, the vibe festive, as if the next day were the Fourth of July, not a mandatory evacuation. Abigail saw Ruth sitting close to the bingo board. She had an entire folding table papered with cards.

"Couldn't resist coming to bingo," Abigail told her.

Ruth removed her purse from the chair beside her. "Who can? Had a hunch you'd show. I set aside some cards for you."

The man with the suspenders Abigail had bumped into at Merle's store that afternoon took his position at the microphone and ceremoniously welcomed everyone to the game.

"This here Hurricane Amelia might be bigger than us and faster than us, but she can't out-bingo us," he declared, rousing a cheer from the crowd.

"Keep those cards warm for me for a minute," Abigail said to Ruth. "There's something I have to do."

Denny was standing with his father, waiting in line to order food.

"This is on me," she told the girl behind the counter.

"That's okay," Denny said, still hurt. "I can get my own."

"Denny, please. I apologize for what I said."

"What's going on, Denny?" his father asked gruffly.

"It's no big deal, Pop."

"If it's no big deal, then pay the gal what you owe her and let's get to our table. Game's fixin' to start."

"Denny, I really am sorry. The least I can do is treat you to a hot dog. You too, Mr. Meloch."

Denny's father was so taken aback that he blushed.

"How about some sodas?"

"Whadaya say, Pop?"

"Hold on. What's this about?" his father demanded.

"It's about your son giving me the smartest piece of advice I've ever heard."

It was Denny's turn to blush. "You mean that, Abby?"

"Yes, I do. I'd pay close attention to that son of yours, Mr. Meloch. He could teach you a lot." The perennially stern man was reduced to a perplexed silence that made Denny grin.

"Mustard and relish?" Abigail asked.

"Why not?" Mr. Meloch shrugged.

She left Denny and his father to eat their dinner while she took a hot dog of her own to Ruth's table. Famished, she finished half of it before reaching her seat.

"Watch you don't take off some of your fingers," Ruth cautioned. "You'll need 'em to mark these bingo cards."

Between bites, Abigail said, "I haven't eaten all day."

"Me, I've been carbo-loading like this bingo game is a marathon. I'm primed for a win. I can tell the cards are hot. Tonight's my night."

Five minutes later a teenage boy shouted, "Bingo."

"That's it. I'm not talking about the cards anymore. I'm jinxing myself. No more bingo talk."

The caller started the next game and Ruth went mum.

"How about another topic?" Abigail suggested.

"Be my guest."

Though Sheriff Larner had sworn her to secrecy, she recounted the story of Hank Scokes's death in Ruth's ear, stunning her to the point that she stopped playing altogether.

"You can't tell anyone, Ruth. Not a soul."

"Hand to God, I won't."

"I only told you because I feel certain Nat had nothing to do with it. I don't know how to make Larner see that he's wrong about him."

"I don't think Nat did it either, but it's not my place to say why."

"I don't understand."

She signaled for Abigail to lower her voice. "Hank came to me in confidence. Told me private information. Very private."

"Ruth, you're not a priest or an attorney."

"I'm not a doctor either. Doesn't stop people from asking my advice. If I'm asked, I give it."

"Ruth, please," Abigail implored.

"All right, but don't tell nobody else. Bad enough I'm telling you. Hank stopped by my house one night not long after his wife passed. He hadn't been drinking. He was stone sober. I sat with him on my porch and he told me he was thinking of, well, doing himself harm. He was saying he wanted to be in heaven with his wife. That he didn't have the patience for waiting."

"Do you believe he'd kill himself?"

"He begged me not to breathe a word. Said he was ashamed for even mentioning it. He didn't want anybody else to know. I told him I'd thought about it too when Jerome died. That seemed to make him feel better."

It would have been untrue if Abigail said suicide wasn't a tempting option for her as well. At least the pain would end, she'd reasoned in those first dark days, and then she would be with her husband and son. Logic wouldn't let her go through with it. Paul had wanted her to live. That was why he'd saved her.

"Ruth, you didn't answer my question."

"Because the answer doesn't sit right with me."

"If Hank did this to himself, Nat would try to protect his honor. He'd take the rap for it."

"That's what's making me worry. Have to trust Caleb will see this for what it is."

"He doesn't and he won't. And now he's trying to pin the robberies on Nat as well."

At that, Ruth's resolve hardened. "I'll go and see Caleb tomorrow."

"Thank you, Ruth. Thank you." Abigail meant it more than she could say.

The caller was announcing the next number. "B-9. The number is B-9."

Ruth's eyes fell to her cards and she froze.

"Bingo," she whispered. Soon she was repeating it louder and louder, "Bingo. Bingo. Bingo." She sprang from her chair, waving the paper card.

"We have a winner," the caller hollered.

"What'd I win? What'd I win?" Ruth was hopping up and down like a kid.

"That game was worth fifty-eight dollars. You can collect it after the final round."

Beaming, Ruth had to sit down and fan herself with her winning card. "I haven't won in so long, I can't tell you, Abby. I feel like I'm having a hot flash. Only way, way better."

People came and patted Ruth on the shoulder. She basked in the attention, savoring the moment. Watching her, Abigail caught a glimpse of her future. Ruth had faced widowhood, yet she'd found something that she looked forward to and enjoyed. It wasn't exactly *happily ever after*. The *happily* part might be plenty.

wel‧ter[1] (wel´tər), *v.i.* **1.** to roll, toss, or heave, as waves or the sea. **2.** to roll, writhe, or tumble about; wallow, as animals (often fol. by *about*): *pigs weltering about happily in the mud.* **3.** to lie bathed in or or be drenched in something, esp. blood. **4.** to become deeply or extensively involved, associated, entangled, etc.: *to welter in setbacks, confusion, and despair.* —*n.* **5.** a confused mass; a jumble or muddle: *a welter of anxious faces.* **6.** a state of commotion, turmoil, or upheaval: *the welter that followed the surprise attack.* **7.** a rolling, tossing, or tumbling about, as or as if by the sea, waves, or wind: *They found the shore through the mighty welter.* [1250–1300; ME, freq. (see −ER[6]) of *welten* to roll, OE *weltan*; c. MD *welteren,* LG *weltern* to roll]

◆　◆　◆

Abigail awoke in her bed, uncertain if it was morning or night. The boards on the windows blocked the sunlight, transforming the bedroom into a cave. She pawed the nightstand for her glasses and watch, which sat atop the ledger. It was almost six. She wondered how early the ferry would start running.

"Maybe not this early."

The floor was freezing. Abigail didn't bother with socks. This was her last day in the caretaker's cottage. She wanted to soak it all in, even if that meant cold feet.

She poured a glass of milk and sipped it sitting in the wingback chair. The absence of natural light gave the room the feel of a museum exhibit, a model recreated to show modern people how their forefathers lived. The house was like a time capsule. It had no heat-ing or air-conditioning, no television or microwave, no washer or dryer. The modicum of current-day conveniences it did have, like the plumbing and the oven, functioned poorly. On top of that, everything creaked. And there might or might not be a ghost.

In spite of it all, Abigail felt at home.

Ironically, the part of the house she favored most was the place she'd taken the least advantage of. She hadn't gone into the lighthouse since devising her scheme with the oil pail, and she'd missed her opportunity to take Bert up on his offer to check it for her.

"You could do it now."

She awaited a noise, some discouraging response from the lamp room. The house was silent.

Perhaps Wesley Jasper doesn't mind what you've done with the place.

The answer was based on a bigger question, one that would entail a trip to the lighthouse. With the hurricane quite literally on the horizon, Abigail's courage was in dwindling supply.

"You could check on the pail after the hurricane has passed. That's not an unreasonable arrangement."

For days, she had been avoiding going to the lamp room and facing her fears; however, there would be no evading the storm.

Dark clouds menaced overhead as Abigail loaded the station wagon. The packing finished, it was time to go. She was having trouble leaving. She stood at the front door, staring in.

"I'll be back soon," she said, a pledge to the house and herself.

The grass out front had already grown perceptibly. In another week it would need cutting again. Abigail wanted to be here to cut the grass. She wanted it more than she'd wanted anything in months.

◆　◆　◆

Cars crammed the island's narrow sandy roads. Families were packed into trucks and minivans, luggage strapped to the roofs. Everyone was en route to the ferry, the mass exodus building into a traffic jam.

"This is what it must be like on Labor Day weekend."

Only this was different. This was an evacuation.

Soon Abigail's car was at a standstill. She couldn't see far enough ahead to discern why. She decided to cut around the line by taking a side street and quickly got lost.

"I have absolutely no clue where I am."

She traversed several roads until she saw a landmark she did recognize; Merle's house. His windows had boards on them, and the floral wreath had been removed from the front door.

"You're supposed to be on the ferry." Merle was standing on his dock as she rounded into his backyard.

"I got stuck in traffic. Then I got lost."

"Those are two phrases not normally uttered on Chapel Isle," he said, putting a cooler in his boat.

"Do you think it's wise to go fishing in this weather?"

"What weather?"

"Look at the sky. It's about to rain."

"It's not raining *yet*. And I won't be fishing. I'm checking my nets. Wanna come?"

"Me?"

"Why not? You missed the first ferry as it is. The line for the next is going to be as long as the Great Wall of China. Maybe longer."

"When you put it that way, how could I resist?"

Merle climbed into the outboard with care. Given his size, the boat might have flipped if he got in too fast. With his injured ankle, he was taking it extra slow. As he helped Abigail in, she was already reconsidering.

"If this old tub will hold me, it'll hold you, Abby. You can swim, though, right?"

"Very encouraging."

The rain held off, thunderheads loitering in the sky. Merle headed into the bay with the boat riding low. The wake disappeared as fast as it rose.

"You ever been fishing before?"

"Once. My husband's firm took its employees on a cruise to go snorkeling and deep-sea fishing. There was dinner and dancing afterward."

"That's not fishing. That's yachting."

The details of the company trip had remained sequestered in the recesses of Abigail's mind until that very moment. She recalled being introduced to Paul's coworkers and their spouses. There were hors d'oeuvres and chilled wine and soft music. She remembered being served grilled halibut and having sorbet for dessert. Paul was new to the firm at the time and was occupied making conversation as well as a good impression. He stole a second to come over and tell her how pretty she looked in her white cotton sundress, then kissed her on the cheek. For an instant, Abigail thought she could feel the kiss. It was only the wind on her face.

"Here we are."

Merle slowed the motor when they entered a cove where groups of tall wooden poles jutted from the water.

"What are those?"

"Impoundments."

Maneuvering between the poles, he released the line on one of them and hooked it to a peg on the side of the boat. Merle repeated the process until a net full of squirming fish floated to the surface.

"Let's see what we got."

After raking clumps of sea grass from the net with his fingers, he tossed aside the unwanted horseshoe crabs along with the punier fish. "Fortunately, I don't have to measure like the commercial fishermen do. Any catch over thirteen inches is legal in the bay. Fourteen inches is legal in the ocean."

He selected a meaty flounder, then dropped the net so the rest could escape.

"That's a tremendous effort for one fish."

"I'm an old man. Haven't got much else to do. Say, I'm sorry about earlier."

"Earlier?"

"When I mentioned fishing it seemed to, well, remind you of

the past. I overheard Ruth telling you about my ex-wife and my boy. Wanted you to know it happens to me too. You're going about your day and somebody says something that makes you think of them. Blindsides you."

"Merle, I wasn't prying. I—"

He waved away her concern. "Didn't think you were. I just brought it up because I can commiserate."

Merle placed the flapping fish in a cooler and shut the lid on it as it thrashed. Initially, that struck Abigail as callous. But what other choice did he have? Bludgeon it to death? Slit its torso with a knife? Suffocation was kind by comparison.

"What should I do?" Abigail asked in earnest.

" 'Bout what?"

"About me, my life, what's left?"

He thought hard before answering, as the fish continued to bump around inside the cooler. "I remember the first time I heard that phrase about the only sure things in life being death and taxes. I always took it to mean that what was for sure was that *I* was going to die and that *I* was going to have to pay taxes. Took a while to get it through this thick skull o' mine that what it really means is that none of us goes without losing somebody we love. You can't tell when you're going to go or when somebody you care about will. What you can do is hope it's later rather than sooner."

Despite Merle's fondness for skewed logic, he had distilled the enormity of grief into a simple, objective truth. The objectivity was what Abigail grappled with.

Dictionaries were intended to be impartial and exact, yet the act of defining a word reflected the passions and prejudices of the definer. Dictionaries required the faith of the user, faith dependent on the belief that the dictionary was beyond subjectivity, but the best dictionaries had come from those with the strongest personalities, the zealots and idealists who sought to teach and to preach, to politicize and to moralize. Abigail could try to be objective about her grief and acknowledge it for what it was, or she could define it by her own biases and feel it as it came. Either way, the definition didn't make the hurt subside any faster.

"How do you do it, Merle? All I can think about is before and all I've got is after. What do I do *after* after?"

"Want me to tell you the secret?" he asked as he rehitched the lines to the poles.

"There's a secret? What secret?"

"You positive you want to hear?"

"Yes, of course. What is it?"

"It's shoes."

"Come again?"

"Shoes."

"Your secret to getting over your ex-wife is shoes?"

"Scout's honor."

He sat down to explain, and the small boat rocked at the change in weight. "Every morning I would wake up and I'd hate knowing I was awake. I would stay in bed for hours trying to go back to sleep. Took weeks for me to get out of bed. Took even longer for me to be able to put my clothes on. For a while, I couldn't do much else. I puttered around the house in my slippers. Couldn't leave. 'Cept I knew if I could eventually put on my shoes, I'd make it. Didn't happen right off the bat. I left them in the closet and wouldn't open the door. Then one day I took out a pair of loafers and put them on and walked outside. Went to the end of my dock. That was it. That was the farthest I could go for a while. Over time, it got easier. Just kept putting on my shoes. "

"Merle, I have my shoes on. I don't feel better."

"Point is, Abby, you got 'em on."

No more noise came from the cooler. It sat motionless. So, it seemed, did Abigail's heart.

Xe•nod´o•chy´, n. [Gr. ?.] Reception of strangers; hos-
pitality. [R.]

X

◆　◆　◆

Merle walked Abigail to her car. She wanted to tell him what Ruth had
confided about Hank Scokes, but she wasn't supposed to have told
Ruth about Nat Rhone in the first place. Merle and Hank had been
friends, though they'd chosen different paths. Merle was still walking along his, his shoes laced tight.

"You moving away?" he asked, regarding the giant duffel bag in
the backseat of the station wagon.

"Did I pack too much?"

"These storms usually blow over in a day or so. And they don't
have a dress code at the shelter. Won't be serving high tea or
nothin'."

"I wasn't certain how long I'd be gone."

"Not long," he assured her. "Better try to catch the next ferry. If
you thought traffic here was congested, wait 'til you get to the
mainland."

"Thanks."

"For advice about the ferry?"

"No, for taking me fishing."

"My pleasure, Abby."

At the main road, she merged in with what had become an exceedingly lengthy line of cars. Traffic crept across the island. Abigail's speedometer topped out at ten miles per hour. Forty minutes later, the dock finally came into sight. A man in uniform was presiding over the procession, a patrol car parked nearby. It wasn't Sheriff Larner, so it had to be his deputy.

Dozens of vehicles awaited a spot on the ferry, which hadn't returned from the mainland. The trip back and forth to Chapel Isle took more than an hour. Since the ferry held a finite number of cars, Abigail calculated that she'd be waiting until late into the afternoon for her turn.

The minutes dripped by. While children played by the dock and adults decamped from their cars to stretch their legs, Abigail stared at the clock sullenly. Once the ferry arrived, the deputy waved the cars at the head of the line aboard, then the ship departed, making a small dent in the swarm of people waiting to get off the island.

Even after the ferry returned three more times, Abigail was nowhere near the front of the queue. With every passing second, she grew more irate with herself, because she realized she had left her books behind.

"What if the hurricane demolishes the lighthouse? What if your books are lost? You'll have nothing."

As she debated what to do, the cloud cover darkened and down came a steady drizzle. Parents who'd been chatting with one another hastened their kids to their cars. Abigail wasn't at the end of the line, although she was nowhere near the middle. If she left, she'd lose her space. She didn't care. She angled out of line and sped away.

"This'll take fifteen minutes. Maybe ten. You'll probably get back before the ferry does."

Rain tapped on the roof of the station wagon, the wipers hurling water from the windshield. To save time, she took a side road, confident it crossed the lane closest to the lighthouse. Except she was wrong. Abigail couldn't tell where she was, and the weather was exacerbating matters. She tried another road, willing it to intersect with one she knew. It didn't. In her haste, Abigail wound up in the tony enclave of large, modern homes Merle had sent her to inspect when she was handling his rounds for Lottie.

"Think. You've been here before. Merle marked the houses on the map. Wait. The map."

She pulled over and put the car in park. The map wasn't in the seat pockets, under the seats, or behind the visor.

"It's got to be at the house. With your books."

The windows were opaque with condensation. Even if she could see through them, Abigail was lost.

"You got yourself into this mess. You're going to have to get yourself out of it."

She shifted gears, depressing the accelerator. The station wagon wouldn't budge.

"Oh, no. Please don't be stuck."

When she gently upped the gas, the wheels whirred. Thinking a jolt might give the car momentum, she floored it. The tires hissed and buried themselves in sand.

"You're definitely stuck."

Donning the hood on her windbreaker, she ventured into the rain. Her rear tires were embedded in a rut, which the rain was rapidly turning into a sinkhole.

"So much for shortcuts."

A blast of wind peeled away her hood, drenching her. She scrambled inside the car. There would no shortcuts for Abigail, not around the island or around her bereavement.

"You have two choices. Seems to be a running theme lately. Stay here or start walking."

Walking won. In preparation, she changed out of her wet sweater and into another from her duffel bag. Her one essential, her glasses, she tucked in her pocket. Jacket zipped, hood pulled tight, Abigail faced the rain.

"Lovely day for a stroll."

Trudging through the mud, she monitored for signs of life. This area of the island was summer rentals exclusively. Despite the grand scale of the homes as well as their luxury and cost, Abigail was definitely in the wrong part of town. What had been a twenty-minute drive from the lighthouse during her route for Merle was about to translate into a punishing hike.

She hunched her shoulders and held her head low, humming in Latin as she went.

"*Ambulo, ambulare, ambulavi, ambulatum.*

Erro, Errare, erravi, erratum."

At an intersection, Abigail had to choose which way to go next. She would have to rely on her sense of direction, and that hadn't proved very reliable of late.

"This is a crapshoot. With the emphasis on *crap*."

She had been caught in the rain, literally and figuratively. Yet this rain would stop. If Merle was right, her personal storm would too. She had her shoes on. She just had to walk.

◆　◆　◆

The terms *day* and *night* ceased to have meaning. The rain was so hard, the clouds so thick, and the sky so dark, it could have been midnight. Abigail couldn't see more than a few paces ahead. Her feet ached, her teeth were chattering uncontrollably, and her clothes were soaked through to her skin.

She kept trudging until she recognized the houses in the distance. She was on Timber Lane, the road where the most recent robbery had occurred.

"Thieves are less likely to commit crimes in inclement weather. I think I read that somewhere. Nobody wants to do heavy lifting in the rain."

Timber Lane crossed a main route that Abigail could take to the lighthouse or straight into town. From where she was, both were equidistant. Finding someone to assist her with her car was a priority if she planned to leave the island. Except she was anxious to go to the caretaker's cottage and get her books. Need swayed her judgment.

An hour later, she reached the lighthouse. In her front yard, where her Volvo normally would have been, was Sheriff Larner's police cruiser.

He must have found your car. Maybe he can radio to Denny so you'll catch the ferry.

The cruiser was empty. The front door to the house was ajar. Because of the boards on the windows, she couldn't tell if the lights were on.

Oh, God. You were robbed. The sheriff's come to see what was stolen.

Abigail nudged open the door. The light in the upstairs hall was on, illuminating the staircase. Her CD player was piled on top of the hand-carved end table, which had been inverted and was resting on the mahogany desk chair from the study.

If you were robbed, why is everything still here?

Footsteps sounded from the second floor. She was about to shout to Larner. However, her voice wouldn't cooperate.

What if that isn't him?

She had to find somewhere to hide. The living room and kitchen were too open. The basement door would squeak. Abigail made a dash for the lighthouse, slipping inside as footfalls descended the stairs.

The lamp room.

Abigail took a step onto the spiral staircase, bypassing the bottom one because she remembered it creaked. Reason wrenched her body to a stop. The lamp room was the last place she wanted to go, because then she'd be trapped. And if she accidentally stepped on a stair that did creak, the burglar would hear her.

The lamp room or the burglar. The rock or the hard place.

Darkness pooled in the well of the lighthouse. Her eyes were dilating, and so was her fear. Through a crack in the doorjamb, Abigail could see out into the living room. A figure rounded the stairwell. It was Sheriff Larner. He had a stack of Wesley Jasper's ledgers in his arms. He put them on top of her CD player, readying to move the items to his car.

Ceding logic, Abigail burst through the lighthouse door. "What are you doing?"

Larner's hand flew to his holster. Abigail froze. The events surrounding the robberies fell together for her. Larner had stopped her the evening of one break-in. He hadn't been at his office the night of the next.

"Merle was right. He knew it was a native, someone from Chapel Isle."

Larner bristled at the suggestion that somebody suspected him. He glanced at the telephone. A knot tightened in Abigail's stomach. He had a gun. She had nothing to protect herself with, no weapon, only words.

"Merle thought whoever was robbing the houses needed money. Did you need the money? Is that why?"

"Does it matter?"

That answer had too many meanings, none of them positive.

"Was it for your daughter?"

Taken aback, Larner didn't answer.

"Ruth told me she's sick. That she can't pay her medical bills."

He lowered his chin for an instant, yielding a little.

"Rental properties are covered by insurance. The owners wouldn't lose any money. You knew that. You guessed there'd be expensive antiques here after what Denny said at the Kettle. The furniture might be worth a few hundred bucks, though I doubt you'll get much for my radio or those ledgers."

Unflinching, he stared at Abigail, refusing to speak.

"I can't let you take these things, Caleb. I don't have a lot left in this world, and even though most of it isn't mine, I can't let you have it."

Larner stiffened.

"So I'm going to make you a deal."

"*You're* going to make *me* a deal?"

Abigail gulped air to get past the threat in his voice. "I'm not going to turn you in to the authorities on the mainland, and you're going to let Nat Rhone go."

He squinted at her in disbelief.

"I don't care about what you stole or why. I'm not from here, but I want to stay. If that means I keep your secret, then you've got to do something for me."

"I'm listening."

"Ruth told you about Hank today. Did you believe her?"

Larner shrugged, loath to tip his hand.

"She has no reason to lie."

"Nat does."

Abigail looked at the pile Larner had amassed in the middle of the living room and said, "We all have reasons to lie."

"You want me to trade my career to let a possible killer go free."

"No, I want you to trade one mistake for one misunderstanding."

He chewed the inside of his cheek. "If I agree, how's this going to work?"

"I'm not sure. I haven't done this before."

"Do we pretend tonight never happened?"

"That's a reasonable place to start."

"You don't have any proof. You can't blackmail me later on."

"I'm not interested in blackmailing you any more than I already am, Sheriff."

"Shake on it."

Abigail was reticent. If Larner was going to try anything, it would be when he had her in his grip. Chancing it, she relented and shook his hand. He let go first.

"You in love with him? Is that why you're doing this?"

"Not in the least."

"Then why?"

Abigail had spent almost ten years with her husband and only four with her son—not enough, but more than some. She'd lost them sooner rather than later. Nat's parents had been taken from him too young, far sooner than he deserved. If she could look out for him in a way fate hadn't, that was what Abigail was going to do. In exchange, fate might return the favor.

"Does it matter?" she replied, echoing what he'd said before.

Abigail trusted that Larner would be true to his word, that he would release Nat. In the grand scheme of things, it didn't matter why she'd done it. What mattered was that it was done.

yare (yâr *or, esp. for* 1, 2, yär), *adj.,* **yar•er, yar•est. 1.** quick; agile; lively. **2.** (of a ship) quick to the helm; easily handled or maneuvered. **3.** *Archaic.* **a.** ready; prepared. **b.** nimble; quick. Also, **yar** (for defs. 1, 2). [bef. 900; ME; OE *gearu, gearo,* equiv. to *ge-* Y- + *earu* ready; c. D *gaar,* G *gar* done, dressed (as meat)] —**yare´ly,** *adv.*

◆   ◆   ◆

*The rain had gone from a downpour to a deluge, battering the win-*dows and beating on the roof of the caretaker's house like a drum. The wind was gusting hard enough to make the plywood boards quake in the casements.

"You shouldn't stay here on your own," Larner said.

"My car's stuck in a ditch on the other side of the island. I can't go anywhere. I have supplies. I can wait out the storm here."

The second Abigail finished saying that, the lights snuffed out. The house had lost power. Larner switched on his flashlight.

"How about I take you to stay with Ruth? That way you're not alone."

"Sheriff, you were about to rob me. Forgive me if this sudden wave of concern seems a bit phony."

"It wasn't personal, Abby."

"This island is too small for it not to be personal. Isn't that what you told Merle?"

"You're one of those people who remembers everything, aren't you?"

It was true. Abigail's memory was her finest asset. It was also the source of much of her pain. Regardless, she was thankful for it.

Wind rocked the patrol car as Larner steered a course across the slippery roads. The windshield had become a sheet of gray. The thrumming of the rain was punctuated by the cracking of tree limbs.

"This is dangerous, isn't it?"

Larner nodded and radioed in to the station. "What's the latest, Ted?"

"Bad news is we lost power," the deputy radioed back. "The good news is the state police issued a report that the hurricane is gonna miss us. Radar is saying it's already turned and heading to sea."

There would always be good news and bad news. Probability dictated there would be equal parts of both. Of late, the odds had not been in Abigail's favor. But math didn't lie. She was due some good news and she'd gotten it. The hurricane would not hit Chapel Isle.

"Can I come with you to the station? I want to be there when you let Nat out."

"Is that smart? We don't need him suspecting you had a hand in his release. Him or anybody else."

Abigail thought it over. "How about I say I flagged you down after my car got stuck?"

Her intentions clear, Larner acquiesced. "I still think you should go to Ruth's. It's going to be a rough night."

"Maybe Nat could give me a ride there."

"That'd be the least he could do."

◆　◆　◆

Rainwater overran the cobblestone square, and the boats tied to the pier were sloshing violently in the surf, caterwauling dolefully. A gale blew off the water, nearly knocking Abigail from her feet. Larner caught her by the arm and aided her into the station.

Ted was hunched over the radio as if he could warm himself by it. His wet hair was dripping down his neck and collar. "Happy you're back, Caleb."

"Ted, this is Abby Harker. She's the new caretaker over at the lighthouse."

"Nice to meet you, ma'am." He wiped his hand on his trousers. "Sorry. Everything's wet."

"I know the feeling." Abigail shucked off her sopping windbreaker.

"Hadn't heard there was a new caretaker."

The fact that her arrival hadn't reached Ted's ears convinced Abigail that her pact with Sheriff Larner would remain in confidence. Secrets escaped only when their keepers let them, when they personally had nothing to lose. Neither she nor Larner would allow that to happen.

"Have a seat, Abby," he said, then Larner took Ted aside and whispered to him. Abigail heard him mention Ruth's name and something about Hank taking his wife's death hard.

"Oh," the deputy responded. "Guess you'll be wanting me to let him out, huh?"

"Yeah, that's what I want you to do."

Ted disappeared into the rear of the station. Soon Nat staggered out with him. He'd been asleep. His hair was mussed, his clothes rumpled. Abigail gave him a wan smile, and Ted handed him his personal belongings, including his hat, which Nat tugged onto his head like a disguise.

"You releasing me?"

Larner nodded, unwilling to admit aloud that he'd been wrong. "You need to sign some papers before you can be on your way."

Nat scribbled his signature. "That's it? Can I go?"

"You can go."

"Mind if I get a ride with you?" Abigail asked. "My car got stuck."

Nat eyed the other two men.

"I'd ask them, but they're swamped, what with the power being down on the island."

Too tired to argue, Nat motioned her along with him. He strode brazenly into the rain while Abigail battled the whipping wind to keep pace.

"Truck's by the pier."

Hank's truck was the lone vehicle in the parking lot. Nat took a deep breath and got inside. Key in the ignition, he hesitated before starting the engine.

"Larner tell you what happened?"

"Yes. I'm sorry about Hank. I know you were close."

"What'd he say?"

"That Hank went over with the net. Intentionally."

Hearing it stung Nat. "If Larner believed that, I wouldn't have been in lockup."

"You're free now."

"Does everyone know?"

She shook her head. "They had the hurricane on their minds."

Rain was pelting the hood of the truck, and each gale sent tremors through the cab. The vacant parking lot was a dangerous place for them to be. They were sitting targets. Nat couldn't bring himself to start to the motor.

"Hank tried once before," he confessed. "He took pills. I found him. He'd thrown them up. Jeez, was Hank pissed about that. He was going on about how his body wouldn't let him die." Nat's jaw clenched, as if he was fighting the words he spoke. "It was his idea to go fishing that morning. Claimed the storm would kick up a stellar take. I told him to forget it, but he wouldn't drop it. I saw him letting out the nets. He was staring at the water. I turned away for a second. One single second. Happened so fast. I thought he was getting better." His voice wavered. "I thought he was getting over it."

There were things people had the right not to get over, but that they had the duty to get past. Not everyone could do it. Abigail had to try.

She put her hand on Nat's shoulder. She could have told him she understood, that she was in the unfortunate position of knowing exactly how he felt. She didn't. It wouldn't have helped. Neither Nat nor her.

"I think you would rather have people believe this was your fault than that Hank did it to himself."

He blinked, an affirmation.

"Except I don't think that's what Hank would have wanted. Do you?"

At last, Nat turned the key, started the truck, and drove into the wind.

◆　◆　◆

Ruth Kepshaw's house had a wide front porch, and Nat pulled as close to it as he could.

"Are you okay?" Abigail asked. "For the storm, I mean. Do you have candles and food and—"

"I'll be fine," he said.

Abigail realized she was treating him the way her parents treated her. She was fully aware that being badgered by other people in the name of sympathy wasn't fun. Abigail also knew that what awaited Nat made the hurricane pale in significance. With Hank's death came countless duties, from making funeral arrangements and notifying next of kin to stopping his mail and dealing with his personal effects. There would be much to do. The first travail would be going home to the apartment over Hank's garage, where everything would remind Nat of his friend.

"Thanks for the ride."

Nat said nothing. Abigail understood. There was nothing either of them could say.

Hood on, she hurried from his truck to the porch and rang the doorbell. Nat didn't leave until Ruth came to the door.

"I'm going to have Denny's head on platter," Ruth growled, ushering Abigail inside.

Candles were burning in the living room, which made the oak

paneling glow. The furniture smacked of a bygone era but was well maintained, giving the house the feel of a seaside rental rather than a permanent home. A can of diet soda and a book of crossword puzzles sat beside a lounge chair.

"Small change in plans," Abigail explained.

"You don't say? Give me those wet clothes and I'll find you something dry to put on. Bathroom's at the end of the hall."

Abigail hung her soaking sweater and pants over the shower rod and stood shivering in her underwear in the bathroom until Ruth opened the door a crack and offered her a flannel nightgown.

"Ain't pretty, but it'll do."

She slipped into the extra-large gown, then returned to the living room, where Ruth appraised the outfit.

"Better you look frumpy than continue dripping on my carpet. Take a load off. You look beat."

Abigail dropped onto the couch. "I feel beat."

"Saw that was Nat Rhone who dropped you here. He figure out you're the one who freed him from the slammer?"

"Nope."

"And that's how you want it to stay?"

"Yup."

"Consider my lips sealed," Ruth said, sipping her soda.

"Thanks for talking to the sheriff."

"Funny—this morning Caleb didn't care a lick about what I had to say regarding Hank. He must have had a change of heart."

"That's what it must have been."

If Ruth sensed what Abigail had done, she wasn't letting on. For that, Abigail respected her even more.

"So, you think you'll stay here, Abby, after everything Chapel Isle's put you through? A fight at the Kettle, a suicide, a hurricane, bingo?"

"If you were me, what would you do? Would you stay?"

"Depends." Ruth put aside her soda and folded her hands in her lap. "Have you heard of the *Bishop's Mistress*?"

"Have I? It was the ship that sank when Wesley Jasper was the caretaker."

Abigail realized belatedly that it was a loaded question. As usual, Ruth already knew the answer.

"That ship was named after a real bishop. He'd been a sailor, an old salt through and through. Gave up sailing to preach the gospel. According to legend, after years of being a priest, he missed the ocean so much that he was going to leave the clergy. Only he couldn't do it. The Lord was his first love. The sea would have to be his second. Whether you stay here on Chapel Isle or take the next ferry home, it won't make a bit of difference. It's like trying to serve two masters. You've got the grief and you've got your life. The one you choose to serve is up to you."

Having a choice hadn't occurred to Abigail. She still had an opportunity to decide.

Ruth coughed and reached for her drink. "Sheesh. This serious talk done dried my throat. Now listen, hon, I've got a spare bed. Why don't you go lie down and leave a gal to her puzzles."

"Are you sure you don't want me to stay up with you?"

"Positive."

"Night, Ruth."

"Night, Abby."

That had become her name, and Abigail was okay with that. She had only begun to get acquainted with *Abby,* but she liked her so far. She was willing to take a chance and get to know her better.

zetetic "proceeding by inquiry," 1645, from Mod.L. *zeteticus*, from Gk. *zetetikos* "searching, inquiring," from *zetetos*, verbal adj. of *zetein* "seek for, inquire into."

◆ ◆ ◆

Abigail rarely remembered her dreams. However, when Ruth roused her the following morning, she was certain what she'd dreamed about had been pleasant.

"Better put on your clothes," Ruth warned. "You have a guest."

Nat Rhone was sitting in the living room, looking nervous. He stood when Abigail entered. He even took off his hat.

"Last night you said your car was stuck. Thought you'd need some help."

"Um, yeah. I'd appreciate that."

"I've got some of Jerome's old tools and such if you need any of 'em." Ruth led them to the garage, where Nat selected a shovel and some scraps of wood.

"These'll do." He headed out of the garage toward his truck, saying to Abigail, "You coming?"

She deferred to Ruth, who shrugged.

"Thanks a lot," Abigail muttered.

Ruth was grinning. "No problem, hon."

"So where's your car?" Nat asked as she buckled in.

"That's an excellent question. I don't have an answer. I was lost when I got stuck in a ditch."

"You were lost? On this speck of an island?"

"It's not that small."

"Stay here long enough and you'll see how small it is."

A tangible silence filled the truck, pushing each of them further apart while they cruised from lane to lane in search of Abigail's abandoned Volvo. Nat was leaning into the driver's side door. She was huddled at the far corner of the cab.

"You like your job?" he asked, seemingly trying to make conversation.

Abigail began to worry he'd inferred the part she played in his release. "You mean as caretaker at the lighthouse?"

"No, your real job. The lexicography."

"Yes, yes, I do. Or I did."

"Did it pay good?"

"The salary was decent."

"Long hours?"

"Manageable. Why? Are you changing careers?"

"Just wondering why you stopped. And why you came here. Chapel Isle isn't the lexicography capital of the world."

"Change of pace. Change of scenery."

"Uh-huh."

"I'm not on the lam, if that's what you're insinuating." Abigail regretted her choice of phrasing.

"In my experience, people usually move to get away."

"Some move to get closer," she contended.

Nat had been ready to take the rap for Hank's death in order to honor him. Abigail had fallen victim to a similar pretense. Following flawed logic, she'd moved to Chapel Isle, convinced she could honor the memory of her husband and son by loving the place Paul had loved, terrified that no matter how hard she tried, she wouldn't be able to do their lives justice. Nat Rhone proved the opposite was true.

In the distance, Abigail saw her station wagon. Leaves were

plastered to the windows, and the rear tires were sunk deep in a ditch, tilting the car on a steep slope.

"There it is."

"When you said stuck, you really meant stuck."

Nat got out to inspect the car, mud sucking at his boots. He shoveled aside some debris, then wedged pieces of wood under each tire.

"Start the engine and press the gas real slow."

Abigail hopped into the Volvo. When she depressed the accelerator, the wheels whirred. In the rearview mirror, she could see Nat leaning into the bumper, pushing with every ounce of his might.

"More gas. Gentle. Gentle."

She applied steady pressure to the pedal, and the car began to creep forward.

"A little more," he told her as he strained.

Suddenly the station wagon bucked free, spraying a stew of mud and sand all over Nat's clothes. Abigail pulled onto firm ground and hurried to him.

"I'm so sorry."

The expression on his mud-spattered face was priceless. She clamped her hand to her mouth, stifling a laugh.

"You think this is funny?"

He wiped the muck from his cheek. Abigail forced a straight face that crumbled as she cracked up. Nat relented, his grimace loosening into a guarded smile.

"It is sort of funny."

They stood in the middle of the muddy road together, laughing like people who could be friends, if not at that very moment, then someday.

◆　◆　◆

Merle's truck was parked in front of the lighthouse when Abigail returned. He was on a ladder removing the plywood boards from the second-floor windows.

"I must be more popular than I thought. People keep surprising me today."

"Last couple o' days have been full of surprises, I'll say that much." Merle climbed down from the ladder. "I heard about Nat Rhone. Strange how Caleb Larner changed his mind," he said knowingly.

"Stranger things have happened."

"They always do."

"Hey, you fixed my shutters. They look great."

"Glad you like them, because you're not going to like what I have to tell you. Lottie's on her way over here."

"She found out about the furniture and the paint?"

"No, ma'am. She called me from the mainland to say she and Franklin were okay and mentioned she'd be stopping by to give you some more of those romance novels o' hers."

"What am I going to do? The changes aren't exactly subtle. Though she did lie about the condition of the property. This should make us even. In a weird, Chaple Isle-ish sense. Right?"

"Appears to me, Abby, you have a knack for getting people to do the complete opposite of what they want to do, so I feel supremely confident you'll be able to get Lottie to overlook any . . . rental indiscretions. Especially if you were to, say, allude to the fact that she might not have declared the antiques to her insurance company, in order to avoid paying more for coverage," Merle suggested with a smirk. "While you're at it, you might propose she make some overdue repairs to this place too. That is, if you're going to be around to enjoy it."

Abigail had made her decision. She was going to stay.

"I will be."

"Good."

Merle collected the plywood boards he'd removed from the windows and volunteered to haul them to the basement.

"My, my, my." He was admiring what she'd done with the house. The pile Sheriff Larner had gathered the night before remained in the center of the living room. "Not finished rearranging?"

"Close."

"You did a fine job," he said, patting one of the wingback chairs as if it were a long-lost friend.

"Now I get it. You put the antiques in the basement. You didn't want me or anybody else to find out about them, because of the robberies."

"That's why I like you, Abby. You're the logical type."

"Chapel Isle logic is the only kinda logic I got," she said, quoting him.

"It's all ya need."

Merle was right. That was all she would need.

"If you moved the antiques upstairs from the basement," he asked, "what'd you do with the rest of that ratty furniture Lottie had?"

"It, uh, found a new home."

He smiled. "Sounds like somebody I know."

◆　◆　◆

Once Merle was gone, Abigail replaced the furniture that Sheriff Larner had moved, putting it back where it belonged. With the boards off the windows, the house filled with the warmth of sunlight. The hurricane had wiped the sky clear. Though the power was still out, Abigail didn't miss it. The sunshine was enough for her.

She put the batteries she'd bought into the radio and turned it on for company while she unpacked for the second time since arriving on Chapel Isle. Dr. Walter was on the air.

"We certainly dodged a bullet with Hurricane Amelia," he crooned. "Call it luck, fate, or divine intervention. Call it whatever you want. We're grateful to be here to tell the tale of the hurricane that never was. And what tales we have to tell today. Our topic is elderly drivers. Should they have their licenses revoked? Should there be an age restriction? Phone in and tell us what you think. You have a say. Your opinion matters."

"That's right," Abigail agreed. "I do have a say."

After she finished unpacking, she went downstairs and tidied the dining room table, storing the army of batteries and flashlights in the kitchen with the hope she wouldn't have to put them to further use in the near future. That done, she had one task left to do. Check on the oil pail.

The whitewashed walls of the lighthouse tower gleamed in the daylight. Abigail climbed the stairs briskly before she could change her mind.

"You can do this," she told herself. A faint echo resonated through the lighthouse, repeating the phrase.

The view from the lamp room was stunning. The Atlantic was placid and glassy. The horizon was a plain line between the sea and the limitless sky.

Abigail closed her eyes and pivoted to face the spot where she'd put the oil pail. Fear was making her dizzy. She could feel how high up she was, how far away she was from the ground. She took a deep breath and opened her eyes.

The oil pail was right where she had left it, askew under the plaque.

In that instant, the proof she had been seeking no longer interested her. Proof wasn't what counted. What counted was everything except the oil pail and what it signified. Whether Mr. Jasper existed or not, he had loved the lighthouse. He belonged there. She belonged too.

Abigail had indeed been haunted. She'd been haunted by *never*. That was what she'd defined herself by: the husband she would never grow old with, the son who would never blossom into a man, the life she would never recapture. It was up to her how she labeled what was to come. From the top of the lighthouse, with the whole world to behold, *never* was suddenly besides the point. It was only a word.

ACKNOWLEDGMENTS

Many hugs and much gratitude are due to my friends for all of their encouragement and support. Alphabetical order has never seemed so appropriate. Thanks to Sarah Baldassaro, Ann Biddlecom, Ruth Blader, Claudia Butler, Alice Dickens, Anne Englehardt, Beth Foster, Debra Keeler, Amy and Brad Miller, Alex Parsons, Grace Ray, Sally Smith, Heather Stober, Caroline Zouloumian, and Sue Zwick.

None of this would have been possible without my amazing agent, Rebecca Oliver, and my talented editor, Danielle Perez. A thank you is also in order to the many real-life lexicographers who have come and gone because without the dictionary my job would be far harder and considerably less interesting.

The
LANGUAGE
of
SAND

Ellen Block

A Reader's Guide

AN INTERVIEW WITH ELLEN BLOCK
CONDUCTED BY THE
MAIN CHARACTER, ABIGAIL HARKER

It's a rare opportunity for a character to interview her creator, so I, Abigail Harker, hope to learn something about the author of this book while letting you, the reader, get to know more about the person who brought me to life.

Abigail Harker: You crafted my character to be logical to a fault, then you had me live in a supposedly haunted lighthouse, a concept that flouts reason and common sense. That begs the question: Do you believe in ghosts? Or did you just want to see me sweat?

Ellen Block: Both! I've always been fascinated by the paranormal. Less for the fright factor and more because of the bigger issues raised in the debate—life after death, the existence of the soul sans body, and the subject of why a ghost would choose to remain in a place that was no longer its own. Your job as a lexicographer, albeit fictitious, is to pin down words and hone definitions to perfection. My job as an author is the exact opposite. A novel is intended to encourage open-ended deliberation and discussion, to get readers thinking about ideas they might not normally wonder about in their daily lives. Haunted houses are usually seen as Halloween attractions or scary movie fare. What if there was some credence to the notion? What if hauntings were commonplace? Would that make a "haunted" location more or less scary?

AH: Um, hello! You stuck me in that creaky, creepy old house, and yes, it was unnerving at first . . . though the horrible décor and rickety furniture was just as terrifying, quite frankly. Thanks for that too, by the way. So, would you live in a haunted house?

EB: I might stay the night to see if anything weird would happen, but no, truth be told, I doubt I'd take up residence. I prefer plotting out spooky sequences to actually being spooked.

AH: Speaking of weird, why on earth did you make bingo the beloved pastime of Chapel Isle's residents?

EB: Bingo is a great game! It's not about skill, competition, or squashing your opponent. It's about luck, a theme that's woven into the story. Plus, I played bingo once while visiting the island I based the setting on and won a fishing trip. So how could I *not* put it in there?

AH: While I wasn't happy about everything you wrote in the book, including turning me into a hammer-wielding security guard and forcing me to face how my life had changed after the house fire, you did allow me to meet a number of amazing, often quirky, characters on Chapel Isle. Which of them was your favorite? Besides me, of course.

EB: Of course! Well, that's a tough one. It's hard to choose. I love Merle Braithwaite's sense of friendship, Lottie Gilquist's from-the-heart laugh, Bertram Van Dorst's humble brilliance, Ruth Kepshaw's hilarious, off-the-cuff candor, Sheriff Larner's desire to do right by his family, Denny Meloch's innocent exuberance, and Nat Rhone's loyalty. A good character is like a good friend. Sometimes you love them for their endearing qualities. Other times you want to throttle them for their flaws. But most of the time, you're just happy to have gotten the chance to know them.

AH: Since you made my character an ardent lover and champion of words, I have to ask: What's your favorite word?

EB: I'd pick "ebullient." It's from the Latin *ebullire,* "to bubble," and as an adjective, it means having or showing liveliness and enthusiasm. It can also mean boiling or agitated. Such a stark contrast in a single word is pretty impressive, yet it always sounds upbeat to me, which is why I like it so much. To be full of life, vitality, and enthusiasm is great for a word, and it's also a great way to be.

THE STORY
BEHIND THE STORY

The idea for this novel came from a collection of happy memories as well as a single, heartrendingly sad one.

Grief defies description. The colossal awe experienced in the wake of the attacks on September 11 simply cannot be compacted into words. In the aftermath of such a monumental catastrophe, language seemed painfully insufficient. For a writer like myself, that was a difficult and confounding feeling. A week after the attacks, I saw a woman from my hometown of Summit, New Jersey, being profiled on *60 Minutes* as she went from hospital to hospital, searching in vain for her husband, who had been killed in the Twin Towers. She was a woman I'd passed by in the grocery store countless times, and there she was on national television, crying, scared, bereaved, a victim.

Like so many, I was deeply affected by that day's events. I couldn't comprehend the magnitude of one survivor's grief, let alone that of thousands. Since the attacks, I'd wanted to create a character whose life was dedicated to language and definitions, but who must deal with that which cannot be defined. The character who evolved was a lexicographer named Abigail Harker, a widow who has lost her entire family in an accidental house fire. Haunted by the death of her husband and child, she volunteers for a position as caretaker at a lighthouse on a remote island called Chapel Isle. There she discovers that the lighthouse may be haunted by the ghost of its former keeper.

This fictional isle is loosely based on Ocracoke Island in North Carolina's Outerbanks, where I spent summers during my childhood. I remember my trips there fondly and always wondered what the island would be like once tourists like me went home. The sense of separation and intense isolation coupled with the close-knit camaraderie of a small community made it an ideal destination for a character at a crossroads and an apt setting for a woman at odds with her own nature, a connoisseur of words grappling with indescribable sorrow.

People often wonder what an author has in common with her characters. In this case, my protagonist, Abigail Harker, and I share one main preoccupation. As a lexicographer, language is the foundation of her career. As an author, it's the lifeblood of mine.

In order to cope with her grief and with the possibility of a resident ghost at the lighthouse where she lives, Abigail must challenge the sanctity of language, thereby challenging herself. Her dogged pursuit of definitions has almost eliminated the necessity to feel. However, moving to Chapel Isle forces her to face her emotions, posing the questions: What's real? What isn't? and is it words that make the difference?

I believe Abigail would agree that words are both limiting and limitless all at once. In the process of writing *The Language of Sand*, I attempted to display language at its most capable and lush while trying to show its many infuriating inadequacies, a contrast that breeds conflict as well as insight. What are books—and words—for if not that?

READING GROUP QUESTIONS AND TOPICS FOR DISCUSSION

1. How did the setting affect the plot and why?

2. Would you want to visit Chapel Isle?

3. Are there situations and/or characters you can identify with? If so, how?

4. Do you feel as if your views on a subject, such as ghosts or grief, have changed after reading this novel?

5. If you could change something about the book, what would it be and why?

6. What motivates a given character's actions, such as Abigail's, Sheriff Larner's, or Merle's? Do you think those actions are justified or ethical?

7. Which characters grow or change during the course of the novel? In what ways?

8. Who in this book would you most like to meet? What would you ask or say?

9. Which character do you like the most and why? The least, and why?

10. What passage from the book stood out for you?

11. Is the novel plot- or character-driven? In other words, does the plot unfold quickly or focus more on the characters' inner lives?

12. Did you expect the book to end the way it did or were you surprised?

13. If you could rewrite the ending, would you? What would you change?

14. Can you pick out a passage that sums up the central theme of the book?

15. If you were to talk to the author, what would you want to know?

16. Were the characters' struggles addressed in a believable way?

17. Why do you think the author chose to tell the story in this manner?

18. What is your favorite scene and why?

19. Does Abigail learn something about herself or view the world differently during the course of the book? If so, what does she learn?

20. What is the central conflict of the plot? Is it internal to a particular character (a psychological conflict), or is it external, having to do with character vs. character?

21. If one or more of the characters made a choice that had moral implications, would you have made the same decision? Why or why not?

22. How would the book have been different if it had taken place in a different time or place?

23. What are some of the themes in the novel? How important are they?

ABOUT THE AUTHOR

Ellen Block is currently at work on the sequel to
The Language of Sand. She lives in Los Angeles.

ABOUT THE TYPE

This book was set in Perpetua, a typeface designed by the English artist Eric Gill and cut by The Monotype Corporation between 1928 and 1930. Perpetua is a contemporary face of original design, without any direct historical antecedents. The shapes of the roman letters are derived from the techniques of stonecutting. The larger display sizes are extremely elegant and form a most distinguished series of inscriptional letters.